TRUE GRIFT

TRUE GRIFT

JACK BUNKER

Published by Brash Books LLC
12120 State Line #253
Leawood, Kansas 66209

ISBN 10: 1941298869
ISBN 13: 9781941298862

For the Bar

I also will laugh at your calamity…
Proverbs 1:26

ONE

After another grueling day of slipping through the grasping fingers of creditors, all J.T. wanted to do was go hit some range balls. It didn't seem that much to ask. A bucket of balls. Maybe a couple of drinks afterward. Had the chiffon-yellow Lincoln Navigator of Frankie Fresh not glommed J.T.'s usual parking spot, the errant Titleist that flew the eighteenth green never would have reached the windshield of his beloved Mercedes S600. But the web of cracked safety glass sparkling in the setting Riverside County sun told J.T. Edwards that the breaks in his life were taking a different direction.

The lot didn't have reserved parking, but J.T. had always thought of it as *his* spot. Technically spots, as he usually parked across two spaces to make sure no one dinged the doors of his Mercedes. Meanwhile, the yellow Navigator still sat empty, idling on the blacktop, a stream of A/C condensation flowing on the ground beneath the engine.

"Are you kidding me?" J.T. roared at the sky. In the center of the windshield, right above the wiper, cracks spun out in all directions in a twelve-inch radius. J.T. saw the offending golf ball nestled in some ice plants a few yards away. He picked it up and heaved it as far as he could into the scruffy hills that surrounded the parking lot.

A couple of spaces away, a slim guy in his early forties, with thinning hair, bad skin, and a cheap polo shirt, sat on the bumper of a bronze Camry, removing his golf shoes and slipping on untied sneakers. "You got a separate windshield deductible on that?"

"Excuse me?" said J.T.

"Your windshield. You're looking at eight hundred bucks minimum to replace that. Who's your insurance carrier?"

J.T. kicked at an ice plant. "I don't know…um, State Farm, why?"

The guy got up from his car and walked over toward J.T. "You're gonna get hammered, aren't you?"

The guy looked familiar. J.T. must have seen him around the course before, but he'd never talked to him. "Probably. You a windshield salesman or something?"

"Al Boyle." The guy stuck out his hand. "I'm a senior claims manager at GSAC. For the time being, anyway."

J.T. was only too familiar with the Golden State Assurance Company. "You got some rat bastards in that legal department."

"You must be a PI lawyer," said Al, nodding toward J.T.'s license plate that read DELICT.

J.T. shook the guy's hand. "J.T. Edwards."

He used to call himself John Edwards back when he'd opened his practice, happy to let some dopes on the phone mistake him for the plaintiff's-lawyer-turned-politician. Until all the scandal and the love child and the angry, dying wife. Then it became a liability and he became J.T. Edwards.

But J.T. didn't flinch from the epithets "plaintiff's lawyer" or "personal injury" when his classmates smirked at reunions. He embraced them like he used to embrace the wooden steering wheel of his convertible XK8 as he tooled up the PCH for a balls-out weekend in Santa Barbara. Or the way he embraced a fiberglass rod when he was fishing for marlin off Cabo. Or the way he embraced a $500 Margaux in his wine cellar…before Stephanie got the house.

All 420 pounds of Francis Xavier McElfresh squeezed through the door of the club's bar and grill, the 19th Hole, and out to the parking lot. He spotted Al and started waving like he was flagging a beer vendor at a ball game. "Al! Al! How you doing, Al? You get out today?"

Al looked up, his eyes fixed on the dimpled knees that supported Frankie's bulk. "Hey, Frankie, yeah." Al lifted a golf shoe from his bumper as if to prove he'd actually gotten out on the course. "You gonna be around? I've got something for you."

Frankie giggled. "Sure, Al, sure." He pointed to J.T.'s shattered windshield. "Boy, looks like someone really wanted to play through!" Frankie threw his head back and laughed, his pelican gullet bobbing up and down.

J.T. gritted his teeth and squinted. He knew Frankie hadn't actually hit the ball that wrecked the windshield, but J.T. couldn't forgive him for his role in the causal chain of events. He made a point of pulling his phone from his pocket as an excuse not to engage in small talk.

Frankie continued on toward his idling Navigator. *"Play through!"* he laughed to himself again.

Once the threat of conversation was past, J.T. jammed the phone back in his pocket and looked once more at the windshield.

"Listen, I know a guy," Al said, clearing his throat. "I mean, I'm assuming you don't want to go with some non-OEM crap on a car like this, right?"

"Almost as much as I don't want to pay eleven thousand bucks to get it replaced."

"Anyway, it's not a GSAC claim, so I can tell you: this guy… good dude, does good work. He's in Riverside. You take it to him and tell him I sent you. He'll hook you up."

"How do you mean?"

"I mean he'll gross up the cost of the windshield to work around your deductible. He'll use the real glass too."

J.T. looked at the windshield. "Thanks." He shook his head. "Hey, I was gonna head inside and get a drink. You want to join me?"

"Sure, why not? Thanks. I need to get something to eat anyway."

The two men started across the parking lot in silence. J.T. looked back one more time over his shoulder at the cracked windshield. Down the lot, Frankie Fresh turned off his SUV, closed the door, and began waddling back toward the clubhouse.

TWO

A window the length of the wall framed the view of the base of the San Jacinto Mountains hard by the parking lot less than a hundred feet away. The golf course was surrounded on three sides by defeated lumps of ochre, scrub-covered rock peppering hillsides that offered no shade but reflected and radiated the desert heat like a convection oven. This was the *vista* of the Mira Vista Golf Resort.

The original developer had either a sense of humor or a limited grasp of Spanish. Maybe both. When they first put down the signage at the course, the landscaping crew laughed and called the place *Mira Chiste*. The developer, who'd dreamed of a big resort back before the Crisis, was pained to learn *chiste* was Spanish for joke, but the damage was done. The nickname stuck.

Across the room, beneath the TV, laughing men finished their beers and began moving for the door. A few more sweating golfers entered as they completed their rounds. Shadows from the clubhouse stretched against the broiling stony backdrop of the dusty hills outside.

"Here you go, Al," said Wanda, the barmaid, smiling as she set a vodka rocks on the table.

Al nodded his head toward the men's room where J.T. was washing up. "This guy? This is the PI lawyer you mentioned, right? You know him from outside the club?"

"His firm represented my mom and me when I was in high school and our SUV rolled over. Fractured my pelvis. Wrecked my mom's back."

"How'd that go, your case? You win?"

"It was a statewide class action. My mom got her surgical expenses paid, and we got sixteen grand in the settlement. She thought we'd won the lottery. In Mexico she'd have had to pay the car company."

"So it worked out okay, then."

"There were four thousand plaintiffs in California. The class settled for like, a hundred and five million. A handful of lawyers split thirty-six million bucks and my mom's in a wheelchair. Guess it worked out okay for somebody."

"Still. You could've opted out."

"Yep, that's true. We could've opted out. My mom barely speaks English, and I was seventeen years old. What did we know? Our lawyers said it was a good deal."

"How'd the opt-outs do?"

"I dunno. I heard a guy with bad dreams from PTSD got a million two. Now he has a B and B in Tahoe."

J.T. approached from the hallway, stopping to pluck a cocktail napkin from the bar. He wiped his forehead and continued walking toward the table where Al was sipping his vodka.

"So, anyway," said Wanda, "haven't seen you in a while."

"Yeah, work stuff. They're trying to transfer me."

"Really?"

"Enh. GSAC's being bought out by San Antonio Insurance. They want to consolidate and cut loose everyone they can, the bastards."

J.T. pulled out his chair and sat down. "At least you're keeping your job." He took a sip from the sweating glass of scotch Wanda had waiting for him.

"I got seventeen years in with these guys. Those jerk-offs know better than to just kick me to the curb." Al took a sip of his drink. He drew his lips tight across his teeth. "They want to send me up to Weed to run a regional claims desk. You believe it? Friggin' Weed, California."

"Never heard of it," said Wanda.

"I thought they were messing with me. I didn't believe it was a real place. But it sure as shit is."

"It's nice up there," said J.T. "Right near Mount Shasta. Quiet. Beautiful country."

"Snows up there, doesn't it?" said Al. "Screw Weed. You can have it."

Wanda excused herself to go wait on a codger waving to her from across the room.

"I'm sure to a lot of people it doesn't sound like a big deal," said Al. "But I'm underwater on my house by at least a hundred grand. I couldn't sell it if I wanted to."

"Yeah, well, let me know when you're underwater on two houses by a good two hundred each."

"Ex?"

"She got the house. I figured no big deal, I'll hop into one of these monsters they were throwing up and flip it in a year."

"That year happen to be 2009?" said Al.

"Like every septic tank in California exploded at once."

Planting his flag in the Inland Empire had been J.T.'s design from the get-go. Riverside and San Bernardino Counties—respectively, the eleventh- and twelfth-most populous in America—meant more than 4.2 million potential plaintiffs. The area of those two counties alone made the Inland Empire, that twenty-seven-thousand-square-mile chunk of nowhere between LA and Las Vegas, bigger than Ireland.

"So what's your big plan to get out of going up to Weed?" asked J.T.

"I can't really call it a big plan yet. More like a dream."

"You jumping ship?"

"What I want to do is get my own ship."

"You want to open your own insurance agency? In this market? That does sound like a dream."

Al sipped his vodka and grimaced again. "Who said anything about an agency? What I'm talking about is consulting. I've done some homework on this. Plenty of opportunities, I think. Just a matter of making the right connections."

J.T. crunched the ice from his empty glass and sipped a little scotch from his new one. "How so?"

"Okay, well, let's say you're a lawyer and you got a claim. Not a rock-solid, drunk-city-bus-driver-ran-over-a-pregnant-neurologist, but a slip and fall. Maybe you know what the reserve is, you shape your offer one way; you know whether it's a no-consent policy, you make a different offer. You see where I'm going?"

J.T. nodded slowly and sipped his drink.

"Now, let's say you got access to a database that gives you every single settlement over the past ten years, with all the facts available—internal notes, the works. You think that's worth something?"

J.T. realized there was no sense telling him plenty of services already provided legitimate insurance settlement data. Sure, it would be nice to have GSAC's internal notes, but the poor bastard was going to hear crickets from the plaintiffs' bar.

"So you're talking about obtaining GSAC's files. Stealing their proprietary information."

"Nobody said anything about stealing."

"You didn't take it?"

"I didn't say that either. I just said nobody said anything about stealing."

"Sounds like you got all the moves figured out."

"Not all of them. Before I can set up my operation, I need to get a little grubstake first."

A gaggle of sweaty golfers drinking in the far corner broke into a collective guffaw. Seeing Frankie Fresh leaning over the table, slapping backs, his face flushing purple, reminded J.T. of his shattered windshield.

"Yeah, we could all use a little cash injection at that, couldn't we?" said J.T.

If it wasn't for George Bush and that stupid tort reform. It had really put him in an ideological bind. The Republicans were taking away his livelihood; the Democrats were taxing it away. If somebody didn't hurry up and invent another Agent Orange, the ass of J.T. Edwards was going to be fitted for a Chapter 7 sling.

"Shit, you're a lawyer," said Al. "What've you got to worry about?"

J.T. crunched some more ice and looked off into the distance. This guy couldn't begin to imagine J.T.'s nut. A strip mall in Norco he bought a few years ago sitting half empty and hemorrhaging money. Economy goes to hell and those shit-kickers just go to Little League games instead of restaurants. Ten grand a month alimony. A grand a month on the Mercedes out in the parking lot. Office rent on half a floor of the Inland Empire tower in Riverside. Still got to come up with campaign contributions for every judge from Calexico to Barstow. Claims hanging fire, some of them, for years now. Goddamn insurance companies doing their war-of-attrition bullshit.

"Believe me, pal, you ain't the only one could use a boost."

Another shout went up from the corner. The TV was replaying the Red Sox batter getting hit in the elbow by a pitch. The replay flashed over and over. In one shot, the camera zoomed in on the displaced flesh at impact; on another, the rictus on the batter's face.

Al waved at Wanda. "This one's mine," he said to J.T.

J.T. rolled a piece of ice around in his mouth. "So where are you getting this grubstake? You go to a bank?"

"Please. Those bastards are getting money interest-free from the Fed and you think they're lending any of it? Shit. They're just stuffing it into their mattresses, waiting for the next bubble. You go in with a legitimate business plan, they don't give you the time of day."

"Yeah, I'm not sure legitimate is the *mot juste* there."

"You know what I meant. Anyway," Al said, hunching forward over the table. "I do have an idea about a clean little transaction…."

THREE

The chatter from the corner grew louder as the TV showed the benches clearing after the Red Sox hitter charged the mound. The Angels' pitcher wrestled the batter to the ground within a frenzied scrum of uniformed players and coaches appearing agitated.

J.T. leaned back from the table. "So this transaction…."

"Watertight. Catch is…" Al looked around and lowered his voice. "I need somebody on the other side. Somebody dependable. Trustworthy."

"Need somebody for what?"

Wanda brought the steaks to the table. "Here you go, boys. You need anything, you let me know."

Al's eyes darted across the table to J.T. and up at Wanda. "I could use another," he said, shaking his glass.

"Same here," said J.T.

"Back in a jiff," Wanda said. She turned sideways to step among the maze of tables on her way back behind the bar.

"I told you I was a senior claims manager. Means I have two-hundred-thousand-dollar settlement authority. On my own."

"Is that right?" J.T. shifted in his seat.

"I got a roster of policyholders in a geographic area, I draw certain cases. Let's say, hypothetically, someone were to bring a claim for a soft-tissue injury. You with me so far?"

J.T. nodded. He looked at Wanda smiling as she approached, lifting first Al's vodka, then his own scotch from her tray. The glasses left dark circles on the tray's cork bottom.

"Here you go, gentlemen," said Wanda. She stood by the table, her arm relaxed with the tray at her side as she studied the batting statistics flashing on the screen.

Al looked at J.T., then at Wanda, then back to J.T.

"Could we get some ketchup for the fries, hon?" J.T. asked. "I'm sorry. I should've asked you when you went back for the drinks."

"Not a problem, señor," she said, and walked back to the bar for a bottle.

"You were saying," J.T. said.

"I was saying there's a nice, easy, untraceable buck to be made under the right circumstances."

Wanda returned, shaking a bottle of ketchup. "Anything else for you fellas?"

"No, thanks. I think we're good, sweetheart," said J.T.

Wanda hovered in the area, wiping off a table in big slow arcs as she watched the Angels run off the field for the bottom of the third.

J.T. looked at Al.

"Hey, Wanda?" said Al, scratching his chin. "On second thought, you think I could get a side salad with this?"

Wanda looked up, startled from her gazing at the game. "Sure thing. Be right back."

Once Wanda was out of earshot, J.T. raised his eyebrows.

"Okay, hypothetically now," Al continued, "let's say there's a victim injured in some minor accident on the property of one of GSAC's insured here in Riverside County. I'm not talking about maimed or paralyzed or anything, just your garden-variety soft-tissue injury."

"With all its attendant symptoms," said J.T.

"Your insomnia. Your nightmares. Physical therapy; pain and suffering. You got the idea."

"So were somebody to bring a case like this, you could guarantee a quick settlement?"

"You get the right policyholder, the right victim, and the right claim, yeah, I can guarantee a quick settlement."

J.T. chewed his lip. "And you've got two-hundred-grand settlement authority?"

"Hold on now. Yeah, technically I can sign off on that, but if I were to approve an obviously bullshit claim, there'd be FBI and half of Sacramento crawling around in my BVDs. My granddaddy used to say, 'Pigs get fat; hogs get slaughtered.'"

"So you got something different in mind," said J.T.

A few more old-timers stood up from their table, creaking and huffing, then hobbled out to the parking lot.

Al wiped his lips with a cocktail napkin. "I'm saying it's soft tissue. Whiplash. Strained meniscus. Some bullshit like that. That's not a two-hundred-thousand-dollar injury. But you get some good backstory? Maybe a doctor that'll play ball? Some way of building it up so there's a chance the fucking thing *might* go to trial? Maybe then you're looking at a buck and a quarter."

In spite of having skipped lunch, J.T. ignored the smell of the T-bone sizzling on his plate beneath sautéed mushrooms and onions. "So how do you see the settlement breaking down? That is, assuming you were able to find the right claim."

"Well, first off, the lawyer always gets his cut off the top, am I right?"

"I know this one does."

"Okay, let's say it's one twenty-five. Forty for the lawyer, maybe five for medical expenses. Maybe we get a couple of opinions, you know what I'm saying? Need to spread a couple bucks around. That leaves eighty. Half for the victim; half for me."

"So the victim only gets a third?"

"Only?" Al huffed. "He's not even hurt, remember? Soft tissue? Means it doesn't show up on an X ray. Keep him up for a couple of days before he sees the doc. Get an erratic heartbeat. Some dark circles under the eyes. Even a legit doctor will have to admit that's consistent with acute pain causing insomnia."

J.T. stretched his neck and looked at the screen across the room. A rangy guy in his twenties, blond hair parted down the middle, came in wearing dusty work boots, grease-streaked jeans, and a faded Mira Vista golf shirt. J.T. recognized him as the kid who worked in the greenskeeper's shed. The blond kid let the door swing closed just as another young guy was walking into the 19th Hole. Another maintenance guy. Black. The club manager didn't want maintenance staff in the place during the day, but on Friday nights he left early. With most of the members and daily-fee players gone, the staff in the 19th Hole looked the other way when the guys came in for beer or a hamburger.

Wanda approached carrying Al's salad on her cork-lined bar tray.

Al drained the last of the vodka in his glass. "Thing is, I don't have a lot of time to screw around. I'm stalling on this transfer thing, but if I get shipped up to Weed, I'm out of the loop. I need to move on this."

Wanda arrived at the table and put Al's salad down. "Blue cheese, right? You didn't say, but I remembered you ordered it before."

Al nodded. "Yeah, that's fine, thanks."

Wanda stood by the table. "I remember back when I was a paralegal, there was a lawyer used to order salad with blue-cheese dressing every single day without fail. Every time I smell it I think of that guy." She blew an invisible curl from her face and wiped her forehead with her wrist.

J.T. looked at her with a polite smile. She had nice skin. White, even teeth. Big dark eyes. Huge tits. She was too tall for him, but if she lost some weight she wouldn't be half bad.

"What do you think, guys?" she said. "One more round?"

"Sure, why not?" J.T. said, his smile widening.

She cocked her finger at him and started back to the bar.

Al poked at his salad with his fork. "So? What's the verdict, counselor?"

"I think I wish we had more time to set up a few of these."

"Unh-uh," said Al. "I'm one and done. I'm not looking to be greedy here. Just enough to get my grubstake and go out on my own."

"Where you'll be mining the database of Golden State's proprietary information."

"Beats the shit out of transferring up to Weed," Al said through a mouthful of salad.

J.T. was looking at the bar. The maintenance guys were on barstools, watching the game with the sound off. The white kid was nibbling something he'd pinched from the bar.

"So you got any thoughts on a potential dummy?"

Wanda approached again with her tray, trading fresh drinks for empties. As she turned around, she spied the white kid reaching over the bar and grabbing a handful of olives from the bartender's fruit tray.

"Hey!" Wanda shouted. "Get your grubby hands out of there!" The kid was laughing as Wanda approached and swatted him with a bar towel.

J.T. crunched the ice in his glass as he watched the tableau at the bar. "Maybe," he said. "Maybe."

When Wanda returned to clear the plates from the table, J.T. told her to buy the guys at the bar a round. She set two draft beers down on the bar and pointed at J.T. and Al in the corner. Both maintenance guys raised their glasses to J.T., who waved the pair over to the corner table.

"Thanks for the beers, sir," said the blond kid.

"Yeah, thanks, man," said the black kid.

"Hey, forget it. You guys been doing a great job." J.T. extended his hand. "J.T. Edwards."

Mack and Buddy took turns shaking hands with J.T. and Alvin. "Mack McMahon." Mack tilted his head toward the black guy. "This here's Buddy."

"You guys work on the carts, right?"

"Yes, sir. Carts, tractors, mowers, pumps, compressors... pretty much whatever needs doing, I guess."

"Yeah," said Buddy.

"Well, I see you fellas out there in that hot sun. I remember what it was like. I used to work outdoors myself back in the day," said J.T. "I know what it was to knock off on Fridays with a couple of cold ones."

"So what do you do, Mr. Edwards?" asked Mack.

"I'm an attorney." J.T. reached into his wallet and handed each of the young men his card.

Al stood up. "If you all will excuse me, I need to hit the men's room."

J.T. gave him half a wave. "So where you fellas from?"

"Van Horn, Texas," said Mack.

"Originally from Two Egg," said Buddy.

"Where?" said J.T.

"Two Egg. It's in Jackson County, Florida. We call it LA for 'Lower Alabama.'"

"You're a long way from home," said J.T.

"Yes, sir," said Buddy, sipping his beer. His eyes met J.T.'s, then he turned to look at the ball game on TV.

Al Boyle was washing his hands when the door opened and Frankie's presence filled the men's room.

"Whaddaya say, Al?" asked Frankie, moving toward the urinal. "Didn't expect to see you in here tonight. You said you got something for me?"

Al nodded. "Frankie." Al reached for his wallet and pulled out two twenties and a ten. "Yeah, had a date, but got stood up."

"That sucks." Standing at the urinal, Frankie leaned his head back and rolled his neck around.

"Yeah," Al said, and laid the bills on the counter. "Here you go."

Frankie zipped up and moved to the sink to wash his hands as Al crumpled up a handful of paper towels and lobbed them into the wastebasket.

"You want to get something down on the Belmont?" said Frankie, washing his hands. He nodded toward the fifty dollars on the counter. "Press?"

"Think I'm gonna pass. Thanks, though."

"You bet." Frankie chuckled as he dried his hands and scooped up the bills. "How 'bout that? Get it? *You bet.*"

"Yeah, Frankie, I get it," said Al as he opened the door to exit the men's room. "That's a good one."

J.T. waved at Wanda behind the bar and circled his hand for more drinks for the table. Wanda nodded and started drawing more beers.

Al stopped at the bar and intercepted his drink while J.T. talked to Mack and Buddy. He watched Wanda behind the bar. Beneath a pink men's golf shirt, the band of her bra was four inches wide across her back. As she went about replacing glasses above the bottles of liquor, Al noticed she didn't even have to stretch to reach the top shelf.

Frankie waddled up next to where Al stood, then plopped down onto a barstool and spun it around so he could watch the Angels game.

In spite of Frankie's company, Al was in no hurry to get back to the table. He didn't have anything against drinking with the maintenance guys. He was just nervous. He couldn't believe he'd actually spilled his idea to J.T., a complete stranger. He'd been thinking about it for years. How easy it would be with the right partners. He didn't want to think of the word *accomplices.* If it hadn't been for the vodka, he would never have had the guts to mention it. Then where would he be? Freezing his ass off in Weed fucking California, that's where.

He watched Wanda bend over and unhook an empty keg, tossing it out of the way like an Easter basket. She picked up the full replacement keg by one handle and then set it down to maneuver it into place beneath the tap. When she stood up, she grabbed the empty keg and walked back to the kitchen, the door swinging back and forth behind her.

Al noticed Frankie had turned to watch Wanda haul the empty keg away.

"Pretty girl," Frankie said, looking sideways over his shoulder. "Could stand to lose a few."

Al sipped his drink. *You fat fuck. Look like you swallowed a goddamned life raft and you're calling somebody fat?* "Yep."

Wanda came out from the kitchen. "You boys going to want anything else?"

Al looked at his watch. Then he glanced around at the guys at the table, all watching the last inning of the Angels game. The picture seemed a little doubled up, so Al squinted with one eye.

"No, we're all done here, I think," said J.T., who now looked at his own watch. "I need to get going anyway."

Mack and Buddy looked at each other and downed what remained of their beers as J.T. and Al pushed their chairs back from the table.

J.T. grabbed the check and gave it a quick glance. No one else made a move for it. He signed the tab and pulled a fifty from his money clip for Wanda.

"They ever give you guys a day off here?" J.T. said to Mack.

"Yes, sir," said Mack. "Usually Mondays."

"You interested in a little part-time work?"

"Yes, sir," said Mack.

"Why don't you come by my office on Monday morning? You know the Inland Empire Tower? Address is right there on the card."

"Sure. That sounds great," said Mack.

Buddy just nodded and didn't say anything.

J.T. gave Mack a wink and walked toward the door. Wanda thanked J.T. for the tip, patting him on the shoulder as he stepped into the warm night. Al followed, grabbing a handful of peppermints from a little basket at the corner of the bar.

When the door closed behind him, Al stepped a little quicker to catch up to J.T.

"You really thinking that's your plaintiff?"

"I'm thinking he's going to be fine. Mack, not Buddy. Buddy's too quiet. I suspect he's also probably a little sharper than Mack, which ain't saying a whole lot." J.T. opened the door to his black Mercedes, the cracked windshield shining white, a baleful snowflake in the darkness. "You see his eyes light up when he thought he might be able to make a little extra money? Probably thinks I want to hire him to shoot a porno for five hundred bucks."

"I can't believe we're even thinking about handing that retard forty grand."

"Nothing's set in stone yet. Let's just consider tonight a preliminary interview. We haven't said anything yet. We're not committed. Let's just see how things go on Monday."

"I don't know." Al was beginning to wonder if he'd moved too quickly. Was he giving away too much too soon? "Maybe we ought to rethink the splits."

"What we ought to think about is logistics."

Now Al started wondering if he might be getting in over his head. Beyond his basic layout of the plan, he'd never given a lot of thought to logistics. "For example?"

"Okay, at least a half-dozen people have seen us together tonight. I think we need to start approaching this like a couple of paranoids."

"What do you mean?"

"God forbid something comes loose, you and I can't have any connection. Okay, so we play golf at the same club. If somebody sees us together regularly, or if there are e-mails or phone calls that can be traced, I don't care what your signing authority is, GSAC will sniff out anything funky."

"Good point." *Of course.* Why hadn't he thought of that himself?

"Here's what we're gonna do. Invest in a couple of prepaid cell phones. Cheap ones. The kind you can use a couple times and throw away. Use cash."

"Jesus, what are you, a fucking Mob lawyer?"

"Should I be rethinking this project, Al?"

"No, no. You're right." Al's buzz was wearing off fast. "I guess things just got ramped up faster than I expected."

"Not too late to change your mind."

Al shook his head. "Fuck it. I'm good."

"What's your locker number?"

"My locker number? Eighty-four, why?"

"Mine's fifteen. We can use each other's lockers as dead drops. Wouldn't be suspicious at all if we're not in there the same time. I'll get a couple of SIM cards, and I'll pass you the numbers into your locker."

"Um, okay." Al's buzz was totally gone now. He had figured J.T. was as drunk as he was, but the guy was spinning out the plan like he was ordering breakfast at Denny's. *Has he done this before?*

"Never call my office or my real cell. Just use the temp phones. We ever need to meet, we can set it up on an ad hoc basis."

"Yeah, okay."

"I want to tell you to relax, but I don't think you should. From here on in, you need to be as alert as you can be." J.T. climbed into his car and lowered the window. "If the kid plays ball, I'll handle things on my end and keep you posted. Just let me know if anything changes."

Al jangled his keys in his hand. "Will do."

FOUR

As he charged the carts and pumped up the tires, all Mack could talk about was what kind of part-time work J.T. Edwards had in mind.

"Wonder if he's shootin' some kinda porno," Mack said to Buddy, who was hosing grass clippings off the carts coming in after early-morning rounds on Saturday.

"I don't know," said Buddy, who had bigger things on his mind.

While Mack flipped through truck magazines and fucked around with dune buggies, Buddy Cromartie had come up with a simple but elegant way to extract golf balls from lake bottoms—without diving. Deploying one of the same compressors they used to pump up golf cart tires, Buddy had rigged up an inflatable bladder. Empty, it could be cast out into a pond, or even dropped over the side of a johnboat, trapped inside a chicken-wire netting Buddy had fabricated himself. Weighted slightly, the netting would sink and spread; when the bladder inflated, the rising contraption would contract, scooping up all the balls on the lake bed as it did so. From there the operator just dragged the bladder to the shore or up over the gunwales of a johnboat.

"Maybe he needs, like, a courier or something. Like, deliver a big bag of cash down to Mexico. You see him tip Wanda a fifty?"

"Yeah."

Buddy had researched the going rate of "experienced" golf balls—balls lost, scavenged, and resold—in pro shops or online.

While golf-ball salvage began as a cottage industry for kids or geezers with unlimited time on their hands, at anywhere from twenty-five cents to a dollar retail, it was now big business. There were whole companies that specialized in diving for golf balls. He might have been from Two Egg, Florida, but Buddy Cromartie had a vision, and he was going to revolutionize a multimillion-dollar industry.

"Shit, man. Fifty bucks just for slingin' a few drinks? Sheeeiit. I bet anything he's got going's gonna have big dollars written all over it."

"Yeah, well, let me know what it turns out to be."

Buddy found this show, *Shark Tank* that ran just about all night every night on CNBC. He'd watched it the first time just because that rich motherfucker who owned the Dallas Mavericks was on there. After that episode, he was hooked. But the more he watched, the more questions he had. Should he patent his invention and then sell it to golf courses? Was there a ready client base with existing salvage companies? What about licensing to another manufacturer? On the show, that bald cat in the middle was always squealing about royalties. Should he take on one of those big golf-course management companies as a partner?

"You ain't coming?" said Mack.

"He was lookin' at you when he said come to his office. I don't think he meant me." Then there was the question of initial capital. Where would that come from? Nobody in his family had any money. He didn't even have a credit card.

"'Sides," Buddy continued, "I gotta take my auntie to the doctor on Monday for her diabetes."

"You don't want to change that? This could be a big ticket, brother."

"My mama'd shit if she ever thought I was makin' a porn movie, man."

Speaking of movies, should he put together a demonstration video? That could help sell it no matter which way he went.

"We don't know it's gonna be porno. That's just a theory. Could be something else. Maybe he needs, like, a fuckin' assistant or something."

"Maybe a lawyer needs two golf course maintenance men to be his assistants. Maybe he want to send us to fucking cooking school too, at the cool-i-nary institute." Buddy shook his head. "Bitch, please."

Dumbass always had his head in the clouds. Here Buddy was offering him a chance to get in *on the ground floor*, and this motherfucker's talking some foolishness about running guns or laundering money or some crazy shit.

"I still think you ought to check it out."

"Look here: you check it out for the both of us. He got some good-payin' gig, you can turn around and invest in my company."

And that was another thing. What was he going to call his contraption? *The ball grabber? The ball sack? Roboscrotum?*

He'd have to give this some thought.

Mack parked his Firebird, piebald with matte blotches of primer, in the covered lot at the Inland Empire Tower on Orange Street. He lifted his chin as the clicks of his boot heels echoed when he strode across the wide terrazzo floor. Looking around the lobby, empty but for a few modern-style chrome chairs and a security guard losing his struggle to stay awake, Mack thought about how this might be his new office. He smiled at a girl watering an eight-foot Ficus tree by the plate-glass lobby wall. He got on the elevator alone and pressed the button for the seventh floor.

When he stepped out of the elevator, the first thing he saw was a frosted-glass wall with EDWARDS & ASSOCIATES P.C. etched in some thick lettering that looked badass. He wondered if he was getting ready to be offered a job as an *associate*. That had a cool ring to it. A smoking-hot receptionist buzzed Mack in and told him Mr. Edwards was expecting him. She walked him down a hallway with some fucked-up art Mack was sure cost a fortune. The girl had long, thin legs. She smelled good too. Like lemonade.

The carpet sank in just a little when Mack stepped on it. Kind of like the fringe around the greens, he thought. A cream-colored crisscross pattern in the carpet hypnotized him as he watched the receptionist's pumps stride down the hall. After a couple of turns past empty offices, they came to the corner office of J.T. Edwards himself. Mack had never seen an office like this in real life. It was like *Dallas* or some shit.

"Glad you could make it," J.T. said, extending a hand. "Buddy didn't come with you?"

"No, sir. His aunt had some medical issues requiring him to attend to."

Mack knitted his brow in an effort to look composed and speak with what he figured should be his best grammar. He wondered if J.T. thought he was smooth enough to be EDWARDS & ASSOCIATES material.

"That's a shame," said J.T. "Just as well. You never know. There might be some possibilities in the future."

Mack declined the receptionist's offer of coffee.

"Coke?" asked J.T. "Water?"

"Do you all have any Dr Pepper by any chance? If not, then ice water will be satisfactorily," Mack said, returning the girl's smile.

"Thank you, Shari," J.T. said. He pointed to the overstuffed leather couch against the wall that looked out over the Inland Empire through a floor-to-ceiling smoked window. "Have a seat, Mack. Make yourself comfortable."

Mack sat down and gazed out the window. He wondered whether J.T. was going to sit on the couch. It hadn't even occurred to him that the guy might be gay. *Holy shit. No wonder Buddy didn't want to come. I bet that fucker picked up on some kind of signal the guy was giving out.* The door was still open. J.T. hadn't sat down yet. Besides, the girl still had to come back with his Dr Pepper. *Holy shit.*

"You look nervous," J.T. said.

"No, sir. Just not used to a view this high." *Nice recovery.*

The girl returned with a tall, thin, sweating glass of ice water. "Sorry. We didn't have any Dr Pepper. I can run down and get some, though, if you'd like."

"No, ma'am, that's okay." *I don't want you leaving the room, much less the building.*

"Thanks, Shari. That'll be all for now."

Shari backed out of the office and closed the door. Mack gulped his water. To his relief, J.T. didn't sit next to him on the couch, but in an overstuffed wing chair that matched the sofa. Mack swallowed his water and exhaled.

"So tell me," said J.T. "What do you like to do?"

Mack wasn't sure where this was headed, but then it occurred to him he was at least twenty years younger than J.T. and in a lot better shape. Shit went down, he'd be able to handle himself.

"I'm into lots of stuff, I guess. Like to go out in the desert. ATVs. Hang gliding. Skydiving. Whitewater rafting. Dirt bikes. Been building my own hybrid ATV in my spare time."

"Is that right?"

"What I really want to do is save up to get my pilot's license."

"Really?"

"Yes, sir. That'll be part of my plan."

"That's right, you mentioned the other night you had a plan. Can I ask what it is?"

"Yes, sir. Two words: Coast Guard."

J.T. nodded and rested his chin on his knuckle. "No kidding, the Coast Guard. Hunh."

"Yes, sir. *Semper Paratus*, that's their motto," said Mack. "Means 'Born Ready.' Kinda my own personal motto too."

"How about that. A man in uniform."

That sounds fucking weird. Mack just nodded back at J.T.

"And pilot's lessons, you say? I understand that's kind of expensive."

"Yes, sir. Been saving to get a new truck too. Kinda slow going."

"I see," J.T. said. "Let me ask you: Do you by any chance have any acting experience?"

Holy shit! It is *porno! I'll be goddamned. Better not be gay shit or I'm out of here.* "Um, no, sir. Not exactly."

"That's okay. Ever thought about it?"

"You mean like porno movies and stuff? I seen 'em. I guess if the setup was right..."

"I'm not talking about porn. I mean acting. Never in any plays in school or anything?"

"Not really."

"Here's the thing. I might be looking for someone to help me with a project. A lack of formal acting training isn't a drawback. In fact, just the opposite."

"Okay."

"If you ask me, it's a scandal what our military personnel are paid. I'd think a young man getting ready to put his life on the line for his country might be able to use a few bucks, you know what I mean?"

"Well, when you say 'a few bucks,' what are we talkin' about?"

"How does fifteen thousand dollars hit you?"

Like a big, sloppy blow job from a high school cheerleader. "Sounds pretty good to me, J.T."

FIVE

Al stopped by Mira Chiste after work. He pulled the small slip of paper with two phone numbers on it from his pocket. He'd bought two throwaway cell phones like J.T. had said. He didn't really understand why one wasn't good enough, but they were only twenty bucks, so he wasn't going to squawk. He went back and sat inside his car with the air conditioning on and called one of the numbers.

"Al?" said J.T.

"Yeah. So how'd it go?"

"Mack's in."

"He'll do it for forty?"

"Locked in," J.T. said, not missing a beat. "Now that we got our plaintiff lined up, we need to figure out who's going to be our defendant."

"Well, we've got a number of possibilities, but I think the best one is Van Slaters."

"The supermarket?"

"Massive reserves. So many locations, the corporate policy's huge."

"I'd have thought they'd be self-insured. Good for us, I guess."

"These guys get slip and falls, bullshit claims for dead mice in their cornflakes, fingertips in the hamburger, you name it. Unless it's one of the managers cornholing the bagboys, they just want us to handle it fast and keep the premiums down."

"You think slip and fall's the way to go? I mean, remember, this kid's in pretty good shape. Told me he's joining the fucking Coast Guard. Might be a tough sell."

Al turned down the air conditioning in the car. He wished he'd thought to stop and bring a beer with him. "I was thinking more like the parking lot."

J.T. was silent on the other end. Al could tell he was using his personal-injury abacus to calculate a plausible scenario.

"Shopping carts," J.T. said.

"They stack those things up, they could get pretty heavy. A big cluster breaks away…gets a little momentum, could easily knock you into a car…knock you down, run over your ankle."

"You ever get a claim like that before?"

"I did a search on the database. We've had a couple over the years. Once with an old lady. Once with a little black kid. Can get some nice bruising for pictures, but a kid like Mack could probably flop and make it look good."

J.T. sighed. "You did a search on the database."

"Uh-huh."

"On your computer."

"Yeah."

"What did I tell you about being paranoid?"

Fuck! Fucking shyster was right. This was careless. This could get him busted. "Shit. I'm sorry, man. I'm not used to this."

"Listen, here's what you're going to do," said J.T. "You're going to go back and do a shitload of searches. Make sure the searches are for old ladies and black kids, you got it?" J.T. sighed loudly into the phone. "Anybody ever asks any questions, you were being proactive. Looking into patterns involving black minors. Looking for trends involving elderly claimants."

"Okay."

"You gotta do a shitload of searches, you hear? It's got to look like the ones you saw just happened to be part of a bigger research project you were doing on your own. Like you were going to write a report or something."

"Sure, okay."

"Do searches for nursing homes, fast-food joints, shopping malls—anywhere there's likely to be lots of old people or little kids, you got it?"

"Okay, I got it." Fuck, this guy was patronizing.

"Let me tell you, this gets fucked up, it's not going to end well, you hear me? I need to know you're one hundred percent on board with what I'm talking about. Para-fucking-noid. You got me?"

"I got you. It won't happen again." Al wanted a quick excuse to change the subject. "Where are we with the doc?"

"I've got a couple of prospects. Need to go back and see who owes me some favors and evaluate."

Al could hear the sound of J.T. clacking away on a keyboard.

"Rotate between phones," said J.T., "yours and mine. I'll check my locker once a day too."

"Okay." Al hung up, deflated. He was pissed at being yelled at by a fucking PI lawyer. Then he felt wet under his armpits. J.T. was right. He was risking going to jail for a lousy forty grand. If they were lucky.

Which they wouldn't be if he didn't start thinking like a scumbag.

J.T. scrolled through his computer. He'd helped out Dr. Mel Phillips with his divorce, suggesting casino chips offered an excellent way to shelter liquid assets. Especially with the Cabazon reservation being just down the 10…didn't even need to arouse suspicion with a trip to Vegas anymore.

He'd lined up expert testimony depositions for Dr. Jeff Cashdan, which was basically free money. J.T. had gotten an injunction against a developer who'd planned to create a subdivision from an orange grove adjacent to Dr. Charles Barber's property. He'd gotten Dr. Willis Thompson off on a second DUI by digging up e-mails from the breathalyzer manufacturer that suggested the machine's readings became less reliable when a patient was obese. He'd put the doc on a steady diet of french fries for two weeks before the evidentiary hearing.

J.T. looked at all these doctors as owing him a favor, but none of them was the kind to approach with this situation. It occurred to J.T. that in spite of the fact that there were now plenty of women practicing medicine, they didn't get sued nearly as often as male doctors. They never went to jail for selling their script pads. Probably because they weren't stupid enough to be degenerate gamblers, drug addicts, or sex fiends themselves.

Which brought him to Sonu Chugh, MD. He'd helped Dr. Chugh close a quick settlement after his receptionist claimed he was walking around her desk with his dick hanging out of his fly. Fucking idiot didn't realize cell phones had cameras in them now.

J.T. made an appointment with Dr. Chugh's office, complaining of a mysterious GI condition. He noticed the new receptionist on duty was every bit as alluring as her predecessor, the one who'd charmed the dusky cobra from the Karachi-born loins of Sonu Chugh.

After taking J.T.'s blood pressure, a still-sexier nurse told J.T. to take off his trousers and wait for the doctor. J.T. ignored her and kept his pants on and hopped up on the paper-covered examining table.

"Johnny!" cried a smiling Chugh as he entered the examination room. "How are you? All is good?"

"All good, Doc. How's the practice?" No sense wasting time.

"Ack! My partners. They steal from me!" He shook his head. "From *me*!"

"It's a hell of a thing when a healer like yourself can't even depend on his fellow physicians to do the right thing."

"The right thing, yes! It is not the right thing, Johnny, the way they steal from me."

J.T. nodded, trying to muster all the empathy he could fake.

"So tell me, you are having gastrointestinal distress? Did you bring a stool sample?"

I'm looking at one. "No, not this time." J.T. felt like an idiot sitting on the table, so he hopped down and leaned in toward Chugh. "Actually, I was wondering if I might be able to refer a patient your way."

"Of course, of course. Always have time to examine a friend of yours."

"This friend of mine…he doesn't use insurance."

"So you have friends on Medi-Cal, Johnny? I am surprised by this."

"No, no, nothing like that." God, he hated being called Johnny. "It's just that my friend likes to pay cash." J.T. leaned in still closer toward Chugh. "That won't be a problem, will it? I mean, your billing department is set up to handle a cash payment, right?"

Sonu Chugh, MD, sniffed and cleared his throat. He threw a quick glance over his shoulder to make sure the door was closed. "Most of our billing is done with credit cards and insurance. But you're a good friend, so I'm happy to make an exception for you." Big smile. "Just have your friend bring the cash with him and tell the receptionist you referred him."

"That's great, thanks."

J.T. shook hands with Chugh and made his way toward the door of the examination room.

"Not at all, Johnny. Not at all. May I ask what is the nature of your friend's medical issue?"

J.T. opened the door and turned around to face Chugh. "Tell you the truth, Doc, I'm not altogether sure myself."

SIX

J.T. swung by Mira Chiste after leaving Chugh's office. He couldn't help but notice Frankie's empty Navigator idling in the parking lot just to keep the air conditioning running.

J.T. had picked up a few toiletries, giving him a pretense for stopping in the locker room just in case anyone was watching. He knew he was being a little over the top, but better too much than too little. He couldn't afford to slip up. Bad enough he was up to his armpits in half-wits. He never got used to it.

He opened the wooden door of his locker. No note from Al. He left the bag of deodorant and talcum powder on the shelf and locked up the cabinet. He looked through the mesh screen and complimented himself on the idea of using the club's lockers as a dead drop.

Wanda was working when he stopped in the 19th Hole for a club sandwich and a beer. She gave him a big smile and almost hugged him when he sat on the barstool. J.T. hoped it hadn't been a mistake to give her such a big tip. Thirty bucks would've been a phenomenal tip on that check, but J.T. had wanted the kid to notice, and the fifty had done the trick.

J.T. watched Frankie Fresh make the rounds. Laughing at this table; whispering at that. The whole time, all J.T. could think about was the fat fuck's Navigator out in the parking lot burning five gallons of gas an hour. That, and when Al had stepped up with the fucked-up windshield.

Finishing his beer, J.T. signed his check for Wanda. He couldn't drop fifty every time he had a club sandwich, but it didn't cost that much to be a hero. He duked her a ten and grabbed a peppermint on his way out the door, passing Frankie on the way as the walking goiter thundered toward the locker room.

Steve Estep, the club's pro, bumped into J.T. in the parking lot, and the two exchanged banalities for a couple of minutes before J.T. climbed into his Mercedes. As he dropped the car into gear and began backing out of the parking space, one of his cell phones reserved for Al rang. He pulled the car back into the space and picked up the phone.

"Hey, Al. What's up?"

"What?"

It wasn't Al. What the fuck was going on?

"This ain't Al, it's Frankie. Who's this?"

J.T. looked into the rearview mirror and saw Frankie plodding through the door and into the parking lot and holding a tiny black cell phone against his ear with his fat, fleshy hand.

J.T. didn't even breathe. He clicked off the phone. What had that fucking idiot done now? J.T. could no longer hear Frankie, but he could see him talking into the phone, looking at it as if that would somehow make it work. J.T. slipped the SIM card from the phone and bent it back and forth like an expired credit card. Frankie had nearly reached the still-running Navigator. J.T. backed the Mercedes out of the parking lot and headed up Gilman Springs Road.

When he got to the 60, the Pomona Freeway, he lowered his window and flicked the mangled SIM card onto the road. He drove for a few minutes, vacillating between pissed off and terrified. Even after the beer and lunch, he felt wired, like he'd just had a half-dozen espressos. He pulled off the 60 and into the big outdoor mall in Moreno Valley. He drove to Staples and bought a couple more phones, paying cash. Then he went back to the car and called Al. The banging sounds of the fumbled phone on the other end confirmed J.T.'s hunch that Al was at his desk.

"Hello?"

“What the fuck is going on?”

Al sputtered on the other end. “What? What? What are you talking about?”

“I just got a call on one of the dedicated phones. There’s one person in the entire world who has that number, Al. You. What I want to know is, why did that fat fucking Frankie Fresh call me on that number?”

“What?”

“You say that a lot, you know it?”

“Wait a minute. Frankie called you on one of those phones? Are you sure?”

“I was at the club. My phone rang. He was on the other end. I fucking saw him while he was talking.”

“I gotta go. I’ll call you back in five minutes.”

Al felt like pliers were gripping his aorta. He stuffed the phone in his pocket and stalked out to the GSAC parking lot and into his Camry, where he called J.T.

“J.T.?”

“What’s the deal, Al?”

“Did you get my note?”

“What note?”

“The note I left in your locker.”

A Nissan 4x4 pulled up behind Al. Al’s heart jumped, but the pickup backed into an empty spot in the next row of cars.

“There was no note in my locker. I was just there fifteen minutes ago.”

“I put a note in there. Van Slaters, Moreno Valley.”

“There was no note.”

“I wrote it on the back of the number you gave me.”

“You’re not hearing me. There was no note. Why is Frankie Fresh calling me?”

The truck door slammed. The driver locked the door with the key fob and Al jumped again at the beeping sound.

"Al…what number locker did you put the note in?"

"Fifty, like you said."

J.T. didn't know whether to laugh, scream, or have a contract put out on Al. He took a deep breath and counted to five. "Al?"

"Yeah?"

"I said fifteen. Locker number fifteen, Al—one-five."

"Oh, shit."

"I'm sorry, but I'm out. I can't be dragged into a clusterfuck like this."

"Wait. Don't do anything, okay? Let me call you back tonight."

"Again, you're not hearing me. This is a fucking goat-rope."

"Listen, please. Just wait until I get off. I'll call you after work." Al's voice cracked. "Please. I'll call you later."

J.T. hung up.

Al was sweating through his shirt. He'd been in such a hurry, he hadn't started the car or turned on the air conditioning. It was stifling inside the Camry. There was no air. He couldn't breathe. He opened the door and swung his legs out. He put his head between his hands and bent over. He thought he might throw up. He sat up and took deep breaths. He couldn't keep his attention on anything for more than a second. He looked around the parking lot. Was anyone watching? He thought about the company. Seventeen years and he was pissing it away. He ought to be grateful they wanted him. Weed wasn't Kazakhstan or Angola. *Angola. Prison.* Jesus, he'd be going to prison if this got fucked up. Maybe J.T. was right. Maybe they needed to pull the plug before this took them all down.

Al got out of the car and took another deep breath. He started walking—soaked—back to the office. *Hold on.* What was really the big deal? *So Frankie called a number. So what?* It wasn't like he knew who he was calling. J.T. would've thrown the phone away immediately anyway. It was a wakeup call, that's all. No harm, no foul. He'd have to be more careful, though. God, he hated J.T. being right. He could be a smug fuck. He was no dummy, though.

Al thought about the serendipity of meeting J.T. in the first place. Al had seen J.T. around the course before—the big black Mercedes parked across two spots in the club's lot; the bag tags from Congressional and Whistling Straits and Pinehurst No. 2 dangling from a tawny ostrich-skin bag left conspicuously in front of the pro shop.

Al was almost all the way back into the building when his cell phone rang. His personal cell phone. He looked at the number, and once again his pulse shot to the redline.

"Hello?"

"Hiya, Al," said Frankie Fresh. "We need to talk."

"Yeah, it's actually not a great time."

"Maybe you'd rather we met at the Van Slaters in Moreno Valley?"

Shit. "Listen, Frankie, I'm at the office now. I can't talk."

"And yet I've got a feeling you know what a huge fucking mistake it would be not to show up at the 19th Hole tonight. Seven?"

Al buried his eyes in his left hand and wiped his sweating face. "Yeah."

SEVEN

Al stopped by a 7-Eleven after work and bought another phone and a six-pack of Coors Light, then drove back to Moreno Valley to check out the Van Slaters parking lot.

Traffic passed along the 60 like a kidney stone. Al made sure to check the rearview every time he took a sip of his beer. He usually wasn't one for drinking behind the wheel, but goddamn if he wasn't wrung out from this afternoon. He needed to get his head right before he talked to J.T. He didn't even want to think about Frankie.

When Al pulled into the parking lot at Van Slaters, he remembered that he'd been there before. It was in a little run-down strip mall off Perris Boulevard. The sun had bleached the asphalt wasp-nest gray. Al cruised the lot in a slow lap around and parked off by himself in the middle. He finished his beer and opened another. There were more shopping carts in the parking lot than cars.

The lot sloped on a very gentle grade southward from Sunnymead. Al looked around at the other storefronts in the strip mall. A pawnshop. A martial arts studio. A craft store. A brake shop at the west end of the lot next to a Valley Lube oil change station. A black kid in a maroon vest came out of the store pushing a cart for an old white lady. He loaded three bags into the trunk of her Impala, then pushed the empty cart to a pod of other carts thirty feet away. The kid bunched the carts together, pointed them toward the grocery store, and gave them a shove. Just as Al had imagined, the carts picked up momentum from the slope. The kid trotted a few steps to catch up to them, then jumped up on the axle of the last cart and rode them across the pavement. The lot flattened and then rose slightly, blunting the momentum of the carts, and the kid hopped off and pushed them the rest of the way to the sidewalk in front of the store.

Al looked at the spot where the carts had been moving fastest. A big crack in the asphalt crossed two parking spaces directly parallel to the sidewalk where it ended on the west side. He wanted J.T. to have Mack park in the best place to sell the runaway cart story. The guy was such a dumbass, Al wondered if maybe he should get out and paint a big fucking **X** on the spot.

He took a swig of his beer and called J.T. from his new phone.

"Hey, it's Al."

"What a refreshing change."

Fucking smartass. "Listen, I'm sorry about the confusion on the lockers. In my defense, it could've happened to anyone."

"I'm just not sure you appreciate the gravity of what fucking this thing up will mean."

"I hear you, but let's hold on a second. First of all, you didn't tell Frankie it was you on the phone, did you?"

"Of course not."

"You shit-canned the phone too, didn't you?"

"Yep."

"Okay, so before we throw away what I still think is a viable score, let's assess what the real damage is. Frankie called a number that no longer exists. He doesn't know who answered. No one told him anything. We're out one phone. That's it."

"The problem is that I'm walking around barefoot, and every time I turn around, you're breaking glasses on the floor."

Al thought about that for a minute and tried to understand what it meant.

"What I mean is, I can't afford to get wrapped up in a clusterfuck that's going to send us to prison. Not for forty grand, not for forty million."

"Hey, this is a learning curve for me. I hear what you're saying, I really do. Things are going to be smoother now, I guarantee it. I bought a new phone to add to the rotation. I'm actually at the Van Slaters parking lot now."

"You are?"

"It's perfect. There's a grade on the parking lot that slopes down toward the store. Three or four carts together breaking away can build up enough speed to knock even a guy like Mack down."

J.T. was silent on the other end.

"J.T.?"

"I'm thinking."

Al gulped his beer. His eyes zipped around the parking lot, desperate for some inspiration for how he was going to deal with that goof Frankie Fresh.

"There cannot be any more fuckups or surprises," said J.T.

"Hey, I'm on top of it. You just need to make sure your end is good. You talked to the doc?"

"He'll play ball."

"What about Mack?"

"He's got dollar signs in his eyes. I thought about this from every angle, though. We need to bring in Buddy to set the wheels in motion. Literally."

"Jesus, really? Are you sure? I don't know, J.T. How comfortable are you with another person being in on this?"

"Without somebody to push the carts, it's going to be an inexplicable flop in the parking lot. Buddy goes in, buys some groceries, and parks near a cluster of carts at the top of the slope. He puts his cart with a couple of others, gives it a push toward Mack fifty feet away, and drives off. Mack's got his back turned, cart bumps him from behind and knocks him over the trunk or the hood or whatever. Big mess. He yells and writhes on the ground for a while. Night manager comes out—"

"You're thinking do it at night?"

"Harder to make Buddy in case someone's in the lot. Harder to tell it's not an accident. Night manager's less experienced than a day manager, so that's a break. Might even be a woman, which could help us."

"Okay."

"So Mack causes a big scene, but leaves under his own power. We get EMTs involved, we lose control."

"Gotcha."

"Next day, he meets with the doc, and our demand letter goes out the day after."

"And the doctor's solid? No fraud shit in his background?"

"I represented him a year and a half ago on an employment matter. He's a perv, but nothing out there to raise suspicion."

Al watched another bag boy ride a shopping cart down the slope toward the store. "So when are you looking to go?"

"Tomorrow night. Going to go over the script with Mack and then we're good." J.T. sniffed. "Assuming, that is, no more fuckups."

"Hey, enough already. I got it." *Prick.*

"All right, then. I'll be in touch when it's done," J.T. said, and hung up.

Al finished his second beer, started the engine, and got back up on the 60. It was time to go deal with Frankie.

EIGHT

Al walked into the 19th Hole and scanned the room for signs of Frankie Fresh. The guy was the size of a Cape buffalo, so it wasn't like he could be missed in an eight-hundred-square-foot room.

Wanda brought a Coors Light and a cheeseburger to Al's table in the corner opposite the TV. Seven o'clock and not a dopey bookmaker in the room. Just as he was thinking he might have caught a break, the door opened and the entrance filled with the flabby mass of Frankie Fresh, who gave Al a big wave and lumbered toward his table.

Jimmy Flynn, a retired Air Force colonel watching the game from the bar, intercepted Frankie as he walked by and clapped the porcine bookmaker on the back.

"Hey, Frankie, you on TV now?"

"TV?"

"Yeah. I saw an ad for a show. *Thirty Stone*."

Frankie threw his head back and laughed, his pelican gullet bobbing up and down. Jimmy clapped him on the back again and Frankie shook his head as he resumed his waddle toward Al's table.

"That looks good," Frankie said to Wanda as he pointed to Al's cheeseburger. "How 'bout you bring me one of those too, hon? Basket of onion rings on the side? Mug of Heineken?"

Wanda nodded and walked back to the kitchen.

Al cleared his throat as Frankie pulled out his chair. "Frankie."

"Hiya, Al, whaddaya say?" Dark symmetrical crescents of perspiration formed on Frankie's golf shirt beneath his man boobs.

"You called me, remember?"

"I did, didn't I?" Frankie leaned in and picked a french fry from Al's plate. "You mind?"

"Knock yourself out."

Frankie pulled out a chair, the wood creaking as he filled the seat. "Found a note in my locker this afternoon."

"Is that right?" Al lifted his chin and cracked the joints in his neck as Frankie started picking fries two at a time from Al's plate.

"So on one side of this note, it says 'Van Slaters' and 'Moreno Valley,' and on the back there's a phone number."

"How about that?"

"Yeah, so I call the number, and a guy says, 'Hi, Al.' Just that. 'Hi, Al.'"

"That's quite a story."

Wanda set a foaming mug of beer in front of Frankie. "Food'll be right up, Frankie."

"Thanks, hon." A few locks of strawberry-blond hair stuck to sweat still beading on Frankie's forehead. He sipped his beer as he watched Wanda return to the kitchen. "So here's what I'm thinking, Al: I'm in for a taste."

"What are you talking about?"

"Look, I know everybody sees the spare tire and thinks I'm some kind of glutton, but I'm really only looking for a taste."

"A taste of what? I don't know what you're talking about."

Frankie sipped his beer again. He wiped a few bubbles of foam from his lip with the underside of his thumb. "I know you're not a degenerate gambler like a lot of bums I take action from. You're a straight shooter. No crying about being short this week, none of that. So even though I don't know you well, I always had a kind of respect for you as a stand-up guy, a guy who settles up, you know what I mean?"

"Thanks."

Wanda set the food in front of Frankie, who had by this point consumed nearly half of Al's fries. She disappeared behind the bar without a word.

"But here's the thing. The world is divided up into zones, territories—call 'em whatever you like. Riverside County's a zone inside California. California's a territory inside the U.S. The U.S. is part of North America, you get me?"

"Not really. Where's this heading?"

"You got something going in my zone."

"What are you talking about?"

"I seen you the other night with that shyster, what's his name...Edwards, and those two mutts from the greenskeeper's shed." Frankie unscrewed the cap on the ketchup. "I get an anonymous note. Probably a mistake, but whatever." Frankie pounded the bottle until fat splats of ketchup coated his steaming onion rings. "I got a strange phone number; I call it and somebody's expecting you. On the phone with you, I drop the line about Van Slaters, Moreno Valley, and you don't even flinch."

Frankie popped a slimy red onion ring into his mouth. "Now look at me. Look past the weight. Look past the fat and tell me: Do you see a fucking dumbass?"

Al had never liked Frankie. He loathed Frankie's love of hopeless puns and hated how he giggled at his own lame jokes and banal observations. He was four or five clicks past morbidly obese and laughed about it. Before Frankie sat down at the table, had anyone asked whether Al thought he was a dumbass, Al would've said sure, no question. But there was no Celtic twinkle in Frankie's blue eyes. There was no mirth in his taut grin. All at once Al realized the bluff hail-fellow-well-met act was bullshit. Under the now-dimming lights, Al had a sickening revelation: Frankie McElfresh was a dangerous guy.

"Frankie, I don't—"

"Before you insult my intelligence and tell me again you don't know what I'm talking about, I want you to think about something." Frankie sipped his beer and smacked his lips as he put the mug back on the coaster. "I'm a small-time bookie, okay? I take bets in a semipublic golf course in broad daylight. We got law enforcement and retired law enforcement in here all the time." Frankie picked up a pair of onion rings and took a bite. "It ever occur to you that nobody seems to fuck with me?"

Al thought about that.

Frankie kept picking at the ketchupy onion rings. "The reason nobody fucks with me is because just like Riverside County is a zone within California, my little turf or whatever is a zone within the territory of a guy named Vincenzo Fegangi. This is a name you've heard."

Al had. As Vincenzo Fegangi, the owner of Alimena Trucking was just another old guy with a modest business in San Bernardino. As Vinnie Fangs, his "friendships" in Los Angeles were mutually profitable arrangements affording him a comfortable home in Rancho Mirage and a healthy skim of bookmaking in the Inland Empire. Collecting on Super Bowl or Final Four bets was rarely a concern. People who crossed Vinnie Fangs wound up fed to hogs or stuffed in drums of industrial solvents. Vinnie Fangs was a man even scarier than his nickname.

Not only could Al not speak, he couldn't even open his mouth. He was no longer looking at the elephantine Frankie Fresh as a half-witted bookie but now, under the still-dimmer light, as a very thick spoke in a wheel of organized crime.

"So, Al," continued Frankie, putting his heavy mitt on Al's shoulder, "I'm not telling you this because I want you to be uncomfortable. Just the opposite. I want you to appreciate the realities of the situation so that *everybody's* comfortable, okay?"

"Okay."

"Now," Frankie smiled, "what's the scam?"

"It's small-time, Frankie. No shit." Al tried to swallow. He reached for his beer, but Frankie laid his hand on Al's forearm.

"There'll be time for that in a minute. You were saying?"

"Look, I'm a square, okay? I bet a game or a horse race here and there, but like you said, I'm no degenerate gambler. I'm just a nine-to-fiver."

"My ass is starting to go to sleep over here."

"Okay. I'm out the door at the insurance company where I work. We got one little slip-and-fall score so I can get some cash before I get laid off. That's it, I swear."

Frankie rolled his neck around. He looked at Al and didn't say anything.

"It's strictly a one-off. A small-time bump."

"How small are we talking?"

"Like nothing. Like…" Al paused. He knew Frankie would demand a piece, but the piece would be smaller if the score was smaller. "Like twenty-five, thirty grand tops—for everybody."

"Jesus."

"What?"

"After the whole speech about insulting my intelligence and everything, you're gonna play a game like that with me? C'mon."

"What?"

"First of all, your shyster buddy, Edwards? Crooked as that fuck is, he ain't about to risk his license and going to the can for even half that, much less a third, is what I got him figured for. You might be that stupid, but he ain't."

Al tried to swallow again as he watched beads of condensation sliding down Frankie's beer mug.

"Second of all, that skel ain't got two nickels to rub together, so he can't take his eye off the ball for some shitty ten-grand score."

"What do you mean? He's broke?"

"You didn't know that? Fucking guy's got half a floor of the Inland Empire Tower and not a single attorney working there.

His 'associates'? They all jumped over a year ago. He doesn't have a debt under a hundred and eighty days past due, and he owes everybody from the copier guys to court stenographers. Two ex-wives taking him to court for back alimony." Frankie separated half his cheeseburger in one bite. "Yeah, ten grand's not going to make a dent with that slob."

"Okay, it's just that—"

"And Al?" Frankie wiped the corners of his mouth with his napkin and raised his eyebrows. "Make sure you don't lie to me again, okay, pal?"

"A hundred grand," Al said. "That's the score." He wasn't really lying, he told himself. They hadn't filed anything yet, and there was still a chance it might be a hundred. At least this way, if they got north of a hundred K, Al could skim a little. Fat fucking Frankie Fresh. Goddamnit.

"See? That wasn't so hard was it?" Frankie took his hand off Al's arm. Al reached for his beer it and gulped like a man stumbling out of the desert. Frankie smiled and massaged Al's shoulder. The enormous bookie plucked another goopy red onion ring from the basket with his free hand while he kept kneading Al's trapezius.

"Okay, here's my proposal." Frankie pulled his hand from Al's shoulder and wiped his fingers on his green linen napkin. "And by proposal, I mean explanation." He wiped the napkin across his mouth. "Now, a standard finder's fee is ten percent, but I'm a reasonable guy, so I'm only going to take eight."

Al set his beer down and started to speak. "But—"

"Now, before you say anything, I want you to just think of two things. One, just think of me as a partner, okay?" Frankie smiled. "And two, ask yourself whether Vinnie Fangs will be satisfied with eight grand out of a hundred-grand scam on his territory. A scam you plotted and planned to execute without his permission or knowledge." Frankie took another huge bite of his cheeseburger and again wiped his mouth with the napkin he pulled from his lap.

Al felt like his head was in a vise. "Got it." His appetite was gone.

"See? It's going to be a good deal all around. In fact, here's what I'm going to do. I'm going to front you the cash for incidentals and expenses to keep things moving smoothly."

"What do you mean?"

"I mean if it's a slip and fall, I know the ambulance chaser's got to be paying off some doctor, am I right?"

Al's eyes shifted left to right. He looked into his beer as he brought the glass to his lips.

"That's what I thought. So seeing as how that asshole's flat broke, and the last thing you want is to stiff the piece of shit that could blow up the whole scam, I say make sure the doc gets paid."

"Makes sense." *God, just get me out of here.*

Frankie tossed a thick envelope on the table. "Here's five grand. Point-a-week vig on top of first dollar return of the principal. That's on top of my eight points at the back end. You can tell Clarence Darrow the vig gets paid weekly. No sense you footing the bill alone for an expense that ultimately benefits everyone, am I right?"

"Yeah." *Now, God. Please just get me out of here right now.*

"There you go. We'll just settle up the points and the principal when the check gets cut."

Al pushed his chair back from the table. "So, Frankie, are we all done here? I kind of got some stuff I need to do."

"Sure, Al, sure." Frankie clapped Al on the shoulder, then pointed to the remaining fries on Al's plate.

"You gonna eat those?"

NINE

Al took the envelope with the cash back to the locker room and counted it. Five grand. His breathing became shallow. Sweat rolled down his sides from both armpits. He felt like he was getting some kind of rash on his right side. *Vinnie Fangs. Jesus Christ.* A stupid fucking slip and fall now had him one degree removed from a guy who made Vlad the Impaler look like Don Zimmer. Scam or no scam, Al wanted no part of Frankie's $5,000 on him. *Jesus. Vinnie Fangs. Fuck it. Let J.T. do some worrying for a change.*

Al went to locker fifteen. He'd never make that mistake again. He ran his hand across the locker door. There was no way he could slide the envelope between the cracks, and no way he was going to roll up fifty hundred-dollar bills and push them one by one through the holes in the mesh screen. He stood up on the bench and looked over the top of the lockers. There were ventilation slits, but still not big enough to stuff the envelope through. His hair felt damp, like he'd played twenty-seven holes wearing a rubber hat.

He hopped off the bench. His pulse was throbbing. How stupid had this been? Why not just call it off? He opened Frankie's envelope. Once he got on the other side of this, he'd never need to be involved with guys like Frankie again.

Al took one last look at J.T.'s locker. He felt around the mesh screen. At the top right corner, the screen was detached from the door. It wasn't much, but when Al pushed it, it gave way. He thought he heard someone coming. No, just a noise from the hallway. He pushed the screen in and bent the wire mesh backward. It was tight, but he was able to squeeze the envelope through. He heard it land at the bottom of the locker. Using his car key, he bent the mesh back into place and pulled the screen almost exactly to where it had been before.

The following morning, Al, cautious now to camouflage his research, had crunched some more numbers. The highest soft-tissue settlement he'd been able to find anywhere was $122,000. One twenty-five was going to be cutting it too close for Al. He called J.T.

"Listen, we've got a little issue. Nothing major, but we're going to have to rework out numbers a bit."

"Okay, you've got my attention. Don't lose it."

"I was able to do some more research on our claim on the computer of a new kid we're training. I made it look like a random session. No worries about it being traced back to me."

"Okay, now you're thinking. What does that have to do with the numbers?"

"The settlement's going to have to be more conservative."

"What? Why? You said you could settle it for a buck and a quarter."

Al knew if he told J.T. about Frankie, he'd freak. Al was freaked himself. He'd decided just to build Frankie's end into the payout, then settle it a little higher at the last minute. Frankie would be taken care of, and J.T.'s expectations would be managed. He'd have to tell him about Frankie eventually, but not until GSAC cut the check.

"First of all, you're the one that's preaching paranoia twenty-four-seven, so just hang on. This research I did? Turns out the highest we've ever paid out on a claim like ours is..." Al hesitated just a second. "One fifteen." He wondered if J.T. had caught it.

"Shit," said J.T. "that does suck, because I got some bad news too."

"What?"

"You know how we budgeted five K for the doc?"

"For the doc and *all* the incidental expenses."

"Yeah, well, I thought I could get him to do it for four. He wants six."

"Are you kidding? Six grand for one exam?"

"Well, yeah, but remember, that includes X rays, depositions, courtroom testimony, and everything else. Remember, a straight doc's going to push for an MRI. Even if Mack's on Medi-Cal, a legit MRI's going to show it's a bullshit claim."

"Fuck," said Al. There went more of the margin. "I was only able to come up with five." No sense freaking J.T. out as to where the money came from. "I already left it in your locker last night. Should we try to get another doc?"

There was a pause. Could J.T. have figured out where the money came from? Of course not. That was just more of his surging paranoia.

"At this point? No way. First off, the guy knows something's up—he could come back at us for the cash anyway. Also, we may need a second opinion, and I have a finite number of pervert MDs I can go to."

J.T. was jumpy all afternoon. He told Shari, the receptionist he couldn't afford, that he'd be gone for the day. With a quarter of a tank in the Mercedes, he'd be able to get out to Mira Vista to hit a bucket of balls, maybe play a quick nine, and still make it back to the house. He decided he'd finally sit down that night with a bottle of wine and sort out what must be $1,500 in change he'd accumulated in various jars and urns. Hadn't paid his quarterly taxes in a year. Still, he wasn't lonely enough to plug in his home phone just to talk to collection agents. If he could only hang on a few more weeks.

He'd already started pulling off his shirt when he opened his locker and saw the envelope fall to the floor. It was too thick to have squeezed through any slits or holes on the cabinet door. *How the fuck did he get it in there?* Reflex made him look around the locker room, but the place was empty. He sat on the bench and picked up the envelope. *Five grand. What do you know?* The putz had really come through with some expense money. This was a terrific development, because he hadn't figured out how he was going to pay Chugh for Mack's exam. Problem solved.

Once he'd changed into shorts and a golf shirt, he no longer felt the need to go bash golf balls in the late-afternoon heat. He took the five grand from the locker and walked it out to his car, pulling out two hundred before locking the rest in the console of the Mercedes. He went back into the air-conditioned 19th Hole, gave Wanda a big smile, and ordered a double Johnnie Walker Black, rocks, as he plopped down on a barstool.

Sipping his drink and surveying the room, J.T. relaxed. His mind drifted from the CNBC desk on the TV to how he was going to chart his career resurgence. All he'd needed was a little breathing room. Get the creditors off his back. Loosen up his cash flow. One of his cases was bound to settle. The defendants didn't want to go to trial any more than he did. Not that he hadn't gotten a jolt from beating the shit out of those guys in front of a jury back in the day. It was just so much work. Once all those ungrateful bastards at his firm walked out on him, he didn't have anybody to help him with the heavy lifting. When the first real settlement came in, though, all that would change again. He'd get back on top.

He crunched the ice in his glass, spun his stool back around, and smiled at Wanda. Pretty face. Jesus, she had big shoulders, though.

"How about another, Wanda?"

"You got it," she said with a wink.

Yep. It was all going to be fine. A month from now, this whole rough patch would be a memory.

Something hit J.T. on the shoulder, something heavy like a sandbag. J.T.'s neck turned with a sharp jerk.

Frankie Fresh was now kneading J.T.'s shoulder. "Howdy, partner."

J.T. didn't know what was happening, but he was pretty sure nothing good was going to come of it.

"I'm sorry?" he said to Frankie, who was trying to wedge his blubber onto the barstool.

"I said howdy, partner. You never seen a western on TV? That's what they used to say all the time. 'Howdy, partner.'"

"Oh. Gotcha." *False alarm. Fat goof's just trying to be amiable.*

Frankie clapped J.T. on the shoulder again and resumed his deltoid massage. "Yeah, I figured since we're partners and all now, we might get to know each other a little bit."

"What are you talking about?"

"Well, counselor, what do you think I'm talking about?"

J.T. played it cool. "I don't know what you're talking about, but I tell you, I'd appreciate it if you'd get your fucking hand off my shoulder."

Frankie pulled his hand away. He smiled at J.T. "Hey, hon," he said to Wanda while still smiling at J.T., "can I get a Heineken?"

Wanda drew a pilsner glass of beer and put it on a coaster in front of Frankie.

J.T. sipped his drink. *Why is this fucking turnip smiling at me?*

Frankie just kept looking at J.T. and smiling. J.T. knew the routine. He'd done it himself in countless depositions and cross-examinations. Ninety-nine times out of a hundred, the other guy will say something just because it's so awkward. The silence. The gap in the conversation. The urge to fill the hole with something—chatter, anything—just to restore some kind of social balance. It was a reflex. Something polite people did. Litigators knew this. They made their living by it.

But the lawyer realized that Frankie knew it too—that if he looked at somebody long enough, somebody who owed him money, eventually the mutt would remember where he might be able to get some cash by the end of the day.

J.T. had had enough. He knocked back what remained of his second scotch, reached across the bar to grab his check, and signed it. He started to reach for his wallet to leave Wanda a tip, but then he remembered he only had the two C-notes in there. *Oh well. Tough shit.*

He got up from the barstool, fighting the urge to say something to Frankie. He turned his head slightly as he pulled the door open.

A smiling Frankie raised his beer in salute.

"So long, partner."

TEN

Buddy drove to the Van Slaters first. He felt like an asshole parking so far away from the store with five hundred spaces closer, but Mack had insisted it had to go down this way. Buddy had never gotten an exact figure as to what Mack was getting out of this. Every time he raised the topic of investing in his ball-retrieval company, Mack changed the subject to how he was going to buy a new truck or some shit with his windfall.

Buddy went into the store and loaded up a half-dozen bags of chips and a case of Coke into a cart. He expected Mack to be in the lot by the time he checked out. No Mack. Goddamn, that boy was stupid. Probably got lost on the way. Buddy started to push his cart as slowly as he could out to his Monte Carlo with the blistered and faded blue-gray paint.

He took as much time as he could loading the groceries into the car. While the trunk was still open, he slipped to the far side of the car and grabbed an extra couple of carts. With his, that would make three. That would have to do.

Just as Buddy was about to close the trunk, Mack pulled into the parking lot, gunning his engine. As he reached the spots where he was supposed to park, he came screeching in with some asshole move where the car slid sideways the last few feet like in those stupid racing movies. Buddy shook his head. Dumbfuck was doing everything he could to draw attention to himself.

He wondered if that other guy at the club, Al, was a part of this, or if it was a straight-up J.T. deal. Buddy knew that if Mack was involved, there was an outstanding chance it would get fucked up. On the other hand, if it did come off, then Mack would be able, if not obliged, to invest in Buddy's project. It wasn't like a handout, Buddy told himself. The guy would get a piece of something with some real potential. Not like pouring his ten bucks an hour into that deathtrap of a dune buggy he was always fucking with.

Mack got out of the car and put his hand on the roof. That was the signal. Buddy didn't know why there needed to be a signal, but he didn't argue. Tired of Mack's foolishness, he gave the carts a much harder shove than he needed to. The carts took off.

From the corner of his eye, Mack saw the carts coming his way. He had his flop all worked out. He'd let the lead cart clip him on the ass, then he'd jump against the Firebird and roll over the hood like a fucking stuntman or some shit.

Mack could hear the tin carts rattling. They were getting closer. He took a deep, slow breath and looked straight ahead as he walked in tiny steps toward the store. He'd only get one shot at this. He felt himself tensing for impact. Just when the carts seemed to be ready to nick his left butt cheek, Mack left his feet and dove toward the car.

What he hadn't counted on was that a crack in the pavement ten feet behind him had slightly altered the course of the speeding carts. Instead of a glancing blow off Mack's left leg, the carts, weighing fifty-five pounds each and rattling downhill at eight miles an hour, struck Mack square in the back, his feet already off the ground at impact.

Mack didn't make it over the hood. His head banged off the front bumper of the Firebird and he laid out flat on the asphalt. The carts jerked right and smashed into the car's driver's side headlight. The momentum of the sudden turn, coupled with the wheels blocked by Mack's torso, caused the 165 pounds of carts to flip over on Mack's prostrate body.

Mack was pinned beneath the carts. They came to rest on his right shoulder, with his arm extended. He couldn't get any leverage to push them off because they were wedged against the Firebird's bumper. It hurt a lot more than it was supposed to.

A Mexican kid wearing a maroon vest came trotting out of the store, and a tall, lanky redneck twenty yards away walked over with long, hurried strides. The redneck got there first and pulled the carts off Mack. The little Mexican kid, maybe five-three, helped Mack to his feet.

"You okay, man?" the Mexican kid said.

"Fuck no, I ain't okay, man," Mack said. "You see what them fuckin' carts did? Jesus Christ, they damn near killed me."

"I seen the whole thing, brother," said the redneck. "Another six inches, those fuckers mighta run right over your neck. You're lucky to be alive, boy."

Mack's face felt scratched from the asphalt. He felt around for blood. Something was wet. Bingo. He walked around to look in the side-view mirror. His face was a mess. He had a lump the size of a golf ball on his forehead from where he'd hit the bumper. Mack turned his head. Fucking thing looked like something from *The Flintstones*. He picked the gravel out of his cheek. He must've landed on his elbow. He looked. It was bleeding. Hurt like hell, but not as much as his shoulder.

By now a couple more shoppers had wandered over to the spectacle. Mack leaned against the quarter panel on the driver's side. He bent down to look at his broken headlight. Goddamn. He ought to send J.T. the bill for that shit.

The night manager, a thirty-five-year-old woman with rolls of motherhood stuffed into a too-small blouse beneath a maroon vest, hustled as fast as she could toward the commotion. Her name tag said "Jenny."

"Are you okay, sir?" Jenny asked.

"No, as a matter of fact. No, I'm not." Mack frowned at the woman. "My head's cracked open, my elbow's busted, my shoulder's hurtin' like a son of a bitch, and I th'owed out my back." He groaned as tried to stand upright. "So, no. I ain't okay."

"I'm really sorry. I already called 911. They're sending an ambulance right away."

Mack's eyes widened. "I ain't gettin' in no ambulance." He remembered J.T. saying that under no circumstances should he let EMTs examine him. Of course, that was when he was supposed to be fake-hurt. He really was fucked up now. Still, he didn't want J.T. yelling at him. "Listen here, what's your name? Jenny? Jenny, I got somewhere I gotta be. I'll be takin' this gentleman's contact information, and my lawyer will be in touch. You can count on that."

He turned to the redneck. "You got a bidness card on you, hoss?" To Mack's surprise, the guy, a glazier, did have a card. "'Preciate it."

The pain was getting more acute by the minute. Mack climbed slowly into the Firebird and drove out of the lot. Once he got up to the 60, he called Buddy.

"Holy shit, man, you fucked me up!"

"Sorry 'bout that, man. They wasn't but three carts, so I had to make sure they'd make it to where you was at."

"Those motherfuckers liked to killed me, man," Mack said, laughing. "Hey, let's go get some wings."

"You serious?"

"Fuck yeah. I need to get some beers in me. Shit, feels like I got dropped outta the Goodyear blimp."

"I don't know. Shouldn't you be callin' J.T.?"

"I'll call that motherfucker, don't worry. Nobody said we couldn't get something to eat, though, did they?"

"All right."

"Meet me at Hooters. We'll get us a coupla pitchers."

—

The driver's side headlight out, Mack's Firebird roared down Canyon Springs Parkway. Just as he turned left onto Campus, a Riverside County sheriff, lying in wait in front of LA Fitness across the road, hit his lights and followed Mack into the Hooters lot.

Looking up through the windshield, Mack saw Buddy, who had already arrived and was looking back at the Firebird and shaking his head.

He lowered the window as the cop approached. "Evenin', deputy."

The deputy didn't react other than to say, "License and registration."

He took Mack's documents and went back to the cruiser, returning a minute later holding his aluminum citation pad.

"D'you know why I pulled you over, sir?" the deputy said, handing Mack back his license and registration.

"No, sir."

"Your front headlight's out."

"That just happened five minutes ago. Swear to God. I got run over by a bunch of shopping carts over at the Van Slaters back there."

"Yeah, well, it's dark and you're driving with one headlight."

"But I got a whole bunch of witnesses'll tell you this just happened five minutes ago! Look here at my face. Them things fu— messed me up, man."

The deputy shone his flashlight on Mack's face. "Looks like you got your ass kicked."

"That's what I'm saying. Buncha damn shopping carts run me down. They's gonna be a lawsuit, I promise you."

"Well, make sure you put in for the cost of a new headlight. Maybe even this citation if you can get it."

"How am I supposed to get it fixed at night if I can't drive to get it fixed?" Mack was satisfied he'd out-logicked the deputy.

"Yeah, they're fixing headlights at Hooters now, are they?" The deputy tore the ticket off and handed it to Mack. "You drive this thing away from here tonight, don't let me be the one to see you." The deputy started walking back to his cruiser. "You have a good night now," he said over his shoulder, and climbed back into the cruiser and drove away.

Mack walked up next to where Buddy was standing.

"If that ain't a motherfucker," Mack said.

ELEVEN

Buddy followed Mack into the bar. Lee-Anne, a Hawaiian-looking chick with what Buddy thought were pretty small tits for Hooters, brought them a pitcher of Foster's.

"What happened to you?" the girl asked Mack as she set the pitcher on the table. "You been in a fight?"

Mack winced. Tiny bits of gravel were still embedded in his scalp. "What if I told you I was training in MMA? That means mixed martial-arts."

"Yeah, I know," the waitress said. "My boyfriend is an MMA fighter."

Mack slunk down in his chair.

The girl's eyes widened, her mouth forming into a soft O. "I mean *ex*-boyfriend. It's only been a few days. Just a habit, I guess."

Mack straightened up. Buddy shook his head and poured himself a beer.

"Can I get you guys some wings or anything?"

"You sure can, darlin'," Mack said. "Make 'em hot as hell, and bring us some a them curly fries too, would you?"

Lee-Anne touched Mack on the arm. "You got it, tough guy." She winked at him before she pivoted and walked away in orange shorts sized for a nine-year-old.

"You see that?" said Mack. "That little hottie's into me, man."

Buddy sipped his beer and squinted at the hockey game on TV. He was waiting for an appropriate window to broach the subject of Mack's prospective investment in the golf ball salvage business. "Uh-huh."

"I'm serious, man. She ain't much in the way of titties, but she's got some beautiful eyes. Like she's from fuckin' Samoa or some shit."

"Uh-huh." Buddy wondered how much he should press for. He knew from his Internet research that prosecuting the patents alone would cost thousands. He'd need to file papers to get his LLC established. That shit wasn't free. The prototype was functional, but if he was going to try to market this thing to golf course management companies, it would have to be more camera ready.

"I tell you I got the McMahon 3000 just about ready for its maiden voyage?"

"Naw." Should he seek out an incubator? It'd mean giving up equity, but then again, with the right connections, it could be worth it if he didn't have to give up too much.

"Yup, that sumbitch is gonna be a fuckin' monster out in the desert. I mean *indestructible*."

"All right." How could he open up a line of credit? He didn't know the ins and outs of that, but he did see a lot of those motherfuckers on *Shark Tank* talking about it like it was important.

"Gonna see if they'll let me keep it in the shed when I ship out to Cape May."

"How's that?" Buddy looked up from the TV showing a picture of some white boy with a fucked-up haircut and some crazy name Buddy couldn't even read, much less pronounce. Manufacturing? Should he outsource that shit or keep it here where he could keep an eye on it?

"Cape May, New Jersey, numbnuts. Where Coast Guard training is? I only told you about that shit about five thousand times."

"Oh, yeah."

Mack continued to swamp Buddy under waves of information establishing unequivocally that the future was the Coast Guard. It was of little moment that at twenty-seven, he was years older than the typical Coast Guard recruit. Through the magenta lens of Mack McMahon, this was not a setback, but a triumph.

"It's like I fuckin' red-shirted already," he told Buddy. "They want guys like me. Mature. Not like some fuckin' bedwetter never been away from his momma's tit. Plus I got experience. Life experience. That's what they want. See, everybody wants to be a fuckin' SEAL. That's the beauty of it. Not only am I older and more experienced, I'm competin' with a bunch of wannabes, man."

He explained how getting his pilot's license would open the gate to yet another Coast Guard bonanza. "Shit, you got your pilot's license, you got no worries. You know how many pilots there are in the Coast Guard?"

"Nope." Buddy gnawed the meat from a chicken bone.

"Shit, tons of 'em. These guys fly all the fuckin' time, man. You get a day off, you go up with these guys, build up your hours easy. Get trained on all kinda different aircraft, not just fixed wing."

"What's fixed wing?" said Buddy.

"Fuckin' plane, man. Your fixed wing is a plain ol' airplane. Then you got your helo. That means helicopter. See, on a plane, the wing is just fixed right onto the plane. Don't move or nothin'. A helo's got all kinds a rotors and blades and shit."

"So listen, shouldn't you be calling J.T.?"

"Yeah, you can't put a price on that kind of experience, man," Mack continued, ignoring Buddy. "You know what else is the beauty of it? Fuckin' Coast Guard is domestic, man. None a this out to sea for six months and winding up in fuckin' Somalia. I'm talking about getting a place...Huntington Beach or Cape Hatteras or something, and just picking the honeys up off the sand."

"What if you get stuck somewhere shitty?"

Mack leaned back on his stool as if he'd already considered this possibility. "The chances are remote." He winced when his shoulder bumped a wooden beam. "I mean sure, in theory you could get shafted with Maine or some Great Lakes bullshit. But do the math. Everywhere there's water, there's beach. The whole coast is just one big fuckin' fiesta, man."

"What about Alaska?"

Mack rocked back to the table. "Oh, I'll grant you there's a lot of water up there. But there's no fuckin' people, man. Who is there to rescue? You think there's a big Eskimo interdiction program? Motherfuckers trafficking in seal pelts or some shit? Fuck, man. Give me Pacific Beach. Give me Caladesi Island. They don't need fuckin' Coast Guarders to rescue fuckin' salmon, man."

Buddy hadn't gone a day past high school, but he knew there had to be ten thousand miles of coastline in the United States, and this motherfucker was sure he was going to be stationed in Southern California. Serve his ass right to get stuck up on Lake Huron or something.

"Those guys are all gonna be replaced by drones, man. Show me a drone that can do a sea rescue, though, or interdict a boat full of refugees without blastin' 'em all to shit. If that's what they think is gonna win 'em friends in the UN, then by all means, fire away. Sheeeiit."

Buddy turned his head to the TV and rolled his eyes.

Mack winced again as he leaned forward onto his good elbow on the table. "Anyway, I'll probably get stationed at Long Beach or San Diego, so it makes sense just to keep it out here close to the desert anyway."

"Shouldn't you be calling J.T.?" Buddy asked again.

"I told you, I'll call that motherfucker in a little while. What's the rush?"

Lee-Anne resurfaced with another platter of wings and a bowl overflowing with curly fries. She leaned on Mack as she set the wings down on the table, mashing her small left breast against his triceps. When she'd set everything down, she leaned on the table on her elbows, her cutoff T-shirt opened up at the neck.

"You sure you're okay? That bump looks painful." With a long pink nail, she traced around what was now a purplish lump the size of a golf ball.

Mack winced. "Yeah, I'll live. Probably just a concussion or a contusion or something." He looked sideways down her shirt. "Speaking of living, you live in Moreno Valley?"

"No, I actually live in Loma Linda. I go to UCR." A bell dinged on the back counter. Lee-Anne popped up off her elbows. "Oops! That's me, gotta go!" She winked at Mack. "You guys need anything, you just holler, okay?"

Even though Buddy had switched to Diet Coke, Mack ordered another pitcher of beer, then another. Lee-Anne popped by every fifteen minutes to flirt with Mack. At one point Buddy thought she was going to hop in his lap. Finally, just before eleven, she said she was going off shift and would they mind settling up. She winked at Mack, who swiped the check off the table.

"You bet, honey." Mack handed Lee-Anne his Visa card. "What are you doing after you get off?"

"Oh, I got a Pilates class first thing in the morning. I'm just going to go home and take a long shower." She winked at Mack again and took his credit card with the check.

"Hey, look here," Mack said to Buddy. "You remember when ol' J.T. tipped Wanda fifty? Watch this shit." He put a fifty-dollar tip on a seventy-dollar tab, going over the fifty three times with the pen in case there was any chance she wouldn't see it.

Lee-Anne put her hand on Mack's shoulder. "Ohmigod, thank you!" she said when she picked up the check.

"So I was thinking I could use a shower myself, darlin'," Mack said, leaning toward her.

"You're cute," she said, and turned and disappeared back toward the kitchen.

"You hear that?" Mack said. "This shit is on, brother."

"Uh-huh."

"I'm serious. I'm gonna hook up with this chick."

"Uh-huh."

"You didn't see that? All the touching my arm? All the rubbing her titties up against me? The winking? That chick is into me, man, I'm not kidding."

"We'll see."

A minute later a blond waitress with a pock-marked face and blue eye shadow came up to the table and asked if they needed another pitcher. Her name tag said "Sara."

"No thanks, darlin'. Lee-Anne was taking care of us."

"Yeah, she just finished her shift, though," Sara said.

The unmistakable roar of an accelerating Harley Davidson rumbled outside as it sped past the restaurant.

"That's all right, I think she was going to come out with us for a drink."

"Um, I don't think so," said Sara. "I just saw her leave with her boyfriend on his motorcycle."

Buddy looked at Mack and shook his head.

Sara tapped her pad on the table. "So you guys are all set?"

Mack finally gave in and called J.T.

"Where have you been? Why didn't you call? Did everything go all right?"

"Well, I got good and fucked up by those shopping carts, if that's what you mean by all right."

"What do you mean? You didn't let the EMTs examine you, did you?"

"No, sir, but them carts knocked me into my car. I cracked my head open on the bumper, fucked up my elbow and my shoulder. Back hurts like hell too."

"That's great!" J.T. caught himself. "I mean, sorry you got roughed up, but in the long run, this is much better, you'll see."

"Yeah, well, on top of that, got a fuckin' ticket for driving with a busted headlight."

"Wait. You got pulled over by the cops?"

"Yeah."

"Where?"

"Right here in the Hooters parking lot in Moreno Valley."

Of all the fucking morons. "You were in an accident that we're going to claim is worth…thousands of dollars, and you went to fucking Hooters afterward?"

"Shit, I got a knot the size of a fucking baseball on my head, I reckoned I was due a couple of cold ones."

"Did anybody you recognize see you there?"

"Naw. Just Buddy."

Holy shit. What a fucking retard. "You went with Buddy? Are you shitting me?"

"Yeah. He's right here. You want to talk to him?"

"You're still there? You're telling me you're still at fucking Hooters *and* with the guy that caused your accident? Are you fucking shitting me?"

"What's the big deal?"

"Jesus Christ."

J.T. hung up.

TWELVE

How had he ever gotten mixed up with such a pack of mindless turds? He was pulling the plug on this bullshit in the morning, that much was for sure. What had he been thinking?

He thought about driving straight to Al's house, even though it was midnight. That cocksucker didn't return *his* calls? The guy that put this whole thing together? Fuck Al.

Then J.T. remembered the five grand from the envelope. He'd already decided Al was only getting four back. Then it hit him. He'd just call Al in the morning and say he'd given the doc the money already. *Can't ask for it back; the guy would just blackmail us if we tried to pull that one. No, tough shit.* This thing was a clusterfuck from the word go.

J.T. Edwards was done.

After a couple tumblers of vodka and the cell phone forgotten in the console of his car, Al just zoned out until 1:00 a.m., flipping around watching movies. When he finally did get up to go to bed, he still got no sleep. He would have carved his skin off with a steak knife if he could. The rash had now come into full bloom. Tiny blisters were erupting all over his ribcage and down to his waist.

He thought about calling in sick to work, but he was so punchy from the lack of sleep, he'd forgotten it was Saturday. He also remembered he'd never heard from J.T. What was he hiding now?

He noticed the car keys on the counter where he usually left his cell phones. Shit. He'd left the phones in the car all night. He went out to the garage. Sure enough, a missed call from J.T.

"I called last night. You didn't call me back."

"Yeah, sorry. I was in the shower and then got distracted. I got some kind of rash—"

"Save it. You playing golf today?"

"No chance. I told you, I got this rash and—"

"Whatever. You might as well meet me at the 19th Hole. I'll be there at nine."

"What are you talking about? You said we should never meet."

Al grimaced as he reached for a coffee mug. The blisters felt like they were popping open and hot grease splattering his entire torso.

"That was before," said J.T. "I'm out."

Al got to the 19th Hole first. A few players were grabbing breakfast before they went out; others were loading up on screwdrivers and bloody marys in big white Styrofoam cups. As usual, Wanda was behind the bar.

"Jesus, don't you ever leave here?" said Al.

Wanda smiled as she looked up from stacking mugs behind the bar. "Morning, Al. Doesn't seem like it, does it? What can I get you?"

"Coffee, please. Black."

Wanda turned a mug over and poured a cup of coffee. "Yeah, back when I was a paralegal, I used to get nights off, weekends off, had a dental plan—the whole works."

Al lifted his mug. The right side of his torso felt hotter than the coffee. "Uh-huh."

"I can't afford to take a shift off now."

"Yeah, well, recession hit everybody."

"I'm just saying I wasn't always a waitress is all."

Al popped two more Advil in his mouth. He'd already taken two an hour ago. He pulled the waistband of his chinos away from his hip. The little blisters were now raised purple spots. Al ground his molars and winced. Wanda kept babbling.

"I remember once we had a case, some guy fell down an escalator at the San Bernardino mall. Broke his arm and his collarbone and busted his spleen. Had one of those braces on his arm out to here." Wanda held her arm up at a ninety-degree angle. "We sued the mall and the escalator company. The guy not only got a jury verdict, his wife got her own claim for loss of consortium. You believe that?"

Al's eyes were watering from the pain. He couldn't believe he had to sit here and listen to this big heifer ramble.

"Jesus, you liked being a paralegal so much, why don't you just go back to it?"

"Whoa. Somebody got up under the wrong rock this morning."

"You realize every time you open your mouth, it's about how you used to be a paralegal?"

"Okay, Al. I hear you." Wanda's eyes glistened. She blinked a couple of times and walked back to the kitchen. She returned a minute later with two plates of eggs that she took to some old-timers sitting by the window. She returned to the bar and continued putting away glasses.

Al shifted in his seat. God, they were all so fucking sensitive. "I'm sorry. I just—"

The door opened and J.T. walked in and straight to the bar.

"Wanda, can I get a cup of coffee, please, sweetheart?"

Wanda looked at Al, then back at J.T. "Coming right up." She managed a weak smile as she poured the coffee.

J.T. took his coffee and headed for an empty table in the corner and sat down facing the wall. Al followed him.

"What's going on?" said Al. "What happened?"

"What happened is that pinhead blew up the whole fucking thing, that's what happened." J.T. sipped his coffee. He was breathing fast through his nose like he'd just run in from the eleventh hole.

"How?"

"After he got hit by the carts, he went out drinking with Buddy...the supposedly random guy that accidentally hit him with a bunch of shopping carts in the Van Slaters parking lot."

"Jesus." Al sighed. Even that hurt. He hung his head and stared into his coffee. "Maybe nobody saw him."

"The carts busted his headlight. He got a fucking ticket five minutes later for driving at night with his headlight out. Driving, I might add, to the fucking Hooters to drink beer with his assailant."

"But if nobody can put them together—"

"You're not hearing me, Al. I'm out."

"But the five grand—"

"That's gone. I had to pay Sonu up front."

"Who?"

"Dr. Chugh. The guy that was going to play ball with us on the medical. I gave it to him last night. You remember—when you declined to return my call last night?"

"Listen, you need to get that back."

"I can't go back to him now. He knows what's up. He'll just blackmail us for more if we fuck around with him."

"Blackmail us for what? Nothing's happened."

"I appreciate that you didn't go to law school, but you do watch TV, right? You know how they always talk about conspiracy? It's a real thing. This bullshit right here? Me, you, Mack, Chugh? That's a conspiracy. You go to jail for that shit." J.T. blew across his cup and sipped his coffee. "No. We are not fucking around with Sonu Chugh for five grand." He sipped his coffee again.

The door to the 19th Hole opened and yellow daylight spilled into the room. Then it got dark.

"I think we got a bigger problem," said Al.

"What's that?"

"Howdy, partners."

THIRTEEN

The chair that Frankie Fresh pulled up to the table groaned as he sat down. J.T. was sure it would splinter like a model airplane, but it held fast.

"Hey, Wanda?" Frankie hollered over his shoulder. "Can you set me up over here?"

Wanda gave Frankie a thumbs-up and turned to carry the order back to the kitchen.

J.T. looked at Al for some hint as to why this asshole was sitting at the table.

Frankie leaned forward onto his elbows. "So, boys, how's ol' Operation Flop Shot this morning?"

"Not good, Frank," said Al.

"That doesn't sound right." Frankie clapped J.T. on the back, nearly causing him to spill his coffee. "That sound right to you, pard?"

"What the hell are you talking about? Why do you keep calling me partner and pard?"

"Well, why not? We're all friends here, aren't we? All co-venturers in a for-profit enterprise."

J.T.'s lips parted. He looked again at Al.

"Um, Frankie's kind of on board with the scam," said Al.

"Now what are *you* talking about? What scam?"

"Easy, counselor," said Frankie, "we're all adults here. Better you keep your voice down, lest any of the duffers get the wrong idea."

"Al? What the fuck?"

"Frankie's in for eight points. Plus he's fronting us expenses."

"For a modest consideration," Frankie added.

"Yeah, for a modest consideration," Al repeated.

J.T. sneered with the sardonic smile he used to give juries when he was cross-examining some defendant's damages expert. He relaxed as it dawned on him that no matter what this idiot thought, J.T. himself would have no more responsibility for this farce. "Well, that's great, but eight points of nothing is still nothing. I told you. I'm out."

"Not so fast, counselor." Frankie put his hand on J.T.'s forearm. "Why don't you tell me what's bothering you and maybe I can help straighten out any kinks in the tactical approach."

J.T. threw a blank look back at Frankie. "I am out."

Frankie stared into J.T.'s bloodshot eyes with the same unblinking gaze he'd given Al the day before. "I'm sure I must not have been clear. Let's start over, because there seems to be some confusion about things."

Wanda came over with her tray and rested it on an adjacent table. She served Frankie a plate of six eggs over a double order of corned beef hash, plus a basket of toast, a side of hash browns, a glass of orange juice, and a cup of coffee.

"What, you're out of wildebeest?" said J.T.

Frankie exploded with a deep bellow and slapped the table, shaking it. "*Wildebeest!*" He clapped J.T. on the shoulder, laughing. "That's a good one."

Wanda picked up the carafe of coffee and warmed J.T.'s cup. Al slid his cup toward her to be topped off too. Wanda ignored him and walked away.

"Wildebeest," Frankie said, still chuckling, still jiggling. He picked up a piece of toast and speared one of the egg yolks resting on the steaming mound of hash. "You are a funny guy, counselor."

"Thanks," said J.T. Al fidgeted in his seat like ants were crawling on him, annoying J.T. still further.

"Here's the deal, Ace," Frankie said. "Your friend and I had a long talk yesterday about spheres of influence, zones of enterprise, and the like. Bottom line is, I will be participating in your score. Boyo here says you're looking to bag a hundred large." Frankie stirred some ruptured yolk into a crispy edge of corned beef. "A typical finder's fee is ten percent. I'm a fellow golfer and sportsman, so I'm only taking eight." Frankie used a piece of toast to push a heap of hash onto his fork and looked up at J.T. as he shoveled it into his mouth. "As I explained to young Alvin here, I can assure you that my own associate, Mr. Fegangi, would himself insist on a far, far larger share." Frankie speared another egg yolk and crammed the triangle of toast into his mouth. "A *far* larger share."

And there it was. The magic word. *Fegangi.* The terror J.T. could now see in Al's eyes now not only made sense, it paralyzed J.T. himself. *Jesus, Mary, and Joseph.* J.T. had never even considered that Frankie was really connected. How could J.T. have been so stupid? How could he have been taken in by that idiotic Irish blather act? Of course if he was making book, he had to be Mobbed up somehow. Why had he never seen it? *Vinnie Fangs. Fuck.*

"I hear you," said J.T., his pulse throbbing inside his collar. "I really do. But you've got to believe me, this is a total fuckup. You don't want any part of it. Our patsy is a complete idiot. He's going to get us all sent to prison."

"Okay, counselor. Now *I* hear *you.*" Frankie scooped up a bale of hash browns with his fork. He shoved the wad into his mouth and chewed a couple of times before he started talking again. "A couple of things." Frankie ran his tongue around his cheek and swallowed. "First, I don't go to prison. Maybe you do, I don't know. But I don't, so let's take that off the table right away." Frankie sipped his coffee. "Second, you tell me this thing is hopelessly fucked up and won't work, I guess I got no choice but to believe you."

J.T.'s shoulders relaxed. Al sighed. Frankie scooped up a mouthful of hash dripping shiny yellow egg yolk.

"But here's the thing. I know you guys saw *Goodfellas.* You gotta know how this works. You don't want to go ahead with the deal, that's your prerogative." Frankie finished chewing his hash and swallowed it. "I still get paid, though." He stifled a demure burp while he gazed at his plate, trying to decide between the hash and hash browns.

J.T.'s jaw dropped. "You're shaking us down for eight grand for a scam we didn't even run?"

Frankie stopped chewing the hash browns that puffed out his left cheek. His eyebrows converged in a malevolent V shape. "I'll give you a moment to reflect on what a poor choice of words that is to impute to your business partner."

J.T. looked at Al. "Say something."

"I got a rash."

J.T. looked up at the ceiling. *Who did I murder in a past life?* He looked at Frankie. "Even if I wanted to go along with this, I don't have eight grand to give you."

"Thirteen."

"Excuse me?"

"Eight plus the five I fronted Patient Zero here."

"What?" *Now what the fuck is he talking about? Am I losing my fucking mind? Is this really happening?*

"The five grand you gave the doc," said Al. "That was from Frankie. Like I said, he's fronting the expenses."

"When were you planning to tell me all this?"

"When you were in a better mood, I guess."

J.T. looked up at the ceiling again. He bit his lip.

"And don't forget the vig, boys." Frankie had inhaled the entire platter of food and was now wiping his plate with his last buttered piece of rye toast. "A point a week on the principal."

Frankie knocked back his cup of coffee and started working his chair away from the table enough for him to stand. He steadied himself as he rose, using J.T.'s shoulder to lean on. J.T. almost collapsed under the weight.

Frankie wiped his mouth with a green linen napkin. "I'll leave you two alone to sort this out." He dropped the napkin in his chair and lumbered out to the parking lot.

Al jumped up from the table. "I gotta go to the bathroom. These things are killing me." He trotted down the hallway toward the locker room. "I'll be right back," he hollered over his shoulder.

J.T. sat alone facing the wall. The greasy carcass of Frankie's breakfast cooled on the table. Wanda came over and topped off J.T.'s coffee.

J.T. couldn't even look up.

FOURTEEN

Al took off his shirt, unzipped his pants, and stood in front of the mirror in the locker room. The rash had now completely covered the right side of his torso. The little red bumps had become blisters, then little purple spots. Not to mention they hurt like hell. Al imagined some kind of jungle rot Marines would have gotten at Guadalcanal. But the closest Al Boyle had been to Guadalcanal was Pismo Beach.

The only thing that distracted him from the discomfort of the rash was imagining the hurt that a disgruntled Frankie Fresh might be willing to lay on him. Al was shamed by the knowledge that if he hadn't been such a chickenshit, he could've held onto that five grand. At least then they wouldn't be thirteen grand in the hole. Christ, if he'd had thirteen thousand bucks, he wouldn't have bothered approaching J.T. with the scam in the first place.

J.T. was going to go nuts now, that much Al knew. He wanted to bail on the thing, and now Frankie's telling him he can't. Al also knew that J.T. would blame him, even though it was *J.T.* who'd been responsible for selecting and then coaching Mack; it was *J.T.* who'd handed $6,000 to Dr. Taliban, no questions asked. Or so he claimed. Al was beginning to wonder: if he was as broke as Frankie suggested, where did J.T. come up with a thousand in cash to make up the difference?

Al stood half naked in front of the mirror, reworking the breakdown of the splits. If they tried again and could settle for 110, but told Frankie it was only 100, that still meant a net of 97. If they split that three ways, that meant a little over thirty-two grand each. It was tempting to try to push the envelope of the settlement, but with all that seemed to be dooming this scam, Al knew, if anything, they should be going lower, not higher.

He thought about J.T.'s lecture about conspiracy. Not only were they in a conspiracy, now they'd even gotten the Mob pulled in with that warthog, Frankie Fresh. It was too bad he couldn't sign off on a higher settlement and stick that fat fuck with his eight points on a hundred grand. Al had been hungry when he woke up, but seeing that gelatinous mass choke down a five-thousand-calorie breakfast had killed his appetite.

He pictured Wanda turning around when he'd stuck his coffee cup out for a refill. What was her problem? It wasn't Al's fault she never shut up. He pictured her holding her arm out like a broken puppet. Then it hit him.

He winced as he zipped up his trousers. His eyes watered when he slipped into his shirt. He gritted his teeth walking back to the table where J.T. sat still staring at the wall.

Al whimpered slightly as he pulled out a chair and sat down. He leaned toward J.T. and said in a stage whisper, "I've got an idea."

"Have you and the universe not fucked me enough for one lifetime?"

"Listen, unless you've got thirteen grand that I don't have, it might be in your interest to pay attention."

J.T. turned his head and glared at Al. "What?"

Al leaned in closer and whispered, "Loss of consortium."

FIFTEEN

In researching the Van Slaters flop, Al had chosen the grocery store as the simplest claim to manufacture. Now that the claim was to be more complicated, the whole strategy was due for a makeover.

"Are you familiar with El Fuente Dorado in Palm Desert?" Al asked J.T.

"Where they used to play that Skins game on TV for sixty million bucks?"

"That's the one. So these guys have a policy with GSAC. They just did a huge renovation. Spent millions spiffing everything up."

"Yeah, so?" J.T. said.

"We just got a demand letter last week because of a slip and fall."

"And?"

"Next to the exit to the pool, there's an elevator bank right inside the lobby. Marble floor."

"Okay."

"The demand letter's claiming the situation was dangerous because people are coming and going in from the pool and just standing there dripping on the marble floor. There's no rug, no sign saying, 'WARNING slippery-as-hell marble floor covered in water you can't see.' Get it?"

J.T.'s personal-injury abacus started clicking away. There were holes in Al's idea, naturally. There would be a lot more moving parts. On the other hand, if they were going to have to go through with this, as the adipose participation of Frankie Fresh indicated, it would at least give them the chance to start anew. The whole Van Slaters fiasco could be treated as a trial run, a warm-up for the main event.

"Who sent the demand letter?"

"Some lawyer from LA. Clint McAuliffe."

"I know that asshole. Thought if he raised enough for whatshername's last campaign, they'd make him a federal judge. Prick just represented one too many gangbangers, I guess."

"Yeah, well, if we could get Mack out there quick, with his back and shoulder already being messed up from the Van Slaters thing, we wouldn't have to worry about an MRI."

J.T. turned things over in his head. "If we could settle before McAuliffe, that would probably screw his settlement up too, wouldn't it?"

"It wouldn't help. If he came in looking for monster dollars, and we'd already settled ours for a fraction of that, they'd hold the line. Take him to trial."

That alone would almost make it worthwhile, J.T. thought.

"It also gives us cover for the loss of consortium claim," continued Al. "We hook Mack up with a girl who'll play ball and not ask any questions. Whip up some backstory. They go to Vegas and get married on the spur of the moment. He and his wife are on their honeymoon at El Fuente Dorado and bam! Right outta the gate, he throws out his back, probably needs an operation on his shoulder, out of work…no chance of banging his new bride."

There was no question it was a more complicated scheme. And by no means cost-free.

"Fuente Dorado's a fortune," said J.T. "The cheapest room in the place is like a grand a night. It's Hong Kong jillionaires and studio heads." J.T. raised his eyebrows and cocked his head. "Is anybody going to believe Mack had a foursome with Harvey Weinstein, Magic Johnson, and Jack Nicholson?"

"They're getting married in Vegas, remember? They won big at blackjack and hauled ass while they were up. They got tired on the drive back and decided to treat themselves to a honeymoon at the spa close to home."

"You got the cash for this?"

"We already got Frankie on our ass. Might as well take on a few thousand more. If it doesn't get fucked up, it would definitely be worth it."

J.T. rubbed his head. Jesus. Going deeper into the hole at a point a week. The saving grace was that the whole thing would be over in a month. Even if they borrowed another five grand and it took six weeks, it would only mean $600 in vigorish.

"All right," said J.T. "You deal with Frankie. The less interaction I have with that fat fuck the better. I'll go have a talk with Mack and give him the good news."

J.T. figured he now had significant leverage over Mack. The idiot still didn't realize how he'd jeopardized the whole plan. Halfway through his second bottle of Malbec the night before, J.T. realized it could've been worse. If Mack *hadn't* mentioned Hooters and the ticket, J.T. could have sent a demand letter and maybe even gotten a payout only to have some in-house rat bastard at GSAC sniff out the scam. Mack's admitting his manifold stupidity might have saved J.T. from a stretch in Lompoc.

Mack would be disappointed that the Van Slaters flop was a scratch, but he'd get over it when J.T. doubled his payday to $30,000. Al wasn't going to have any contact with Mack, so the way J.T. looked at it, Mack's cut was coming out of J.T.'s end. It didn't affect Al's bottom line, so he should have no beef.

J.T. figured a loss of consortium claim, done right, could raise a $120,000 claim up to $190,000. This would mean after, say, twenty grand off the top for Frankie, and another thirty for Mack, there was still close to a hundred forty grand on the table. Al would be counting on Mack pulling in about $57,000. With J.T. pocketing all but Mack's promised $30,000, it made J.T.'s end closer to $85,000. With that kind of cash, J.T. would be back in business.

Among the pesky details, however, was the fact that Mack was single—single with no prospects, as far as J.T. knew. This meant expanding the crew by one. Mack would not only have to get married; some emolument would be required to induce the would-be bride. Assuming one could be found that wasn't as big a fuckup as Mack.

"I don't have to remind you," said Al, "this shit's got to happen fast. I gotta take the transfer to Weed or quit. Either way, the whole thing falls apart. And don't forget, we're still on the hook with Frankie Fresh."

After going over the new and improved plan for twenty minutes, Al begged off, saying he had to find a pharmacy to get something for his rash. J.T. stayed at the club, drinking coffee, doodling on cocktail napkins with circles and arrows representing splits and potential payouts. He was now all alone in the 19th Hole with a wad of napkins in his pocket.

Feeling superstitious about Moreno Valley, Al drove out of his way to find a Walgreens in Hemet. After buying a tube of cortisone cream, he went out to his car and took two Tylenol with codeine he had left over from getting his wisdom teeth removed a year before, and washed them down with a warm Coors Light that had rolled under the front seat last night. He lifted his shirt and rubbed the cream all over his torso. Christ, this was uncomfortable.

J.T. had taken the idea for a second run better than he'd imagined. Al congratulated himself on coming up with the loss of consortium angle. Okay, maybe technically Wanda had planted the seed. He should probably apologize to her. The big cow seemed to have had her feelings hurt. He wondered whom

J.T. was going to be able to bring in on short notice. He didn't know how much time he could buy on the Weed thing, but he knew it wasn't a lot.

J.T. called one of the cell phones he'd given Mack, who answered it on the fifth ring.

"You working?" J.T. asked.

"Yeah. I mean, I'm at work. I ain't doing nothing right now."

"Grab a cart and ride over to my car. Black Mercedes, far end of the lot. Bring a shovel. Anybody asks, tell 'em one of the members saw a rattlesnake."

J.T. was out in the parking lot standing in the grass near his car. "You bring the shovel?"

"Got it right here." Amped, Mack reached into the back of the cart. "Where is it?"

"There's no snake, Mack. That's why I said '*tell* them somebody *saw* a rattlesnake.' I needed to get you out here to talk and we don't have a lot of time."

"So there's no rattler?"

Jesus. "No, there's no rattler. I just want you to hold the shovel and look around the ground like there *is* a rattler, you got it? This way if anyone sees us talking, we have a plausible reason for being together."

"That's fucking smart, man."

"Thanks." J.T. forced a quick, pained smile. "Now listen. Got a good news, bad news deal here. The bad news is, last night's flop is a bust. We can't file a claim."

"But I really did fuck up my shoulder and stuff."

"Yeah. Anyway." J.T. was trying to stay calm. "You see, we just can't take a chance that anyone who saw you and Buddy drinking together might have been able to put the two of you at the Van Slaters parking lot."

"I don't think there was anybody."

"We can't take that risk. On top of that, you went straight from what's supposed to be a serious injury to Hooters, which a jury would see as a glorified titty bar."

"But—"

"Mack, it's a scratch, sorry. Now, that's the bad news."

Mack hung his head and kicked gently at the blade of the shovel, then grunted and grasped his shoulder.

"The good news is we have a Plan B."

Mack looked up, still rubbing his shoulder. "A Plan B?"

God, it was like talking to a dachshund. "Remember the fifteen thousand you were going to get for the gig last night? Well, it just got doubled. Thirty grand."

"You serious? Thirty grand?"

"Yep."

"But I wasn't even supposed to get hurt last night."

"Well, that's true. But come on, you're going to take harder knocks than that up at Cape May, am I right?"

Mack rolled his shoulder and gritted his teeth. "I reckon."

"Listen, just think of it as a mulligan. It's a piece of cake. Hell, you might even enjoy it."

"So what do I have to do for this performance?"

"Nothing. Just enjoy an all-expenses-paid honeymoon."

SIXTEEN

J.T. had to remind Mack a half-dozen times to keep looking at the ground as if they were looking for a rattlesnake. As J.T. unfolded every wrinkle of the plan, Mack would stand upright and lean on the shovel like a fence post.

"So let me get this straight: You want me to go to Vegas tomorrow night. Get married. The next day drive back to Palm Desert, then slip and fall in the lobby by the pool?"

"The beauty of it is, you're already banged up, so it will make the claim that much more plausible."

"You keep saying plausible. What the hell does that mean?"

"It means believable. Like it could really happen. Unlike the whole thing with you fucking up the last one by going to Hooters with Buddy."

"Okay, okay." Mack nodded. "I just didn't know what the word meant's all. I got it now." He squinted at J.T. "So why do I have to get married?"

"This is why you're getting bumped from fifteen thousand to thirty. It makes the claim more valuable if your wife can show what we call a loss of consortium."

"All right, I know you must think I'm a dumbass, but what the fuck is loss of consortium?"

"It means the loss of services, usually between spouses. Let's say you're an old married couple. You're the husband, naturally you take out the trash at night. You cut the grass. You drive to the Home Depot to get a bag of birdseed. But if you're injured or bedridden, you can't do all those things."

"I get it, but if I was married—"

"See, you're not a dumbass." J.T. couldn't believe he had to hold this guy's hand like this.

A pickup drove through the lot down to the cul-de-sac by the pro shop.

"Remember, keep looking down like you're looking for the snake."

As the driver pulled his clubs from the truck bed, Mack looked down at the ground.

"Loss of consortium has another important component," J.T. continued. "It means that you're unable to have sex anymore, or at least like you used to."

"And this will make the claim more plausible?"

"More valuable."

"That's what I mean."

"Yeah. Loss of consortium is what we call a derivative claim. Her *injury* is that she's lost the use of your services. It's tied to the same set of facts, but it's technically her claim."

"I gotcha."

"Now I need to ask you...I don't want you to be embarrassed; I want you to be honest with me, because believe me, if you're not, this whole thing will blow up in your face."

"Shoot."

"You aren't gay, right?"

"Sheeeiit."

"Mack, I'm not judging, I just have to know. If you are, that's your business, it just means you would not be the right guy for this job."

Mack stood up straight and leaned on the shovel. "No, man, I ain't gay."

"Look for the snake, Mack." *Sigh.* "And you're not married, right? No high school sweetheart you hooked up with and just never bothered to divorce?"

Mack shook his head and dropped down into a crouch to examine the bush. "No. Not married, never been married."

"Okay, I had to ask."

Mack looked up at J.T. "To make sure it's plausible."

"There you go." Maybe he was getting it after all.

"So who would I have to marry?"

"Well, if she'll go along with it..."

"Who?"

"You know Wanda from the 19th Hole?"

"You shittin' me?" Mack hopped up on his feet. He straightened his elbow out and grimaced.

"What?"

"Shit, she's bigger'n I am!"

"So what?"

"I got a thing about chicks that can kick my ass."

"Listen to yourself. Wanda's a pretty girl."

"I don't know's I'd call her a girl. She's gotta be pushing forty. Is this what you mean by plausible?"

Down at the bag drop, an old guy J.T. recognized struggled to haul his clubs out of the tiny trunk of his red Kia.

"She won't be thirty-five until December. She's not that much older than you."

"Still, you see the shoulders on her? Godamighty, she's like a fuckin' lumberjack."

"Did you know she almost qualified for the Olympics in swimming? That's where the shoulders come from. She was one of the top high school swimmers in California until she was in a car accident her senior year."

"I didn't know that."

"She's a pretty girl. Smart. Works hard. Besides, nobody said you've got to stay together forever. If this thing settles like I think it will, you'll be going off to Cape May with thirty thousand dollars in your pocket and you two can just get the thing annulled. Like it never happened."

Mack cocked his head, bit his lip, and nodded slowly. "Okay, man. I guess you can count me in."

"Great. Now one more thing. We're treating last night like a scrimmage. We can't have any more fuckups, you got me?"

"The rattler!" Mack jerked the shovel up like a spear.

J.T. jumped a foot in the air. He fell backward on his ass and started scrambling like a crab.

"Oh, wait...nope...hang on." Mack bent down and picked up a lizard trying to hide in the shade beneath a bush. "Just a lizard," he said, smiling.

J.T. scowled, brushed off the back of his pants, and turned to walk back to the clubhouse. *Asshole.*

J.T. stepped out of the bright morning sun and back into the dark room, where he had Wanda set up a bloody mary on the bar. The situation was not ideal. Golfers trudged in and out. Fortunately, no one else sat down at the bar or lingered longer than it took Wanda to pull beers from the cooler.

J.T. pulled up his barstool and smiled. "What are your goals, Wanda? What are your dreams?"

"Pay off my credit cards. Take care of my mom. Buy a little duplex by the beach and rent it out."

"No kids?"

"I think that train's already left the station."

"C'mon...pretty girl like you? I bet you had plenty of chances."

Wanda blushed and sucked in her stomach, causing her breasts to push forward.

"Who are you kidding, J.T.? Why do you think I give Frankie such a big breakfast? That guy makes me look like a gymnast."

J.T. chuckled at that and Wanda smiled back.

"Where are you going with this, J.T.?"

J.T. laid out the barest sketch of the plan. He didn't mention the Van Slaters attempt, and he said nothing about Frankie Fresh being involved. Al was never mentioned as a part of the scheme, but J.T. knew Wanda was bright. She'd read between the lines.

"Look, even if you could talk somebody into marrying me—even for money—that's not really the way I'd envisioned spending my life, you know?"

"First of all, Wanda, let's assume I already have somebody. Somebody you know and like. Somebody who thinks you're pretty."

"It's not one of these old retired guys, is it?" Wanda shook her head and wiped some water off the bar.

"Mack McMahon."

Wanda threw her head back and laughed. "He never told you his 'thing about girls that can kick his ass'?"

"I'll be the first to concede that Mack's not the sharpest pencil on the desk, but deep down he's okay. Besides, you know he's joining the Coast Guard, right?"

"Yeah, what about it?"

"Okay, he joins the Coast Guard, the first thing they do is ship him off to New Jersey for a couple of months. After that he could be stationed anywhere. If this thing goes like I think it will, it'll be over in a few weeks. If you two turn out not to be Gable and Lombard, you just get the thing annulled right after the settlement."

A twosome walked in and asked for some coffee before they sat down at a table across the room. Wanda held up a finger to J.T., then carried a carafe over to the customers.

Returning the carafe to the warmer, Wanda turned around and blew a curl from her forehead. "What's in it for me, J.T.? How does this get me closer to those goals you seemed so interested in a minute ago?"

J.T. knew Wanda would be sharp enough not to take him up on his first offer. "Ten grand."

"What's Mack getting?"

"Yours would just be based on a derivative claim, Wanda, you can't—"

"I'm sure with an offer as attractive as this, you won't have any problem finding someone discreet—especially on short notice." Wanda walked a couple of menus to the players she'd just served the coffee to.

Wanda had him boxed in. What's more, he couldn't even lie to her like he did to Al. The honeymooners would be sure to compare notes.

When Wanda returned to the bar, J.T. said, "Thirty. He's getting thirty thousand."

"Twenty it is, then."

"Jesus, Wanda." J.T. had to look pained to sell it. He knew if he'd come in at twenty, she'd have said forty. "Your *injury* is *not* having to sleep with Mack. You want twenty thousand dollars for that? You've done it your whole life for free."

"No problem," she said, turning around to unload a rack of glasses. "I think there are some girls down at the Pizza Hut could probably use a green card."

"Okay, twenty." He shook his head and smiled. "I wonder if Mack knows what he's in for."

Wanda's smile disappeared. "You just need to remember, J.T., that whatever it is you're ginning up in that little head of yours, when it's all said and done, I'm not going to be jerked around." She stood up straight, towering over J.T., who looked up from his barstool. "I'm looking out for Number One. I *will* be taken care of."

SEVENTEEN

Mack McMahon pulled a Corona from his refrigerator. He sat down on the thin carpeting of his apartment living room with his laptop and started trolling the Internet for F-150 King Ranch edition Ford trucks. They were still expensive, even the used ones. Mack tried to figure after flying lessons how much he'd have left of the thirty thousand.

He switched his limited focus from pickup trucks to flight schools. There was a guy in Corona who could get him his license for $5,199. Another place in Norco would get him qualified for $5,299. It was going to take a couple of months. Of course, if he got the thirty grand, he could probably quit his job a couple weeks early and go for the license full time. That made a whole lot more sense. Mack found a flight school in Riverside with an expedited program that would get him his license in seventeen days. It was $5,600. He'd just have a little less to put down on the truck, but then again, once he got married, he could cut his housing expenses by moving in with Wanda. Hell, he hadn't thought of that. It was like an added bonus old J.T. never even considered. Mack sipped his beer and wondered what Wanda's place was like. Probably smelled good. Better than his place, Mack was sure.

Al Boyle woke up on Sunday morning unsure which hurt worse, his rash or his head. He'd taken Tylenol with codeine every four hours on Saturday. He started drinking screwdrivers at four in the afternoon and continued alternating between vodka and pills until he passed out on the couch at nine. He woke up completely dehydrated at 6:00 a.m. and staggered to the bathroom. The purple spots that yesterday had looked like tiny boils were now black. *This looks like fucking plague or something.* Maybe it wasn't the deodorant he'd already quit using. Had he changed his detergent? The rash was just on one side, the side he slept on. If it were some kind of fever, it would be all over his body. This was local, although covering a big patch on his torso. Mostly it just hurt like hell. He decided to give the cortisone cream one more day to work. He also decided codeine might not be a great idea if he had to drive anywhere.

J.T. gave Mack two thousand of the additional five thousand Al had borrowed from Frankie Fresh. Mack was to drive to Vegas after work on Sunday afternoon. After checking into the hotel of his and Wanda's choice, they were to go to an all-night chapel and get married. The next morning they were to drive back and check into El Fuente Dorado as honeymooners. J.T. told Mack to sell the newlywed angle hard when they checked in. The back story was to be they'd gotten married on the spur of the moment in Vegas, but wanted to spend their honeymoon at a nice, quiet upscale resort in the desert close to home.

If Mack could flop on Monday afternoon, theoretically, J.T. could mail the demand letter as early as Wednesday. Thirty-one days later would be a Saturday, meaning Al could sign off on the claim as early as the following Monday. Add five business days for processing, that meant a check would be cut the following Monday...add a day for courier service of the check to arrive Tuesday from Sacramento...deposit the next morning...it was pushing it, but if he could just hold off a few more creditors a few more weeks…

Wanda drove her Passat through the dusk and into the night. Riding shotgun, Mack didn't talk much on the way to Vegas. He worked his way through his twelve-pack of Tecate as the convertible blurred across the featureless desert. Wanda's hair spread out in a fluffy pillow in the breeze, and every five minutes or so she'd sweep her black curls behind her ear. Mack realized that if he angled his seat just so, he could see nearly Wanda's entire left breast, including her surprisingly large cordovan nipple, as the wind in the open car luffed the top of her sundress.

Nearing Vegas the darkness became more acute and the temperature dropped.

"You want me to put the top up?" said Wanda.

Mack guessed the end of the wind would mean the end of his show. As he saw Wanda's nipples harden, he felt his crotch swelling against his jeans. "Naw, I'm fine."

He was getting cold himself. He was only wearing a short-sleeved golf shirt, but he didn't want to break the spell. He tried coming up with some small talk, but he really didn't have a whole lot in his playbook.

"Boy, them stars are something, ain't they?"

"Yeah. Hey, do me a favor. There's a sweater in the top of my bag on the back seat. Hand it to me would you, please?"

Mack had been intercepted. The game was coming to an end. He rubbed her shoulder with the back of his hand, a desperate Hail Mary. "What's a matter? You really that cold?"

"Yeah."

"Well, here," he said, rubbing her shoulder and arm like he was trying to thaw out a frostbite victim, "let me see if I can warm you up." For the first time, Mack noticed that her unblemished skin was the color of toasted coconut.

Wanda kept looking straight ahead. "You know what would be great?"

"What's that?"

"If you could hand me my sweater."

Defeated, Mack fumbled with the zipper on her bag and pulled out a big black cardigan and handed it to Wanda. She slid into it one arm at a time, but she didn't button it. At first the sweater covered up her chest, but gradually, as the wind pushed it aside, Mack was once more able to see the rising breast of his prospective bride. The crotch of his jeans tightened uncomfortably.

In the distance the blue-white lights of Las Vegas seeped onto the horizon.

"You give any thought to where you want to stay?" Wanda asked.

"Not especially," said Mack. "Lady's choice." He grinned what he'd hoped was an endearing rather than threatening smile.

He'd had to agree with J.T. that the girl had a pretty face. Like J.T., he caught himself thinking of her as a girl as opposed to a middle-aged woman. Mack had flirted with her at the club, but he had never seriously considered trying to hook up with her. He didn't want to guess her weight, but he was pretty sure she weighed more than he did. Still, if J.T. was telling the truth about the swimming, that might account for those shoulders that were easily wider than his.

"Well, if it's all the same to you, I'd kind of like to stay at the Corcovado."

"Sure." Mack shifted again in his seat. He was feeling the wind now, but he still didn't want to alter his view from the passenger seat. "Thought I might as well try a little blackjack while we're here, what do you think?"

Wanda smiled. "Fine with me."

As they checked into the Corcovado, liveried staff wandered through the lobby with blue or scarlet macaws on their arms or shoulders, followed by hotel photographers snapping pictures of tourists feeding the brilliant parrots. A floor-to-ceiling aviary the size of a jai alai fronton surrounded the elevators on three sides with still more macaws and screeching emerald conures.

Mack grabbed a double Jack Daniel's from a waitress as they stood at the edge of the casino floor, their small overnight bags at their feet. A sixty-foot replica of Rio's Christ the Redeemer statue dominated the casino, standing high atop a base shaped like Corcovado itself, overlooking the tables below. A ski lift rose slowly on cables from a corner of the lobby up and over the casino floor to an observation deck just at the feet of the Messiah. The statue looked to Mack like Jesus was an umpire giving the safe sign at home plate. With a dozen beers inside him, his outlook on the whole plan was increasingly positive.

Up in the room, Mack tossed his nylon duffel bag on the luggage rack while Wanda laid her bag on one of the room's two king-size beds.

"They don't keep minibars in here?" said Mack.

"No, they don't want you staying in your room; they'd rather give you the drinks for free downstairs and have you gamble."

"Well, I don't know about you, but I didn't come to Vegas to snuggle up with the Gideons. I'm gonna go get myself a drink."

"Go for it. I'm going to hop in the Jacuzzi."

Mack thought about offering to join her. He felt a slight unfurling in his boxers. *Fuck it. Plenty of time for that later. She ain't going anywhere. Might as well enjoy my last night as a free man.* "All right then. See you in a few minutes."

Mack went down to the casino floor. He'd been to Vegas once before, but that was staying at a down-at-heel old hotel on the strip. He couldn't even remember the name of it. He'd lost a couple hundred bucks playing limit Texas Hold'em. That was about all he could remember. That and a vague recollection of banging a mother of three from Traverse City, Michigan.

Mack sat down at an empty ten-dollar blackjack table. The name tag on the black vest of the blond dealer said "DONNA, Houston, Texas."

"Howdy, Donna," Mack said. "I'm from Van Horn."

"Well, hey!" she said. "Always a pleasure to meet another Texan!"

She looked to be in her early thirties, her blond hair pulled back in a ponytail. She had a nice buttery color to her, not the kind of dried-up, two-pack-a-day skin Mack usually associated with barmaids and other cash handlers of the hospitality industry.

He pulled two hundreds from his wallet and bought chips. A dark-skinned waitress came holding an empty tray on her fingertips. Her name tag said, "FELICIA, Atlanta, Georgia." Mack ordered a double Jack Daniel's on the rocks.

After being down sixty dollars in less than ten minutes, Mack thought about going back up to the room, drink or no drink. Just as he was about to get up from the table, Felicia reappeared with two doubles and apologized for the delay.

With the drinks in front of him, Mack figured he might as well play two hands, seeing as how he had the whole table to himself. He hit blackjack on both hands. Donna gave him a big smile.

"Look at you."

"How about that? Hell, let's do that again."

Donna dealt two more hands. No blackjack for Mack, but the house busted with twenty-three, and Mack was caught up.

He gazed from time to time at the statue of Umpire Jesus on the top of the mountain. Mack felt calmed by the Redeemer's passive expression. Or maybe it was just the whiskey. Increasing the size of his bets, he played two hands at a time, never losing more than one. His roll continued until Donna's shift ended.

Mack looked down at his stack of chips. He thought of J.T. as he tossed Donna a fifty-dollar chip. She smiled, thanked him, and gave a clap for the cameras—just like in the movies.

An Italian-looking kid with some kind of shit in his hair sat down between Mack and a Japanese tourist. A new dealer came on. He had a moustache and a name tag that said "BRIAN, East Caldwell, New Jersey." Mack had a feeling that none of these portents could be good. He counted up his chips. Thirty-two hundred dollars. Hell, that was more than halfway to his flying lessons right there. He got a couple of glasses of champagne from Felicia and headed back upstairs.

All the lights were off in the room, and some kind of soft Brazilian melody played on the TV's music channel. Mack noticed a thick nine-by-twelve-inch manila envelope on top of a bathing suit and a pair of shorts in Wanda's open suitcase. A muted light was on in the bathroom, with the door open a few inches. Mack was wondering what kind of loser brings paperwork to an overnight trip to Vegas when he heard a splash from the tub.

"Hey! You decent?" he hollered. "I brought you a glass of champagne."

Another splash. "Thanks! Yeah, c'mon in."

The bathroom was enormous. Wanda had her curly black hair pinned up off her neck, with thick iridescent white foam covering nearly the entire surface of the water. The Jacuzzi's jets were off. Steam fogged the mural mirror above the sink.

Wanda smiled. "You can set it down there," she said, pointing to the side of the tub, bubbles dripping from her forearm. "I thought you were just going down for a drink."

"I was. Then I got to playing blackjack. Guess how much I won?"

Wanda reached for the stem of champagne. "I don't know."

"Three grand! You believe it? More than that—like thirty-two hundred!"

"Wow! That's terrific."

The air in the bathroom was thick with humidity. The bubbles had a nice tropical smell, light but not overly sweet.

"Yeah, my dealer went off shift, so I figured I'd come up and see if you wanted to go down and gamble."

Wanda sat up a few inches. The suds pushed away from her chest a little. Mack could make out some cleavage, but not much else.

"You know, I can't remember the last time I had a night off, much less a hot tub. I think I'm just going to hang out here. But thanks again for the drink."

"No problemo." He smiled, although he was disappointed he didn't get another look at her breasts. "Hell, I'm too jacked up to sit around. You don't mind, I'm gonna go back downstairs. Get another drink."

She smiled again. "That's great about your big win."

Mack peeled off two hundreds and laid them on the counter as he stood up. "Hang onto this. You never know."

EIGHTEEN

After trolling the floor looking for blackjack dealers from Texas, Mack found "JIMMY, Corpus Christi, Texas," dealing at a twenty-five-dollar table. By the time Jimmy's shift ended, Mack had doubled and redoubled his stack.

Mack tossed Jimmy a hundred-dollar chip. The replacement dealer was from Boston, so Mack scooped up his more than $9,000 in chips and went in search of another table.

He had another Jack Daniel's and fingered the chips in his pocket. A couple more laps around the floor revealed no new dealers at the blackjack tables. Mack didn't want to play craps or the other games, just get one more hot dealer from Texas.

The thought of going to another casino crossed his mind, but he wasn't sure what that would do to his luck. Then there was the question of going back upstairs, although Wanda hadn't seemed in any hurry to get anything going. He'd be pissed if he'd walked away from a lucky streak just to get blue-balled.

Mack settled on a ski lift ride over the casino floor. The din from the tables and slots softened as the lift rose, then banked diagonally across the floor on the slow ascent up Corcovado. Concealed speakers piped in the melodies of Tom Jobim and Stan Getz. Ordinarily it wasn't Mack's kind of music, but he had to admit it had a relaxing quality to it. As the lift neared the base of the statue, Mack looked up at Umpire Jesus. As he got closer, he could see that the statue wasn't stone or even concrete, but some kind of polymer like the rocks they use in movies. Mack didn't care. A sixty-foot statue of Jesus in a casino was just badass.

When he got back to the casino floor, Mack found another blond dealer. This one, Vondel from Fort Worth, was just coming on shift at an empty table. By the time Vondel's shift ended, Mack was up more than $20,000. He shared his theory about Texas dealers with Vondel, who told him Jim Don, from Dallas, was at the hundred-dollar table.

Chewing on a straw while he waited on another Jack Daniel's, he weighed the risk of moving to the big tables. Jim Don had probably already been on for a while; he'd likely only have a little time left on his shift. Even if Mack's luck turned, he'd still be ahead for the night.

Another Chinese guy and a really short white dude, maybe five feet tall, were already playing at Jim Don's table when Mack slid onto a seat. He split aces on his first hand and hit blackjack with both. Everything felt just as it had with the other tables. He won after doubling down on eleven and started playing two hands again. He occasionally lost one of the two, but never both. The Jack Daniel's kept coming.

Jim Don's shift ended and Mack tossed him two hundred-dollar chips from chips the black mound in front of him. He glanced up at Umpire Jesus. Mack didn't know how much he was up, but he was looking at a shitload of chips. He checked his watch. Six a.m. As he gathered his chips, a guy in a white blazer stood next to him and smiled.

"You've had quite a night, Mr.…?"

"McMahon. Mack McMahon," said Mack, extending his hand.

"Mr. McMahon, I'm Sam Restivo from the hotel. Are you staying with us?"

"Yes, sir, I sure am. Room nine-fifty-four."

A black guy in a tropical shirt hustled through the lobby with an enormous cerulean hyacinth macaw screeching from his shoulder.

"Well, Mr. McMahon, the hotel would like to upgrade you to a suite at no charge."

"Thanks, but my fiancée and I were supposed to be heading out today."

"Have you seen our suites, Mr. McMahon? I bet your fiancée would be impressed. How about staying over another night as our guest? Maybe take in a show. Perhaps your fiancée would appreciate an afternoon in our exclusive Buzios Spa."

Wanda stirred and rose in the far king-size bed when Mack opened the door with his card.

"Ohmigod, have you been in the casino all night?"

"You damn right. Guess who got us upgraded to a suite?"

"But I thought we were going back today. You know, after…"

"You ever seen one of these suites? I think it'd be worth staying another day, don't you?"

"You really want to?"

"Fuck it. When am I gonna hit a streak like this again?"

Wanda sat up in bed and rubbed her eyes. She looked at her watch on the bedside table.

"Why don't we go get some breakfast while they move us to the suite?" said Mack. "'Cause after that, I gotta get some sleep."

Alvin Boyle, too, was tired. He hadn't slept at all. The searing pain of his rash made his eyes water. After applying the cortisone cream, the little black spots now had little black scabs on them. He had to go to the doctor.

Something had never sat right with Al about J.T.'s doctor story. Without having even seen Mack, J.T. had given the guy $6,000, five grand of which Frankie Fresh would be holding over Al's head. Yet the instant Mack's accident got even a little wobbly, J.T. called off any notion of getting the money back. At 8:00 a.m., Al called the office of Dr. Sonu Chugh and asked for an appointment for later that morning. When the receptionist protested that Dr. Chugh's schedule was booked with existing patients, Al told her, "Just tell him I've been referred by J.T. Edwards and that I'll be there in an hour."

"What was the name, sir?" asked the receptionist.

"McMahon."

"And your first name, sir?"

Al realized he didn't know Mack's real name. He assumed Mack was just a nickname. "Piltdown."

Mack took Wanda to breakfast while the Corcovado staff carried their two overnight bags to the new suite. Wanda mentioned that she really hadn't packed for the extra day. Mack leaned back and pulled three black chips from his pocket. He thought about giving her more but figured they weren't married. She wasn't his girlfriend. He hadn't even slept with her. Not yet anyway. Maybe after he got some sleep, they could go down to one of the chapels on the strip, and then he'd get to tap it for sure.

But he was crashing hard. Wanda teased him for yawning through breakfast. Mack told her about the offer of the comped spa.

"Wow," she said. "You must have been the big winner last night."

Was she angling for a share of his winnings? Mack leaned back and stretched his legs. On one hand he wanted to tell her he was up $40,000—enough that he could walk away from J.T. and his bullshit. For the first time since they'd hit Vegas, his shoulder started to ache. Wanda wasn't even looking at him anymore, just staring off into the casino. Mack watched her in profile. J.T. was right. She was pretty. Maybe the spa would loosen her up, get her relaxed for later.

Goddamn, his shoulder hurt, though.

As he pulled into the parking lot at Mira Chiste, J.T. mumbled aloud the figures he'd worked out earlier. For the first time, he was hoping to bump into Frankie Fresh. With the settlement close at hand, and Frankie all but assured of a nice payday, J.T. figured charging a few more incidentals to the project wasn't altogether out of line.

With the waiting room to himself at the office of Dr. Sonu Chugh, Al figured the full-schedule bit was bullshit. The receptionist looked awfully sexy to be sitting behind a desk answering a phone for some crooked sawbones. Pretty, but hardly enough to distract him from the scorching pain on his side.

A nurse led Al to an examination room. Al raised his shirt and looked at the reflection in a shiny chrome canister on a counter. He looked like a Gila monster. He started when he heard the brushed stainless steel door handle turn. Dr. Chugh was smiling and talking over his shoulder to the receptionist in the hallway.

"Ah, Mr. McMahon," said Chugh, "you are the friend of Johnny's?"

"Johnny?"

"Johnny Edwards. He referred you?"

"Oh, yeah, J.T.," said Al. "Right."

"So what seems to be the trouble today?"

Al raised his shirt. "This. It's killing me."

"I have to say, I'm surprised. Can you remove your shirt please?"

Al winced as he unbuttoned his shirt and slid out of it.

"For some reason I had expected you had a more orthopedic injury," said Chugh, "not herpes zoster."

"What? Whoa. Hold on, Doc." What the hell was this quack talking about? No wonder he was crooked. Guy was probably run out of Waziristan for being a sorcerer. "No way do I have herpes."

"Ah, but I'm afraid you do."

"Impossible."

"Who's the doctor here, Mr. McMahon?"

Good question. "Listen, Doc, there's no way I've got herpes. Besides, how do you get herpes on your ribcage?"

"Ah, yes, now I see the confusion." Chugh nodded and pushed his rimless glasses up to his forehead. "Herpes zoster is not a sexually transmitted disease. It is what we call shingles. You have heard of shingles?"

"Well, yeah. I thought it was something old people got, like... hemorrhoids."

"Yes, like piles, yes. One of the charming British euphemisms, no doubt." Chugh slid his glasses back into place and bent down to examine the rash more closely. "Painful, is it?"

Al shuddered. "Hurts like hell. I've been putting this cream on it." Al pulled the tube of cortisone cream from his pocket.

Chugh had a creepy little laugh like breaking glass. "Oh, ho. You don't want to be putting such creams on herpes zoster." He chuckled again. "That is like giving the little devils vitamins." He pronounced it vitt-a-mins, like a Brit. "Quite literally steroids. It will only make the little buggers grow big and strong." Still chuckling and shaking his head. "Like little tiny linebackers, you understand?"

Al's nostrils flared. *"I got it."* He gritted his teeth. He'd thought the rash was the most annoying thing he'd had to deal with, but this clown was making it close. "So where does this come from? How'd I get it?"

"Veddy simple, actually. You have had chicken pox, of course."

"Sure."

"Herpes zoster is simply a delayed release of the virus. It stays stored in your spinal cord your whole life. This is why you see the breakout in an isolated zone emanating from your spine, see?" Chugh pulled off his glasses and pointed with the frame to the area of the rash. "The reemergence of the herpes is triggered by stress."

"Can you stop calling it herpes?"

"Veddy well. I understand the unsavory implications. The shingles, is that better?" Chugh raised his eyebrows and smiled at Al as he readjusted his glasses. "The shingles can emerge during periods of stress. Tell me: Are you under stress at this time?"

"A little bit. Job stuff."

"I see."

"So what do I do to get rid of it?"

"Nothing, I'm afraid. You should stop applying the cortisone cream. No good." Chugh tsked. "I will give you a prescription for Valtrex. Otherwise, just keep the area as sterile as possible. Avoid stress."

Chugh produced a prescription pad from his lab coat, scribbled on it, and tore off a page he then handed to Al.

Al's eyes watered at the corners as he put his shirt back on. "Thanks, Doc."

"It is my pleasure. Any friend of Johnny's is always welcome." Chugh brushed his nose with the back of his knuckle. "You did not fill out any insurance forms, correct?"

"No. J.T.—Johnny said it was taken care of."

"Yes, that's right. So you have the cash?"

Al winced as he stuffed the folded prescription into his pocket. "Excuse me?"

"The cash? Johnny said the fee would be paid in cash."

Al's head was buzzing. *That son of a bitch.* "There must be a misunderstanding. I gave the cash to Johnny. He didn't give it to you?"

"No. I was under the impression your condition called for a much more...*comprehensive* diagnosis and treatment." Chugh smiled at Al. "As it is, your condition is quite benign, actually. I ordinarily charge two hundred and fifty dollars for the consultation, but as a friend of Johnny's and keeping the insurance companies out of it, why don't we just call it two twenty-five, shall we?"

The audible wheeze that leaked out of Al brought his hand to his mouth. Not only had J.T. lied about the cost of Chugh's diagnosis, he hadn't even paid it. The fucking shyster was skimming six grand off the top of what he was already bilking GSAC. He took a deep breath. He didn't know what J.T. had actually told Chugh. Al's eyes darted around the room. Then it hit him. Let Chugh fuck with J.T.'s mind. Mack was in Vegas; he wasn't even supposed to be seeing Chugh. The only name Chugh had was McMahon. When Chugh explained the rash to J.T., the shyster would put it all together and realize Al was onto him. There was a way Al could use this to his own advantage, he was sure. He just hadn't yet figured out how.

Al reached into his wallet. He had $120. "Um, I didn't bring that much with me. As I said, I'd understood Johnny had already paid for this visit."

"Veddy well," said Chugh. "Not to worry. I'll give Johnny a call. I'm sure he's good for it. I'm afraid I must withdraw the offer of the discount, but that can be our little secret," said Chugh winking. "Can't it?"

"Sounds good to me, Doc."

NINETEEN

Up in the suite, overlooking the pitiable hopefulness of the Las Vegas skyline, Mack McMahon was unable to sleep. He was tired. He was plenty tired, but even with the blackout curtains drawn, every time Mack closed his eyes, his heart raced thinking about the $40,000 in his pocket.

He thought about Wanda. Probably stretched out in the spa on a table getting worked over by some little Vietnamese honey. That'd be a nice little snack right there. Mack sensed the familiar tumescence beneath the sheets. Maybe the little Vietnamese girl would be rubbing those big shoulders. God, if she could only shrink them some. Work her way down…over those big tits with the berry-colored nipples…down under that towel.

Mack's nuts started to hurt. He knew this would happen. He wondered how long Wanda would be in the spa. Maybe he should rub one out. No, then he might only be able to go one time this afternoon once they started their honeymoon. He thought about taking a shower, but he was hoping to take one with Wanda. Get a look at the goods up close and soapy.

He did feel kind of funky. Maybe he should just take a really fast cold shower. That would do it. Then there was the question of washing off his good luck. No, better not risk it. He changed into the clean shirt he'd brought. He made a mental note to go by one of the boutiques in the lobby and pick up a bunch of those Tommy Bahama shirts those rich fuckers wore at the golf course.

He went back down to the casino. Wanda could find him if she wanted to. He asked the first waitress he saw for a Red Bull. He circled the floor looking for a familiar face among the dealers, but of course it was way too early for any of them to have been back on shift.

After ten minutes of watching tables and looking at dealers' name tags, he finally found a guy from Beaumont dealing at an empty twenty-five-dollar table. He sat down and ordered another Red Bull from a hovering waitress. He was surprised how much action was going on in the casino given that it was still only eight thirty in the morning.

Mack still felt the same as the night before. He never lost two hands in a row. He kept ordering Red Bull, he kept sitting with Texas dealers, and his chips continued to mount.

What if he could run it up to a hundred grand? *Wouldn't that be some shit?*

J.T. met Frankie in the men's locker room. Frankie handed over an inch-thick envelope.

"I'm guessing you don't need a receipt," said J.T.

"Don't worry about it, counselor. I know what's in the envelope. You know what's in the envelope. That's pretty much all that matters, isn't it?"

"And a point a week?"

"And first dollar off the top of the payout." Frankie worked a toothpick around a bicuspid. "You know what you're doing, right, partner?"

God, he wished he'd stop calling him partner. It was bad enough Mira Chiste was the only golf he could afford anymore; owing money to this menacing tapir was just a grim reminder that rock bottom was looming closer.

"Yeah. Just squaring away a couple of things so there are no surprises at the end."

"Hey, how was the spa?"

"Ohmigod," Wanda groaned, "it was fantastic." She scoped around the casino floor. "Have you been here since I left?"

"Naw. I tried to sleep but I was too jacked up after all. You feel like getting some lunch?"

"It's not going to mess up your system?"

"Naw, I've been doing a little recon. I don't think any of these dealers are from Texas." Mack watched Wanda's body turn as she looked up at the ski lifts floating overhead. She was graceful for being so thick through her back and shoulders. "How 'bout that Mexican place upstairs?"

"Sure." A slot machine pealed in the distance. "You give any more thought to J.T.'s thing?"

"Yeah." Mack's boot was tapping on the floor. "I reckon we still got time for all that. I don't think it'll take very long. Maybe we can catch a show or something later. The guy said we'd be comped."

"What the hell," said Wanda. "Why not?"

The farther he got from the casino floor, the more Mack's shoulder ached. The knot on his head had gone down, but he could still feel a dull pain under his scalp. He had the waitress bring margaritas two at a time. After his fourth, he switched to tequila on the rocks.

Wanda pushed the basket of tortilla chips away from her. Mack kept scooping up salsa as she talked him through her massage and various spa treatments. He shifted in his seat on the banquette as she described lying completely naked on the table while a young Vietnamese girl, just like Mack had imagined, gave her a sixty-minute full-body massage.

She picked at a taco salad. Mack, ignoring the ache in his shoulder, attacked his enchilada platter. He took one bite of his refried beans, a favorite of his back in Van Horn, then remembered his pending honeymoon and thought better of it. He pushed his plate away and leaned back on the banquette.

"So how much are you up?" asked Wanda.

"I don't know exactly," said Mack, knowing he was up exactly $58,650. Unbelievable. More than halfway to a hundred grand. "A lot, I reckon."

"Maybe you're one of those guys you hear about that goes on a million-dollar run."

"Maybe so," Mack said, leaning forward, "but we ain't married yet. Don't go getting any ideas about community property."

Wanda chuckled and shook her head. "What a charming conversationalist you are."

Mack quit smiling as he saw he'd hurt her feelings. He hadn't really said anything mean, and she wasn't really his fiancée, but he still felt guilty. "Aw, listen, I was just kiddin' around, darlin'. Hell, easy come, easy go, right?"

Wanda nodded with a fragile smile.

Mack didn't know whether it was the lack of sleep, the tequila, or the crashing from all the Red Bull, but he now felt exhausted. "Listen, you mind if I go up and try to take a nap again? I'm 'bout dead all of a sudden."

"Yeah, okay, I guess. I can just wander around."

"Why don't you check out what the shows are and get us some tickets?"

"Yeah?"

"Sure. Look here," said Mack, leaning back and pulling a handful of black hundred-dollar chips from the pocket of his jeans, "why don't you go do a little shopping this afternoon?"

Wanda's eyes widened. "Seriously?"

"Sure. What the fuck." Mack was relieved to see her smile return. "You want to do me a favor?" He pulled two more black chips from his pocket and laid them on the table. “You mind picking me up a coupla them Tommy Bahama shirts I seen in the window of that store off the lobby?”

“Yeah, of course, no problem. What kind did you want?”

“Doesn’t matter. Just use your taste, darlin’. I’m sure you know what you’re doin’.”

TWENTY

Between the platter of enchiladas and the half-bottle of tequila, Mack was finally able to get some sleep. Before again drawing the blackout curtains, he counted his money three times and locked his wallet in the safe. He called down for a wake-up call in four hours, just in case.

Mack awoke disoriented when Wanda entered the suite. He sat up as she showed him the shirts she'd picked out for him. She had a couple of other shopping bags, but he didn't bother feigning interest in what she'd bought.

He was thirsty. Unlike the standard room, the suite had an impressive minibar, and Mack cracked open a Red Stripe. As much as he'd wanted to wait, he decided he had to take a shower. He paused by the bathroom door. Wanda started looking through her shopping bags.

"I'm gonna hop in the shower."

"Okay."

"You feel like joining me?"

"Thanks, but the girl in the shop forgot to put one of my tops in the bag. I'm going to go back for it."

Well, that wasn't a complete shutout. With a little patience... "I can wait, if you want to run down."

"No, that's okay. It's down at the Bellagio. It'll take a while."

"Gotcha." Mack was disappointed but undiscouraged, as Wanda had clearly indicated that it was the *errand* and not an aversion to *him* that was keeping her and those big tits out of the shower with him. "If I'm not here when you get back, you know where to find me."

When he heard the door shut, Mack came out of the bathroom and checked the safe. Still secure. He took a cold shower and hoped that it wouldn't change his luck. He wasn't able to stand the freezing water for more than thirty seconds.

He pulled the tag off one of the three Tommy Bahama shirts. He put it on and checked himself out in the mirror before he went to the safe and collected his wallet.

Downstairs on the casino floor, Mack looked for familiar faces. The lurid cold of the shower had worn off and the fatigue started coming on again. He asked a passing server for a Red Bull and vodka. It was still pretty early for any of last night's dealers to be back on, but then there was always that chance.

He found Bobby, a dealer from Midland, working a twenty-five-dollar table, and he sat down between an old woman with beet-colored hair and a black guy who looked like he was probably in the service. Mack thought about Buddy. He'd lose his mind if he knew Mack was up close to $60,000. Hell, with that kind of cash, he could actually invest some serious bucks in Buddy's little business opportunity. *Ha.* Shark Tank *my ass.*

Not trusting his luck, Mack fingered his stack and watched a hand before he started. The black guy, who had only a few chips in front of him, busted out and left. The old lady followed shortly after, leaving Mack alone at the table.

"So what's the biggest winner you ever saw?" he asked Bobby.

"Oh, we've had guys in here who've been up millions."

"Is that right?"

Maybe Wanda was onto something. Somebody had to be the guy who goes on that million-dollar run. Why not him?

"What's the limit on this table?" Mack asked.

"Five thousand."

"Jesus, people bet five thousand dollars at a twenty-five-dollar table?"

"Well, sure. That's how you make it up when you hit a cold streak. You double your bet every time you lose. That way, when you win, you're sure to win all your money back."

"No shit?"

"No shit," said Bobby. "Of course, that's why the casino puts the limit on there. Otherwise players could just ride it out forever. Two hundred losing hands in a row and they'd still come out ahead on number two-oh-one."

"Is that right?" Mack looked up at Umpire Jesus. Could this guy, a fellow Texan, be bullshitting him right under Christ's watchful eye?

"Yup."

"So what's the limit at the hundred-dollar table?"

"Ten thousand."

Bobby went off shift. Mack had only played a few hands, but he'd still come out a couple hundred ahead. He thought about what Bobby said. It was time to hedge his bets. From now on, not only would he play exclusively with Texas dealers, he'd stick to the hundred-dollar tables so he could make it up, just in case he hit a cold streak. He got up from the table as the cocktail waitress, who looked a lot like the Hawaiian chick from Hooters, brought him another drink. Mack looked up again at Umpire Jesus and gave the girl a five-dollar chip.

Walking around the casino floor, every now and then Mack caught a glimpse of his reflection. He looked good. More importantly, he felt right at home, especially with his tip from his panhandle homeboy. His cell phone rang. It was J.T. Mack stared at the phone, unsure of whether to answer it, when it simply stopped after the fourth ring. *Fuck him.*

Mack couldn't believe how he'd let a measly little $15,000 turn his head like that. He figured if J.T. was now giving him

$30,000, that ambulance chaser was probably pulling in a lot more than that himself. Busted up his shoulder for fifteen grand and now suckered into some crazy scheme to marry Wanda. Marry her and join the fucking Coast Guard. If he ran this thing up to a hundred grand, that was like three or four years in the Guard. And that was three or four years maybe having to live on a base—a base full of dudes—not the Niteroi Suite at the Corcovado Hotel. No, sir. With a sound system of conservative betting, and the occasional inside tip from a real live Texan, Mack saw his future was as bright as that big fucking beam coming out of that pyramid at the Luxor.

Two drinks and another ski lift up to the feet of Umpire Jesus later, Mack found another dealer from Houston, Linda, at a hundred-dollar table. Sticking with his tried and true method, he started off slow. One hand at a time. After winning two hands at a hundred dollars apiece, he lost a hand worth $300. Mack decided to try out Bobby's tip. He bet $600 and Linda busted. He was up $500, just like that. He'd have to remember to give ol' Bobby a nice tip if he saw him again.

With steel discipline, Mack kept to his formula. Just as Coleen, his dealer from San Antonio, ended her shift, Mack saw Wanda out of the corner of his eye. Mack slid two black chips to Coleen across the green felt. Mack's stack of chips was so big, there was no way he could disguise it before Wanda reached the table, and he didn't bother trying. She wore a black cocktail dress with spaghetti straps, and big shoulders or no, she looked fantastic.

"Ohmigod!" Wanda said. "Is that all you? Ohmigod."

"Yes, ma'am. I'm having a pretty good trip, how 'bout you?"

She smiled. "Yeah, I'm having a pretty good trip."

"Well, you sure look good enough to eat, I'll tell you that. How 'bout a drink?"

"Sounds great." Wanda's eyes widened as she did a rough calculus of Mack's winnings. "There's got to be close to fifty thousand dollars there."

Mack cocked his head and looked at the stacks. "Fifty-two five fifty, to be exact." He didn't tell her about the other $40,000 in his wallet. His phone rang again.

"There's J.T."

"You going to answer it?"

"Fuck him. Let's go get that drink." Mack switched the phone off mid ring.

He put his hand on the small of Wanda's back and steered her across the casino floor and toward the lounge. She had some kind of citrusy, lemon-grapefruit scent in her hair. He'd never seen her really dolled up before. Her skin on her shoulders was smooth and tan; the dress scalloped just beneath four inches of cleavage in the front. Mack recognized the shift in his boxers. His phone rang again.

"Maybe it's an emergency," Wanda said.

"Not likely." He clicked the phone on. Wanda winced at the sound of J.T. yelling through the pinholes in the phone's receiver a foot from Mack's ear.

"What the fuck's going on, Mack? You're not taking my calls?"

"Hey, J.T.," said Mack, smirking at Wanda, "you might want to slow down there, hoss."

"What the fuck are you talking about? Where are you?"

"Vegas."

"Vegas!"

Wanda winced again as Mack held the phone from his ear.

"Vegas! You're supposed to be in Palm Desert!"

"Yeah, well, the plan got modified a little bit." Mack smiled thinking about how red J.T.'s face must be by now.

"Since when do you unilaterally change the plan?"

"Hey, I'm on my honeymoon, man." Mack looked at Wanda and smiled again.

"What the fuck is that supposed to mean?"

"Means you might want to think twice about who you're yelling at," said Mack, and he switched off the phone.

TWENTY-ONE

The phone shattered when J.T. spiked it on the russet Saltillo tiles. He paced back and forth across the kitchen. He punched the Sub-Zero refrigerator. It was wood-paneled, so it didn't dent, but now his hand hurt like hell.

Who does this little prick think he's dealing with? J.T. opened a $120 Cabernet he'd bought a few years back. He sloshed the wine into a balloon glass and gulped half of it before the bubbles had popped. He ground his molars as he slugged another mouthful of wine. *That little bastard.*

A hot wave of dread washed over him as he realized if Mack bugged out on the scam, not only was he out the sixty grand or so he'd already spent in his head, he was still on the hook with Frankie Fresh for at least half of $28,000. As he downed the rest of his glass, he assumed the fat fuck knew all too well about joint and several liability. If Mack quit, J.T. would soon be rafting down *el rio de mierda.*

Wanda. Maybe she could rein in the little prick. She had dough riding on this too, although she also had to marry the dumb bastard. Maybe she could be sweet-talked. The important thing was not to let Mack know he held the whip hand.

A tall hostess, taller than Mack or even Wanda, led them to a dark corner table in the Leblon lounge. The band was on a break, and a soft bossa nova rhythm poured from speakers hidden in the ceiling.

Wanda ordered a martini and Mack ordered the same. He'd never been a big martini guy, but here in this swanky hotel, the flashing gin and the cool-looking glasses it came in made him wonder if maybe this shouldn't be his new thing. The first one went down smooth and quick. He ordered another while Wanda sipped at hers, looking around the dark room with wide eyes. Beneath the dim light, her skin was the color of pecans. She nibbled an olive as she looked around the room.

She sure has pretty teeth. "You hungry?" he asked.

"Umm…maybe. A little, I guess." Her fingers drummed lightly to the music, gently tapping the stem of her glass. "I don't want the martini to go to my head."

Mack couldn't imagine one little drink could do much damage to a woman her size, but he remembered she hadn't eaten much at lunch. "No, we wouldn't want that," Mack said, winking.

Wanda blushed. "I'll be okay. It's too early to eat anyway."

They sat listening to the music without speaking. Mack downed a second martini. He felt relaxed. Looking at Wanda's curls in the soft light, he felt the crotch of his pants self-adjust yet again. He was going to have to do something about this soon. A waitress even hotter than the hostess that had seated them brought him another martini without him even asking for it.

Wanda's phone rang. She looked at the number. "It's J.T."

Mack shook his head and sipped his martini as she answered the call.

"Yeah, I can talk," Wanda said, making a shushing motion to Mack. "No, I don't think so. I think he just doesn't want you yelling at him.…Yeah, we're still here.…We got comped for another night.…I don't know, he's been in the casino.…No, not yet.…I don't know…well, when we get around to it, I guess." Wanda pointed to her ring finger and rolled her eyes. "They're open all night, I'm sure. It's no big deal.…Okay, now you're starting to annoy *me*....Will you just relax? We'll leave tomorrow, no big deal....Okay, bye."

Mack chuckled. "He's pissed I blew him off, huh?"

"It's more than that. He's freaking out that you're going to quit."

"No shit?"

"That's not what he said, but I can tell."

"What if I's to tell you I'm thinking about it?"

"Are you really?"

"Look here," Mack leaned closer over the table, "what if I's to tell you I'm up more than ninety grand?"

"Ohmigod! Are you kidding?"

"No, ma'am. Which is why I ain't particularly inclined to put up with J.T.'s bullshit."

"Holy cow. I had no idea."

"Well," said Mack, leaning back on the banquette, "there you go."

"So what are you going to do?"

Mack crossed his boots under the table and looked up at the head and torso of Umpire Jesus through the window behind Wanda.

"Run it up over a hundred. That's it. I don't want to be greedy, but I think I got this thing figured out."

Wanda looked over to the stage as the band returned and was getting ready for their next set.

"I guess you think that's pretty dumb, huh?"

Wanda looked back at Mack and leaned forward with her elbows on the table and her chin resting on the tops of her hands. Her cleavage plunged even deeper as her breasts mashed together. "Here's what I think: I think it's your money. I think that either way, you're always going to wonder, 'What if?' I think that even if you lose everything, you've still got J.T.'s deal in your back pocket, so it's not like you're not coming out of this ahead no matter what."

Mack took another peek at Umpire Jesus, finished his martini, and smiled into his glass.

"I think the odds are against you, but then again, if I'm so smart, why am I a thirty-four-year-old waitress at the 19th Hole of a crappy, semiprivate golf club?"

"Don't go runnin' yourself down, darlin'. I think you're plenty smart. What's your cut on this deal with J.T.?"

"Thirty."

"Really? Shit, that's what I'm gettin'."

Wanda raised an eyebrow. "Well, if you go through with it, I think you ought to get more, don't you?"

"Bet your ass." Mack chewed on the olive from his vanquished martini. "I don't want to let you down or nothin', but if I get to a hundred, I *will* pull the plug on this. I can't give you no thirty thousand, but maybe we can work something out," Mack said, winking.

Wanda leaned forward, her breasts spilling out even more over the piping of her dress. Carmine lipstick accented her white teeth that flashed in the dim light like scalpels. With her grin framed by the deepest dimples Mack had ever seen, she looked like a movie star when she smiled.

She put her chin on her hands again, shot Mack another sultry raised eyebrow, and said, "I wouldn't have it any other way."

The show didn't start until late, and Mack was too geeked up to focus on anything but getting his stake to $100,000. He gave Wanda another $200 to blow in the gift shop and went back to the casino. He ordered another martini and strolled around the hundred-dollar tables, looking for Texas dealers.

A hundred thousand dollars. He couldn't believe how close he was. His daddy had never seen a hundred grand in his asphalt-spreading, forty-year life. Mack wasn't sure how long this streak was going to last, and he didn't want to risk it running out before he hit his hundred K.

He sat down at a hundred-dollar table with Donna, his first dealer from the other night. She remembered him with a big smile. Mack played two hands, $1,000 apiece. He got a pair of eights on one, ten-queen on the other. Mack split the eights and pushed another thousand from his stack. Drawing a queen and a jack on his eights, he stuck at eighteen. Donna had a six showing. She turned over a five, then a king. Twenty-one. Mack was out $3,000.

Mack played another two hands. Afraid of fully committing to the doubling strategy just yet, he nudged his bets up to $1,500. He won both. The system worked. If he doubled his bet after a losing hand, he made it back. Simple. He'd be up to a hundred in no time and could tell old Mr. Plausible to fuck himself.

Mack bet $4,000 on each of the next two hands and lost both. On the next, he pressed his bets to $8,000 per hand. He busted on one hand showing fourteen when he drew a king; he split aces on the other and stuck at soft eighteen and nineteen. When Donna turned over a second jack, Mack had lost $32,000 in three minutes.

His pile of chips now seemed anemic—hardly the stuff of a high roller who was going to slam the Corcovado for a hundred grand. He got a pen from Donna and swapped his $40,000 check for neat stacks of purple and orange chips.

When Mack tried to bet $16,000 on each of the next two hands, Donna reminded him that the table limit was $10,000. He bet the maximum on two hands, winning one and losing one. He'd almost thought his luck had run out, but seeing $10,000 in chips pushed his way convinced him otherwise. He finished his martini and ordered another. He resumed betting the limit on each of the two hands he played at the same time.

By the time Wanda found him, he was down to just under $15,000. She put one hand on Mack's shoulder and covered her mouth with the other. He looked up with a crooked smile and pushed his remaining chips into the two circles in front of him.

"What the fuck, right? At least if I win, I'm up what that asshole was going to pay me anyway."

Wanda tucked her lips inside her teeth and said nothing. She patted Mack on the shoulder and raised her eyebrows as Donna dealt the final two hands, all face cards. House drew a seven on top of its fourteen showing.

And Mack McMahon was broke.

TWENTY-TWO

"You ain't gonna say 'I told you so,' are you?" said Mack, rising from the table.

"Not me. Like I said, it's your money."

Mack stared at the sixty-foot statue of Umpire Jesus rising from the far wall of the casino.

"So what do you want to do now?" she asked.

"I reckon I'm gonna have me a couple more of these," he said, tilting his glass. Mack saw Restivo, the guy from the casino, walking toward him.

"Mr. McMahon," said Restivo, "how are the tables treating you this evening?"

"Not so great. Busted out."

"Well, sometimes that happens. You sure gave it quite a run, though."

Mack squinted at Restivo. He wasn't sure if he was mocking him.

"I was really impressed," continued Restivo. "You couldn't have been counting. The way you kept changing tables...that was some system you had going, I have to give you that."

"Well, thanks, I guess."

"In spite of your turn of luck, I hope you've had a good time with us. We really value you as a guest. Are you at least going to have dinner and take in a show tonight?"

The ski lifts floated overhead toward Umpire Jesus. Mack looked up at the Lord's impassive face, wondering where he'd gone wrong, what signal he'd missed.

"We were going to, but I tell you, right now I just feel like a drink."

"I understand. Well, all the same, we wish you the best on your honeymoon." Restivo extended his hand. "We hope to see you both again in the future."

Mack shook Restivo's hand, and the guy disappeared onto the floor without another word.

Wanda rubbed a couple of circles on Mack's back. "You feel like getting some dinner? There's a steakhouse that's supposed to be really good."

"That's right," said Mack, still dazed. "I forgot you were hungry. Let's go."

Mack took a final martini from the server as he followed Wanda off the casino floor and to the elevator bank. In the restaurant, Wanda ordered a petit filet mignon; Mack, a porterhouse. The waiter brought over an expensive Bordeaux with a note from Restivo, who seemed to Mack to be everywhere.

Mack ignored the wine. He ignored the steak. He ignored Wanda. He sat silently staring into the bottom of successive martinis. Every once in a while he'd tap his boot against the table's stanchion. Wanda didn't say anything.

Alvin Boyle hadn't been informed of Mack and Wanda's complimentary extended stay in Las Vegas. He had figured Mack should be well along in the plan by now, yet Al had heard nothing from J.T. *Fucking shyster knows I'm on to him.*

SAICO was ramping up its due diligence on the takeover of GSAC. Every time Al saw one of the lawyers in the lobby or on his floor, he got nervous. Was there some way to slow down the takeover itself? He wanted to believe that but he knew better. He had one chance to get out of the Weed transfer, and it was riding on a moron with an ambulance chaser in the stirrups.

It was too early to tell if the Valtrex was helping. *Christ, but that's a big pill.*

Mack awoke when the door to the room clicked closed. Wanda walked toward the beds, wearing a loosely tied terrycloth robe, the top half of her bathing suit visible and her hair swept up in a white towel.

"Hey," he croaked.

"Well, good morning, sunshine," Wanda said, smiling. "Doesn't look like married life's agreeing with you too much."

Mack rolled over and propped himself up on his elbow. "Wait. We got married?" His mouth tasted like roadkill. "Where the fuck was I?" He looked around the room. The other king-size bed had clearly been slept in.

"Oh, you were there." Wanda walked over to the armoire and picked up a pile of documents Mack didn't remember seeing before. She selected the nine-by-twelve manila envelope Mack did recognize, and she pulled out a certificate from among a thick stack of smaller envelopes and papers. "See?"

"Son of a bitch. How about that?" Mack tried to swallow, but his throat felt like broken glass. "What's that smell?"

"'What's that smell' like the six gallons of gin seeping through your pores? Or 'what's that smell' like where you threw up behind the curtain?"

"The second one, I reckon."

"It's been quite a honeymoon so far."

He didn't remember the pain in his shoulder until he rolled over on his side. He needed about a pound of Advil. *Shit.* The scam. Now he was back on that asshole J.T.'s payroll and under his thumb after all.

He got another whiff of the smell from behind the curtain. "Sorry about that."

When he saw Sonu Chugh's number appear, J.T. put the phone back in his pocket. He didn't have any idea when Mack would be scheduling his appointment, so there was no sense enduring another inane discussion. There was always the chance that Chugh had gotten in trouble and was calling to engage him, but if that was the case, J.T. figured, the good doctor would call back.

J.T.'s first order of business was to go to La Bodega and pick up some cheaper wine. He'd put off buying wine because he was trying to save cash. Once he did the math, however, he realized that it was cheaper paying Frankie Fresh 52 percent interest on thirty-dollar bottles than drinking up his $150 bottles. J.T. figured a few cases ought to hold him until he got his end from the scam.

He was sick of paying for Domino's with loose change because there was no food in the house. At Whole Foods he loaded up on Manchego, Cheshire, Stilton, Reggiano Parmesan, and Saint-André cheeses. He bought two Wagyu beef filets three inches thick. He threw jar after jar of cornichons, cocktail onions, French mustards, and English marmalades into his first cart; when that filled up, he grabbed a second. He bought $360 worth of acorn-fed *jamón ibérico*, sliced thin. A pound of whitefish, a pound of sable, and two pounds of Nova salmon. Two quarts of kalamata olives and a gallon of Pugliese olive oil. He bought five pounds of Jamaican Blue Mountain coffee at sixty dollars a pound.

He felt better already.

Mack, too, was starting to feel better. He and Wanda stopped at the In-N-Out Burger a couple miles from the hotel and Mack sucked down two double-doubles, fries, and a chocolate milkshake. Wanda had to pay, just as she'd had to tip the valet. By the time she filled her car up with gas, they were effectively out of cash. Mack wasn't worried. If old J.T. wanted this thing done, he'd just have to absorb a few more expenses. Hell, Mack was out almost a hundred grand and nobody heard him bitching.

Wanda drove back to Palm Desert with the top up and the air conditioning on. There wouldn't be any nipple glimpses this trip. Wanda was covered up in some black knit jersey she'd bought on a Mack-sponsored shopping spree. Not that Mack could keep his eyes open anyway. He leaned against the window's warm glass and, still drunk from the past two days, dropped off to sleep.

Mack had only been asleep thirty minutes when his cell phone rang. With his eyes still closed and his face still mashed against the glass, he dug the phone out of his pocket. He cracked one eye open enough to see that it wasn't J.T. but Buddy.

"Whatcha say, Buddy Roe?"

"Tommy told me to call you. Said he couldn't get ahold of you."

"What's his problem? I told him I was gonna be out a few days."

"We been furloughed, man."

"Come again?" Mack sat up and wiped the drool from his cheek. "We been what?"

"Furloughed. Means we got time off now."

"Awesome."

"It ain't paid, man. It means you still got a job, you just stay home a coupla days a week without pay."

Mack stretched his eyes wide and reached for the sweating plastic bottle of Dr Pepper in the cup holder. "Well, that sucks."

"Yeah, no shit."

"So when are you off?"

"Tomorrow."

"Well, shit, c'mon over and hang out with us at El Fuente Dorado."

"Say what?"

"Fuck it, man. If we ain't workin', let's play a little golf. We can play one a these nice resort courses. Put it on ol' J.T.'s tab."

"You sure?"

"Fuck yeah, why not? Hell, I'm supposed to be on my honeymoon. Nobody said I had to be stuck inside watching TV, did they?"

Still leaning against the window, Mack reached down to the console and fumbled with the bottle of Dr Pepper as he tried to find the cup holder with his eyes closed.

"Yeah, all right. You sure it's free?"

"Absolutely. All part of the honeymoon package, brother."

Al was standing next to the Coke machine in the employees' cafeteria when Marino Vargas, his district manager, walked up.

"How's the due diligence going?" Al asked.

"Moving along. Once you get the fucking lawyers involved, you know how everything's going to slow down to a crawl," said Vargas.

"I heard that. They got a time frame on when the merger's going to go through?"

"Shouldn't be long now, assuming we figure out this IT shit before they do."

"What do you mean, IT shit?"

"You know fucking lawyers." Vargas leaned in and lowered his voice. "One of the IT guys was going through the data room they have set up for SAICO's attorneys doing the due diligence. He didn't say anything to them, but it looked like somebody may have hacked in to the central database."

Al opened his Coke. It fizzed through the top of the can and over his fingers. "Are you serious? Why?"

"Who knows? Maybe it's the Chinese. Maybe it's some bored high school kids. Bunch of dumbasses. Go through all that trouble to hack into the computers and do they start wiring money into Cayman accounts? No, these assholes just download a bunch of worthless, encrypted historical settlement data from years ago." Vargas shook his head. "Douchebags."

"So they don't know who hacked in?"

"No, and until this SAICO merger goes through, nobody on our end's saying shit. It doesn't create any liability we have to disclose. As far as our lawyers are concerned, it's a nonissue for the merger. If SAICO's lawyers haven't asked any direct questions about it, we'll just investigate it internally."

Al could feel a new rash blooming beneath his shirt. "Leave it to the Chinese."

"I know, right?"

Mack fell back into a road coma.

Wanda cleared her throat. "So you think that's a good idea?"

"What?"

"Having Buddy come out to play golf. You're supposed to be on your honeymoon, aren't you?"

"Yeah, at a fuckin' golf resort. What's the problem?"

"It doesn't matter to me, I just know J.T. has a lot of ideas about how he wants stuff done."

"Like you said yourself, J.T. wants a lot of stuff. What he needs, though, is to chill out and shut the fuck up. We can walk away from this shit and then where is he?"

"I'd just hate for this to get screwed up."

"You mean like I screwed up losing that money in Vegas?"

"I didn't say that."

"Listen, don't worry about nothing. You just go on and get another massage and relax."

"Whatever you say, Mack. You're the man of the house."

"Yeah, I guess you're right. I never thought of that."

"I'm sensing a pattern."

Mack half raised a sleepy eyebrow. "How's that?"

"Never mind."

Mack reached down, reclined his seat, and crossed his legs. "Hell, maybe you ought to bring one of them little oriental honeys back to the room and we can get a real party going."

Wanda shook her head. "How did a prize like you manage to stay single all these years?"

"Hard to believe, ain't it?"

When they got to El Fuente Dorado, Mack and Wanda checked into one of the poolside casitas. The porter brought in their luggage, which consisted primarily of bags from Wanda's shopping adventure. Mack opened a Corona from the minibar, flopped on the room's single king-size bed, and flipped on the TV.

He was still wiped out. The In-N-Out had helped his stomach, but he was completely lethargic. His eyes were starting to close when Wanda's rustling shopping bags jarred him awake.

"Where you going?"

"Down to the pool. Like you said, I didn't come to stay inside and watch TV."

Wanda stepped into the bathroom and came out two minutes later wearing a white tank bathing suit with a maroon sarong wrapped around her waist.

"I'm gonna take me a little nap," Mack said, yawning. "Maybe I'll come down and join you in a bit."

"Suit yourself." She reached into the minibar and pulled out a can of Amstel. She laid it in a pool bag with a towel and a paperback and shoved her sunglasses from her forehead down onto her nose. “See ya.”

Mack watched her wide shoulders turn slightly as she went through the door. Her already-tan skin looked even darker set off by the white bathing suit. Mack’s swelling member reminded him that they’d yet to consummate this marriage. Tonight would be it for sure.

TWENTY-THREE

J.T. couldn't wait anymore. He called the cell phone he'd given Wanda. She answered it on the third ring.

"Hey, it's me," he said. "Can you talk?"

"Yeah, I'm out by the pool."

"Where is he?"

"Back in the room taking a nap."

J.T. paced back and forth in the kitchen. "So what's the deal? When is he going to have his accident?"

"Jeez, would you relax about that?"

"How can I relax? Do you know how complex this situation is? How much I've got invested in this little project?"

"Yeah, about that."

"What?"

"You're going to need to invest a little more."

"What?" J.T. started to hyperventilate. "What are you talking about? I already gave that jagoff two grand for expenses."

"Yeah, well, that's not gonna cover it. That disappeared in Vegas."

J.T. wanted to spike the phone again, but he was running out of them. He took a deep breath and tried to calm himself. "What are you talking about?"

"The money you gave Mack. It's gone. He lost in Vegas."

"That little prick."

"Listen, you need to get over this. Just send a couple thousand more out with Buddy."

"Buddy?"

"Yeah, he's coming out tomorrow to play golf with Mack."

"ARE YOU SHITTING ME?" J.T. was desperate for something to throw, something to smash, something not too valuable. When he couldn't find anything, he opened the microwave door and slammed it. It pinged when it shut. "That asshole thinks he's playing golf? I ought to drive over there and drown him right now myself!"

"Hey, get a grip on yourself. Take a deep breath and listen, okay?"

J.T. did as instructed, filling his mouth with the thirty-nine-dollar Cab he'd bought at La Bodega.

"First of all, you promised me an all-expenses-paid honeymoon, remember? Putting aside how absurd this whole thing is, I used my credit card when we checked in. There's no way there's enough available credit on there to cover even the minibar tab, so you need to get some money out here."

J.T. gulped his wine. "But—"

"I wasn't finished. Now listen, this whole thing is supposed to be set up as a honeymoon. Is it really plausible for him to slip fifteen minutes after we get to the place? If that's what you were thinking, you should've told me that up front. That's the stupidest thing I ever heard."

Still breathing hard through his nose, J.T. filled his mouth with more wine and let it sit there.

"I'm not asking questions about the moving parts of this," Wanda continued, "because I don't want to know. But I told you I'm not going to get jerked around on this. You said all expenses paid, and that's what I expect."

A lawnmower started up next door. J.T. looked out the kitchen window. His own lawn hadn't been mown in three weeks. His gardener had gotten tired of getting stiffed and finally just quit showing up. Maybe the guy cutting the neighbors' yard would do it for a quick fifty bucks.

"Furthermore," she continued, "you seriously need to dial back how you're talking to Mack. He told me how he already messed up his shoulder on something that wasn't supposed to hurt. You keep talking to him like he's your bitch, he's going to walk away. I'm not kidding."

"Okay, I hear you."

"You sure?"

"Yeah. You're right. Another day does make it a more believable story."

"Just chill. It'll be fine."

J.T. looked in his wallet to see what he had. "Have Mack call Buddy and tell him to meet me tonight at the Home Depot off the Sixty in Moreno Valley at seven o'clock. And Wanda," J.T. said, exhaling, "I'm telling Buddy to give the cash to you. Do not fuck me on this."

"Yeah, yeah," she said, and hung up.

Al was completely unable to focus at work. What if the IT guys figured out the system hadn't been hacked but accessed by someone inside? What if Vargas telling him had been a trap to see how he'd react? Jesus, J.T. was right about paranoia. There was no such thing as too much.

Should he tell J.T.? *No, it's the other way around. That slippery fuck needs to be telling* me *some things.* Al was still looking for the angle to spring the knowledge about the Chugh mini-scam on J.T. Needed to pin him down, figure how to get something out of this. The return of the five grand, for starters.

He hadn't heard dick from J.T. since he sent Mack and Wanda off to Vegas. And the whole loss of consortium angle had been his idea! Well, maybe Wanda had planted the seed, but it was Al who'd saved their asses with Frankie Fresh, and this was the gratitude?

But this Weed thing. Vargas hadn't mentioned anything about it the other day, but it was only a matter of time. Vargas had finagled keeping the job off the HR posting, just because he didn't want to see Al get shafted altogether. Maybe Al could move up there temporarily and rent out his house until the market turned, or until he could work another transfer back.

That was nuts. He wouldn't even cover his mortgage with what he could rent his place for. Both the other completed houses in Tangelo Estates sat empty. He was convinced dirtbags were using the house behind his as a meth lab. Yeah, that'd be a great idea. Rent out a house to a bunch of thugs to raise pit bulls, stage cockfights, and rape teenage girls in the backyard.

No, Al needed Mack and J.T. to come through on this deal.

Wanda walked through the door of the casita and a wave of sweet coconut swirled into the room behind her. Mack, reclining in his boxers and watching CNN, sat up and drained the last of his beer.

"You hungry?" Wanda asked.

"I could eat."

"Let me take a shower and we can go over to Saguaro at the lodge. I saw the menu while we were checking in. It looks amazing."

"Sounds good to me."

Wanda pulled off her sunglasses and laid them on the desk. "By the way, I talked to J.T. You need to tell Buddy to meet him at seven tonight at the Home Depot in Moreno Valley off the Sixty. You know which one I mean?"

"Yeah."

"J.T.'s going to give him the money to pay for the room."

"So you told him Buddy's coming to play golf? Was he pissed?"

"Yeah, at first. Then I reminded him that it made the honeymoon story more plausible if you didn't have an accident on the first day."

"Yeah, he likes that word plausible."

Wanda disappeared into the bathroom. A minute later Mack heard the shower running. Tired as he was, his throbbing erection led him into the bathroom.

Standing in the shower, Wanda turned and looked at him. She didn't say anything, but lifted her chin under the showerhead and began rinsing the chlorine from her hair. Her head seemed to change shape as her normally puffy heap of curls flattened under steaming jets of water. She squirted a handful of gel into her palm and started lathering up her body. Mack didn't know why he'd always thought she was fat; seeing it all at once, naked, she had an awesome body.

He stood in the middle of the room slack-jawed, his member pointing at the shower like a divining rod. Wanda looked over at him, then covered her mouth. An indigo splotch the size of a dessert plate now stained Mack's chambray-colored boxers. He looked down and his erection vanished. Crimson spread from the tips of his ears to his collarbones.

"Hey," Wanda said, still laughing, "it's no big deal."

Mack turned, grabbed a hand towel, and walked out of the bathroom. He stripped off his boxers and pulled on a pair of shorts, commando style. He threw on one of his new Tommy Bahama shirts, snatched a Dos Equis from the minibar, and just before he slammed the casita door behind him, scratched out a note on the desk.

"*Gone to bar.*"

Mack hadn't told Buddy whether he was supposed to meet J.T. in the parking lot or inside. Buddy didn't see J.T.'s Benz in the lot, so he went inside and walked around. A couple minutes past seven, he saw J.T. by the paint section. When their eyes met, J.T. threw his head in the direction of the garden center.

Buddy walked over to the garden center first. J.T. sidled up next to him like he was looking at Weedwhackers and passed him an envelope.

"There's twenty-five hundred in there," J.T. said, looking up and fingering the monofilament line poking through the bottom of the Weedwhacker. "Give two grand to Wanda. The other five hundred's for you."

"For me? For what?"

"I need somebody to count on. So far everybody's falling apart. Mack fucked up the other night at Van Slaters. He should never have gone out with you after."

"I told that fool."

"Yeah, well, seeing as how you're the only one with any fucking sense, I need you to make sure he doesn't fuck up and stretch this thing out for another few days while I'm picking up the tab, you get me?"

An orange forklift beeped as it backed up and turned around. A couple of pigeons fluttered overhead among the rafters.

"I think so." Should he be pitching J.T. as a prospective investor? Got that big Benz out in the parking lot. *Then again, if he's so rich, why's he running around faking accidents at grocery stores?*

"When he starts talking about how much golf he's going to play and how he's going to enjoy his honeymoon, you need to bring his ass back to reality, know what I mean?"

Buddy stuffed the envelope in his back pocket and hitched up his jeans. "Yeah, man, I hear you." Mack was about to fuck up J.T.'s deal and Buddy's business plan with his foolishness. *Not to mention, who wants to go into business with somebody you already know is crooked?*

TWENTY-FOUR

Wanda stepped into the bar wearing backless high heels and a saffron-colored dress with thin straps that crisscrossed. Mack sat at the bar with his back to her, drinking tequila on the rocks with a little salt on the rim.

She walked up behind him, put her hand on his shoulder, and smiled. "There's the happy groom."

Mack licked the salt from his glass. "Hey."

"You call Buddy?"

"He'll be there."

Wanda picked up a menu on the bar and opened it. "You okay?"

Mack motioned to the bartender for another tequila. "I'll live, I reckon."

When he finally woke up the following morning, Mack didn't remember how he'd gotten back to the room. His head was killing him. He scraped the crust off his tongue with his teeth as he rolled over and looked around for Wanda. The bathroom door was ajar, but the light was off.

He made it to his feet and into the bathroom. After brushing his teeth and showering, he saw a piece of paper on the minibar with long, feminine handwriting. "Gone to spa – W." His phone showed a missed call from Buddy and a text: *ON MY WAY.* Mack did the math and realized Buddy should be arriving any minute.

Out of clean underwear, he threw on a pair of shorts and one of his new shirts and grabbed a bottle of water out of the minibar.

Mack called the pro shop. The assistant pro, a kid who sounded maybe twenty-two, said a tee time was no problem. With no tourists around and the heat already at 117, the local geezers would be off napping during midday. Mack and Buddy would have the whole course to themselves.

When his stomach began rumbling, Mack headed down the breezeway to the restaurant for some brunch. He saw Buddy's two-tone, blue-gray Monte Carlo pull into the parking lot far from the valet. Mack could see him reaching for his phone as he stepped out of the car. Mack just whistled and Buddy nodded and started walking through the heat waves rising from the soft black asphalt.

"Yo," said Mack, "let's get us some breakfast before we get out."

"Breakfast? Man, it's after ten o'clock. You just getting up?"

"Hey, honeymoon's a bitch, ain't it?"

"So you hit it, huh?"

Mack slugged the last of the water in his bottle. "Not exactly."

"Say what? Goddamn, you staying in a hotel with that fine Amazon and you ain't hit it? What, you still afraid of her?"

"Shit. I never said I was afraid of her. She's just too goddamn big for me's all."

"I don't know. I'd be nuttin' round the clock I was married to that."

"Yeah, well, we kinda got thrown off track in Vegas. I was up for almost two days straight. Fucked with my system."

"I talked to that fool J.T. He said you better get your system un-fucked."

The air inside the restaurant was more than fifty degrees cooler than the temperature outside. Mack was starting to feel, if not good, better than he had a minute ago. "Fuck J.T. You know my shoulder's still hurting from them shopping carts."

"I ain't giving you no strokes, if that's what you're angling for."

Mack laughed and clapped Buddy on the back. "Fuck it. Let's get fortified and we can work out the strokes on the first tee."

Mack had two bloody marys with his omelet, sausage, and biscuits. Buddy had a screwdriver and some bacon and hash browns. Mack got another bloody mary to go in a white Styrofoam cup before they walked toward the pro shop.

Mack charged both rounds of golf to the room, as well as his rented clubs, a dozen Pro-V-1 balls, and a pair of Nike golf shoes and socks for himself and Buddy.

"Need a couple of hats too," Mack said, and grabbed one off a table. "Pick you one out, man."

"You sure?"

"Hell, yeah, it's all good." Mack looked at the assistant pro behind the counter. "I'm on my honeymoon."

"You two look very happy," the guy said.

"Not with this motherfucker," said Mack. "My wife's up in the spa. This is my homeboy from Moreno Valley. We're just gonna squeeze a round in while the ol' ball and chain gets her mud on."

"All right." The pro pointed out the window to the course. "You got the whole course to yourselves. We've got a little work going on at fourteen and fifteen, so everything inside the paint is ground under repair and you get a free drop." He handed Mack a scorecard from the counter. "Hit 'em straight."

While Mack went back to the grill for a cooler of beer and ice, Buddy strapped his own mongrel set of clubs on the back of the cart next to the shiny, purebred rented irons of El Fuente Dorado.

True to his word, Buddy gave Mack no strokes, although Buddy did allow him a mulligan on the first tee after Mack duck-hooked his first drive. Mack then hit his approach fat and shrieked in pain when the club struck more ground than ball.

Buddy laughed into his hat as Mack grabbed his shoulder and slung his rented eight-iron at the cart.

"Well, this is gonna be a shit round, I can tell," said Mack, reaching into the cooler for a beer. "It's like there's a fuckin' Chinese throwing star in my shoulder."

"Maybe you can get your wife to give you a mass-sage later on," said Buddy.

"Sheeiiiit. I tell you what. She's a big 'un, but she's got some body on her."

"I heard that."

"She was standing in the shower," said Mack, pushing his hat back on his head as he drove the cart behind the green. "All soapy and shit. Got that big bush. Old school, you know what I'm saying?"

Buddy nodded and pulled his putter from the bag. He started walking to his ball, shading his eyes as he tried to read what little break there might be.

"Anyway," Mack continued, "I'm standing there watching her take a shower and just blew it right there in my drawers." Mack felt his pleated twill shorts shifting again as he lined up his own putt.

"Goddamn, man. You need to hit that. If you ain't up to it, I'll hit it."

"Oh, I'm up to it. I just hadn't slept in two or three days. Between that and the whiskey and the blue balls…shit, I'm lucky we didn't both drown in a goddamn tsunami of jizz."

"You a sick motherfucker, you know that?"

After the second hole, Mack pulled another beer from the cooler and gave it a little shake, then pointed it at Buddy as he opened the can. *"Oops!"* Mack laughed as Buddy tried to dodge the spray and almost fell out of the moving cart.

Buddy shook his head and wiped the side of his face. "Asshole."

Considering rented clubs, an alien course, and the mid-day summer desert heat simmering his three-day drunk, Mack was having a good round. He was only a couple strokes behind Buddy, and that he blamed on his shoulder that felt like it had broken glass inside.

"Shit, you ought to come back out tomorrow. We can play thirty-six at this pace."

"Man, you need to be getting back to the job. J.T. said you done strung this shit out too long as it is."

"I told you. I'm on my honeymoon."

"Don't sound like you getting too much honey to me."

Every two holes, Mack pulled another beer from the cooler. Every time, he gave it a quick shake, then opened it with one hand, spritzing Buddy as the cart blazed down the fairway.

As they left the green at thirteen, Mack cracked open another.

"Oops!" he said, laughing.

"Bitch!"

"Man, I hope she brings back one of those little Asian hotties," said Mack, still laughing at Buddy wiping the beer spray from his face. "How fuckin' sweet would that be?"

Mack closed his eyes and thought about Wanda, smelling like coconut oil, making out with a ninety-three-pound Thai masseuse on the bed in the casita. Tumescence had now stiffened into a nail-pounding erection. He'd never gotten a boner before on a golf course, but he knew he needed to take care of it.

Just a little way down off the fourteenth fairway on the right was a portable toilet, a temporary convenience for the guys reshaping the course to keep them from trucking back and forth to the clubhouse and mucking up the resort's facility, or worse yet, whipping it out to take a leak unobstructed by any trees or discretionary shrubbery.

"Yo, man, hold up," said Mack, "I need to go get rid of some of this beer."

Buddy, sipping his own beer and wiping the sticky foam from the side of his face, just nodded. He watched Mack scamper down the hill to the portable toilet below. *Goddamn, white people run funny.* Then Buddy noticed the tractor just behind the elevated tee box.

Watching Mack enter the toilet and pull the door closed, Buddy then glanced up at the tractor again. He swiveled his head as he checked out the area. Twelve-thirty and not a soul on the course. He slipped out of the cart and hustled up to the tractor. The absent landscaping crew had left the key in it. Buddy lined up the wheels so that the back left tire would just nick the toilet and knock it over. *Motherfucker wants to spray beer on somebody, let him get wet for a change.* Without starting the engine, Buddy popped the tractor into neutral. It started rolling slowly at first, then began picking up speed.

Mack had decided his strategy of saving his seed for a double header had been a mistake. That's why he blew his load like a thirteen-year-old watching Wanda in the shower. No, what he needed, he figured, was to rub one out; that way he'd be able to go all night once Buddy was on his way back over the mountains.

It stunk inside the portable toilet, but not enough to derail Mack's erection. He'd stroked himself five times or so when he felt the ground rumbling. *A fucking earthquake?* The rumbling grew more intense. Mack looked around. He had one hand on his joint and the other on the door handle.

When the tractor clipped the corner of the toilet, the force slammed Mack against the fiberglass walls. The little hut upended, dumping its contents all over Mack, who screamed like a bobcat in a croker sack. The toilet shattered completely when it bounced on the ground, shards of green fiberglass spread out in a thousand jagged pieces, surrounding Mack, who lay among them on the grass, moaning in a soggy heap.

TWENTY-FIVE

Buddy jogged up to the scene. *Oops, motherfucker.*

Mack wailed and writhed all over the mess, his navy shorts around his ankles. The smell caused Buddy to pull his shirt up over his nose.

"Goddamngoddamngoddamn..." Mack moaned.

"You awright?" Buddy couldn't suppress a smile under his shirt.

"Ooooh, fuuuuck," Mack rolled over onto his back, his dick in his right hand.

Buddy guessed it was his dick. He'd never seen anything but a knee or an elbow bent at that angle. It looked like some kind of pink fishhook.

"Jesus. That yo' dick? What was you doin' in there, man?"

Mack moaned. He opened his eyes and looked down at his crotch. He yelled so loud Buddy was sure they must've heard it in the clubhouse.

"Ohmigod! What the fuck?"

Buddy's face popped up from beneath his shirt. "That shit looks bad, man."

Mack whimpered.

"Stinks too." Buddy put his face beneath his shirt again. "Goddamn."

Mack let go of his dick, but it kept the same safety pin shape.

"What you want to do, man? Call an ambulance or try to ride back on the cart?"

Mack rolled over on his side and onto one knee. "Uuugghhh." His shorts were soaked with the toilet's contents. He gradually stood up and gingerly pulled them up and over his crotch, holding them closed in his hands without zipping up.

"Just get me out of here and back to the hotel."

Buddy raced back to the pro shop, every bump sending Mack howling in pain. Buddy locked up the brakes and skidded to a halt next to the pro shop. Mack was doubled over and trying to stagger away from the cart. The teenaged kid who cleaned the clubs came running up.

"Is he having a heart attack or something?" the kid said.

"Yo, man, he needs a doctor," said Buddy, and the kid took off sprinting into the pro shop. Seconds later, the assistant pro who'd booked them onto the course came running out.

"Do you want an ambulance?" the pro said as he ran up to Mack. When he got three feet away, like Buddy, he buried his face in his shirt. "What happened? Does he have some kind of IBS situation or something?"

"What's IBS?" asked Buddy.

"Irritable bowel syndrome."

"You mean, like, people shit all over themselves?"

"Something like that."

Mack groaned and tried to stand up.

"That's a common thing?" Buddy cocked his head and looked at the guy. "I thought that was just something little kids and old people did, man. Seriously?"

"No joke," said the assistant pro.

"Fuuuuck," groaned Mack.

"Naw, man. You know that tractor you got up on fourteen? Motherfucker just rolled down the hill, man, and hit my boy while he was inside takin' a piss."

"Jesus," said the assistant pro and the kid in unison.

"Did the tractor run over him?" the assistant pro asked.

"I don't know, maybe."

"Fuuuuckk," Mack moaned again. His shorts dropped down to his socks stained brown and blue-green from the toilet's chemicals.

"Oh, shit!" said the kid, pointing to Mack's crotch. "Look!"

Mack's penis was still bent at a sixty-degree angle, the head shiny, purple, and swollen.

"Looks like a tennis ball," said the kid.

"More like one of those Portuguese rolls you get in the bakery," said the assistant pro, craning his neck to get a better look.

"Those the soft ones or the crusty hard ones?" asked Buddy.

"I think they can be either," said the kid.

"You're probably right," said the assistant pro, "but I was thinking of the crusty kind. You ever have those with just some olive oil? Maybe a little black pepper? Fucking awesome."

Mack moaned again. His eyes were wet. "Call," he said, huffing, "Wanda."

Alerted in the spa to an undetermined emergency, Wanda came jogging out to the clubhouse parking lot. When she got close, her hand went up to her mouth.

"Ohmigod! What happened?"

"Sounds like there was an accident with a tractor out on the course," said the assistant pro.

"I can't believe this! We're on our honeymoon!"

"Those fucking landscaping guys," the assistant pro said, "excuse my French."

"We've got to get you to the hospital, baby."

Mack looked around and realized Wanda was talking to him.

"You want me to call an ambulance?" said the assistant pro.

Mack shook his head. "No ambulance." He started to gag from the smell. "You got a shower in there, right?"

"Yeah," said the pro.

"Get me a clean shirt and a pair of shorts. Thirty-two," said Mack. "I gotta hose this shit off'n me, before I puke. Then I'll go to the hospital."

"Yes, sir, right this way," said the kid. Buddy guided Mack toward the locker room as the assistant pro slipped into the shop and gathered up clean togs and carried them to the shower.

While Mack showered, Buddy pulled five hundreds from J.T.'s envelope before handing the envelope to Wanda.

"Here's the cash J.T. sent. Said give you two grand and keep five hundred. We cool?"

"Yeah." Wanda shook her head. "I'll talk to J.T. when I know what's going on." She gave him a halfhearted wave and turned back toward the clubhouse.

Buddy stuffed the five bills into his front pocket. It was a start. More than enough to cover the filing fees for his company, but still short of what he'd need to prosecute a patent. Shit, from what he'd read on the Internet, he'd probably need multiple patents. He wished he knew what Mack was bringing in from the scam. Of course, now that he was really fucked up, that had to be worth more than a fake back injury.

When he looked at it that way, maybe Buddy had done them both a favor.

TWENTY-SIX

After yet another missed call from Sonu Chugh, J.T. wondered if maybe the doctor didn't have some legal quandary after all. J.T. dialed Chugh's office and leaned back in his desk chair.

"Dr. Chugh," boomed J.T. over the speakerphone, faking the enthusiasm he always did when he planned on keeping a call short. "How are you today?"

"I am veddy well, Johnny. Veddy well indeed. And yourself?"

"Can't complain, Doc. What can I do for you?"

"Yes, of course. About the matter of our last consultation."

"Yeah, I don't know when he's going to call, but I gave him your number." J.T. swiveled in his chair and flipped through an online article about toxic mold resurfacing in Southern California.

"Oh, no, I have already met with Mr. McMahon."

J.T. looked away from his screen and stared at the phone on his desk.

"Excuse me?"

"Yes, I met with Mr. McMahon in my office on Monday."

"Monday?"

"Yes. I have to say I was quite surprised. From your rather cryptic description, I had assumed some sort of orthopedic injury."

"On Monday."

"Yes, Monday. A veddy simple diagnosis. Herpes zoster. Nothing to be alarmed about."

"You saw McMahon on Monday. For herpes."

"Yes, I see how you, too, associate herpes zoster with the sexually transmitted disease." Chugh chuckled. "No, in this case, it's quite a simple case of what we call shingles. Nothing more."

"Shingles."

"Just a rash. Not serious." Chugh cleared his throat. "Ordinarily, of course, I wouldn't discuss a patient's medical condition, but seeing as you referred him in your capacity as a lawyer and so forth.... As we're keeping the consultation private for the time being, I thought we might dispense with the formalities of a release for attorney disclosure."

"Right." J.T. chewed his lip.

"So with respect to the fee for the consultation. We agreed that it would be in cash."

"Right." J.T. thrummed his desk. *Fucking Al.*

"So if you can just drop by with two hundred and fifty dollars, we may consider the account settled."

"Two fifty."

"Yes."

"Did you ask Mr. McMahon for the money?"

"He said he understood you'd already taken care of it. We don't have a misunderstanding, do we, Johnny?"

"No, no," said J.T. "We're all good." Well, at least he wasn't out of pocket much. He shook his head. *Fucking Al.* "I'll drop the money by this afternoon."

"Excellent. Any time I can be of service. You just give me a call. We can keep our transactions discreet this way, yes?"

"Sure, Doc. I'll be in touch." J.T. tossed the phone into its cradle.

J.T.'s first thought had been that Mack had been lying about Vegas. When Chugh mentioned the shingles, he knew it was Al.

Which meant, of course, that now Al knew J.T. hadn't paid Chugh the six grand. J.T.'s gaze bounced among the tchotchkes on his desk and his computer screen. He looked at the walls, then out the seventh-floor window, waiting, as he always had, for inspiration to strike. He called Al on one of the disposable phones. With Al at the office, it would put him off guard and force him to call J.T. back, giving J.T. a little more room to read the situation. He was surprised when Al answered.

"Hey," Al said. "What's up?"

"Just checking in with a status report. I heard from Mack. I also talked to Chugh."

"Talked to Chugh, huh?"

"Yeah, he told me about the shingles. Guess that solves the mystery of the rash." J.T. leaned back in his chair and looked at the haze floating about the San Bernardino Mountains in the distance. "I can't believe that greedy fuck tried to hit you up for more cash."

"More cash?" Al snorted. "You didn't pay him dick."

"He's full of shit. I gave that skel six grand. Hope you got our money's worth."

"He didn't call you for the money for the visit?"

"That's what I'm saying: he was laughing about it. Figured since I'd referred you, he might be able to beat you out of a fee for the consultation. Claim that I'd said you'd pay. Fucking classic scam. I see this half the time I deal with guys like this."

"Seriously?"

"They're fucking notorious. They figure if they don't get caught, no harm, no foul."

"What a scumbag."

"What do you expect from a crooked doctor?" J.T. had regained his momentum. "By the way, aren't you at work right now?"

"No, I stayed home today because of the shingles." J.T. heard the rattling of dishes in the background. "I guess I got a free diagnosis out of it."

"I don't know about free. You realize what this means, right?"

"What?"

"Because you went to Chugh claiming to be Mack, now we can't use Chugh."

"Oh, shit."

"When Mack fucked up the first flop, there was no need to tell him. When we greenlit the second adventure, Chugh didn't know that it wasn't the first one. Get it?"

"Yeah."

"So now, your 'free' medical advice means we have to find another doctor. What that's going to set us back, I don't know. Chugh was my first option."

"Jesus, I'm sorry. I didn't think of that." Al cleared his throat. "So what's going on with Mack?"

"He finally left Vegas. He's at Fuente Dorado." J.T. could tell that Al was still buying the Chugh story. "He pissed away the four grand I fronted him and I had to send another four. That shit's not coming out of my end."

"Absolutely. Hotel's one thing, but this is ridiculous." Al sniffed. "So when is his accident taking place?"

He bought it. "Any time now. I decided that they shouldn't have the accident on the first day. Makes selling the honeymoon story more plausible."

"That's good thinking. I guess it would be kind of suspicious if they checked in and got hurt a few minutes later."

Why didn't you say that when you came up with this plan, asshole? "Anyway, it still leaves us with the problem of paying for another doctor."

"Yeah."

"Any ideas?"

"I guess we could go back to Frankie Fresh for more cash." Al sighed. "God, I hate to get in deeper with that fat bastard, though."

"Well, unfortunately, since you're the one who stirred the pot with Chugh, I don't know what choice you have."

"What choice *I* have?"

"Hey, I'm not the one that fucked up the medical trying to get cute."

"I'll call him and get some more. How much do you think we need?"

"Get ten. Let me recoup some of the cash I fronted Mack and Chugh."

TWENTY-SEVEN

With Mack cleaned up and Buddy gone, Wanda shepherded Mack out to her car and drove the eight miles to Eisenhower Medical Center in Rancho Mirage. After scratching out a medical history on a form, Mack was guided into an examination room where a tanned doctor in his early sixties soon joined them.

"Well, now," Dr. John Garvey announced, rolling a small three-wheeled stool up to where Mack stood leaning against an examination table. "What have we got here? Can you lower your shorts for me?"

Mack let his shorts drop to the floor. The doctor tilted his head to one side, then the other. With his gloved hand he moved Mack's member slightly. Mack's whole body jerked back.

"Hurts, huh?" asked Garvey. "Sorry about that." The doctor looked at Wanda. "What happened?"

"I don't know, I wasn't there."

Mack grimaced as he tried to get comfortable. "I got hit by a runaway tractor."

"It ran over your penis?"

"Not exactly." Mack winced. "I was in a portable toilet on the golf course at Fuente Dorado when—"

"Which course?" asked the doctor.

"Uh…Tesoro."

"That used to be a nice track. Very nice. Too bad it's taking them so long to get it back into shape." Garvey pulled a tongue depressor from his pocket and lifted Mack's penis slightly while looking underneath. "I think they may host the Dinah Shore there next year."

"Uh-huh," Mack said.

"So you play there often?" asked Garvey.

"No. We're here"—Mack winced again—"on our honeymoon."

"Hey, congratulations!" He turned to Wanda. "How about that?"

"Yeah," said Wanda. "How about that?"

Garvey turned back to Mack. "So how bad is the pain?"

"Pretty fuckin' bad."

"Right." Garvey stripped off his gloves and threw them into a plastic garbage can labeled MEDICAL WASTE. He clicked a ballpoint pen emblazoned with the logo of a pharmaceutical company. "Okay, first thing we're going to do is get you something for the pain. I can give you a local; then I'll write you a scrip for some painkillers."

"Great."

"What then?" asked Wanda.

"Well, we need for the swelling to go down just a little bit to determine the extent of the damage. I'll schedule you for an MRI in the morning."

"So what's the diagnosis?" Wanda asked.

"Preliminarily, it looks like a penile fracture. Possibly an early onset of Peyronie's disease."

"Jesus," said Mack.

"So what do you do?" asked Wanda, now gently rubbing circles on Mack's back.

"Leeches!" said the doctor, grinning. "The problem is all that blood trapped at the head of our friend's penis there. Leeches take down the swelling like you wouldn't believe." Garvey walked to the door. "Mary Ann," he hollered down the hall, "can you bring me two of the six-gram leeches, please?"

"What the fuck?" shouted Mack.

Standing erect, Garvey was well over six feet, maybe six-four. He was kind of handsome in a way that reminded Mack of one of those old cowboy shows. His teeth matched his hair—eggshell white—and were set off by his tanned, barely lined face.

Garvey chuckled. "I'm just kidding."

"Thank God," said Wanda.

The doctor leaned in and smiled. "They're not really *that* effective." Garvey stood up and stepped back to the door and stuck his head out. "Mary Ann! Make that *four* of the six-grammers, please."

"Holy shit! You ain't really putting leeches on my cock!"

Garvey threw his head back and laughed. "C'mon," he said. "Frank Sinatra used to come to this hospital. You think we'd really use leeches? I'm just playing with you. Relax." Garvey put his hand on Mack's shoulder. "You're in the best possible hands."

Mack and Wanda started chuckling together until Mack winced.

"So seriously, what happens now?" asked Wanda.

"Well, there are a couple of ways we can go," said Garvey. "Immediate surgery, naturally, is one option. There are possible postoperative effects, however, that a specialist can explain better than I can."

"What kind of effects?" Mack and Wanda asked together.

"Well, for one, there's a risk the procedure will not be successful. Then of course there's always a risk anytime a patient undergoes general anesthesia."

"But what else?" said Wanda, who watched Mack staring at his fractured member.

"Inability to achieve erection and sexual function could be one result. Permanent dislocation another." Garvey picked up a chart on the counter and made a notation. "The most important thing right now is to rule out a ruptured artery or torn urethra. Have you been able to urinate?"

"Hasn't even occurred to me."

"Well, at this point, we'd have to knock you out to insert a catheter anyway."

"Jesus."

"So what were you shooting?"

"Excuse me?"

"At Fuente Dorado. What'd you shoot before the tractor?"

"I don't know. I think I was maybe six or seven over after thirteen. Playing from the tips."

"Not bad. I played in a Pro-Am there with Ben Crenshaw years ago."

Mack shifted up onto his elbow as he leaned against the examining table. "Ben's from Texas, you know."

"Great guy. Not long off the tee by today's standards, but could he putt."

"Yeah, I just fucked up my shoulder the other night too, or I'da been lower."

Wanda nudged Mack.

Garvey made another notation on his chart. "Well, while surgery is an option, my recommendation—at least for this evening, unless there's a sudden negative reaction—would be simply to ice the area down. Give the tissue a chance to ameliorate some of the swelling. If things don't look better by tomorrow, I think a specialist will recommend surgery. He might anyway, but at least it might not be the de-gloving procedure."

"De-gloving?" said Mack.

"Just what it sounds like. They make a cut and then peel back the—"

Mack raised a hand. "Stop. 'Less you want me to puke right here."

Garvey nodded and held up both of his hands.

"What's the risk of waiting?" asked Wanda.

"If there is a tear, things could get bad quickly. Frankly, though, I think if that were the case, we'd be seeing a lot more swelling below the bend here." Garvey pointed with his pen and circled Mack's penis.

"Either way," he continued, "if you opt for surgery, you're going to want a specialist, and that would likely take several hours to arrange anyway. I want to keep you here tonight for observation. You can just chill out, take one of the muscle relaxants and an anti-inflammatory, and ice the area down. If it gets worse, we can operate tonight. If the swelling goes down, we'll take another look in the morning. What do you think?"

"I think this is some shitty honeymoon."

"It's a tough lie, that's for sure," said Garvey.

"You said it, Doc," said Wanda.

TWENTY-EIGHT

Al swung by the club that afternoon to meet Frankie Fresh to take out another loan against the payout. Frankie was in the 19th Hole eating a meatball sub with a basket of fries. Al sat down and Frankie pushed an inch-thick envelope across the table.

"You guys aren't letting your expenses get away from you, now, are you?" Frankie asked.

"No, we're okay."

"If you say so," Frankie said between mouthfuls of sub. "Thirty percent seems like an awful high investment for a hundred-K return like you're expecting."

"Thirty?"

"Your original five, the other five, and this ten, plus the ten the counselor hit me for the other day."

J.T. hadn't told Al about taking out ten from Frankie. "Yeah, that ten he got must've been on his own account. I don't know anything about that."

"Uh-huh. Now I suppose he's going to tell me the same thing about this. Listen," Frankie said, stuffing a wad of fries in his mouth, "I personally don't give a shit who's doing what with the money. If you guys are borrowing at a point a week to buy chicks' underwear, I don't care. Just remember the golden rule." He pointed at his chest with his two greasy thumbs. "First dollar payout. Me." Frankie leaned in so close, Al could smell the potatoes on his breath. His blue irises were darker and cloudier than

Al had ever seen them. Bloodshot capillaries textured the whites of his eyes. "I will get paid, Al. First."

Al's sphincter tightened. "Understood."

"Which raises another point: vig's due."

"Already?"

Frankie wiped his mouth with a napkin and raised his eyebrows. "The first ten you guys took out?" He sipped the iced tea in his right hand and extended his open left palm. "That's a hundred this week and three hundred next week, got it?"

Al reached for his wallet. He hoped Frankie didn't notice the bill tremble as Al pulled out a hundred and placed it on Frankie's swollen mitt.

"Got it."

J.T. had nearly worn a groove in his office carpet pacing back and forth, waiting for a call from Mack or Wanda. Unable to bear it any longer, he called Wanda.

"So, how's it going? Did he execute his gainer in the lobby?"

"Not exactly."

"What the fuck is going on over there? This is bullsh—"

"He really got hurt."

"What?"

"I'm at Eisenhower Medical Center. He got hurt on the golf course. A tractor rolled down a hill and knocked over a portable toilet when he was inside."

"You're kidding."

"He's got a fractured penis. He's lying knocked out on the bed here in the hospital room. He's going to need surgery."

J.T. whooped. "Fan-fucking-tastic! You're not kidding me, right?"

"Nope. He's really hurt."

"Any witnesses?"

"No. It was the middle of the day. Just him and Buddy on the course."

J.T. bounced on his toes. "So you're with him at the hospital and everything? He really got hurt on the resort property?"

"Yes."

"And the fracture? It's been confirmed by MRI?"

"No, the doctor wanted to wait and let the swelling go down. They're worried there might be an arterial tear or a tear in the urethra. At a minimum, he's got to have some kind of surgical procedure done."

"And on his honeymoon! That is just terrific! I knew you wouldn't let me down." J.T. thought about what wine he should celebrate with.

"Nice to see you take such an interest in your client's well-being. You realize he's seriously injured, J.T. Not to mention this means we have to stay out here another day."

"Yeah, sure. Don't worry, I'm coming out tomorrow."

"You?"

"You kidding? I'm the lawyer, babe. The first responder." J.T. pumped his fist. "God, I knew I was overdue for a break!"

"You're not going to shaft Mack on this, are you?"

"Ooh, nice one."

"You know what I meant."

"Don't worry about Mack. You're both going to be taken care of." J.T. shut down his computer and started gathering keys, glasses, and cell phones from his desk. "Trust me."

J.T. hopped around his living room with Warren Zevon's *Excitable Boy* album pouring out of his Bose speakers. In spite of his recent investment in more affordable vintages, he opened a special Pouilly-Fumé and blew the dust out of a Baccarat glass, rather than the huge balloons he used with his reds. He let his wine settle in his mouth—every bit as nice as he'd remembered—while one of the disposable phones lit up on the kitchen counter.

"So when were you going to tell me about Frankie Fresh and the ten grand?" said Al.

"Whoa." J.T. pointed the remote at the armoire hiding the stereo and turned down the volume on Warren Zevon. "What happened to hello?"

"Okay, hello. What the fuck, J.T.?"

"So it slipped my mind. Don't worry, I've got great news."

"Slipped your mind? What kind of fucking scumbag lawyer excuse is that?"

"Hey, last time I checked, when there was cash to be handed to Mack, to Wanda, to Buddy, to Chugh, Big Al was nowhere to be seen. You sure you want to take that dirt road, my friend?"

There was silence on the other end of the line. J.T. imagined Al stewing, unable to come up with a retort.

"All I'm saying is you should've told me," Al said. "We've got a thirty-thousand-dollar balance with that warthog. And he's expecting to get paid, don't forget."

"Al? Listen to me. We are all good, baby. I just talked to Wanda."

"And? Did Mack slip in the lobby?"

"Better. Much, much better."

"What, then?"

"Penile fracture!"

"What?"

"Penile fucking fracture! *On his honeymoon!* At a five-star resort in Palm Desert, California!"

"Jesus, is he okay?"

"You mean aside from a broken dick?" *God, is everybody in the world as thick as cake batter?* "Needs a procedure at least. Maybe a big-time surgery."

"Wow."

"Good news is, now we don't need to worry about Chugh. We'll have the best doctors in Palm Springs lined up to vouch for the injury."

"What the hell happened?"

"I don't know. He was in a portable toilet that got hit when a tractor rolled down a hill." J.T. sipped his wine. "Probably in there jerking off, the dumbass."

"Any witnesses? Anybody from the resort talk to him?"

"I don't think so. Maybe the golf pro." J.T. lifted the bottle and studied the label. He might have to pick up some more of this. "I'm going out there tomorrow morning to get the lay of the land."

"So what are you thinking the claim's worth now?"

"I don't know. A hell of a lot more than a measly hundred K. Jesus, throw in the loss of consortium claim…broken dick on their honeymoon? Forget about it. Monster. Absolute monster."

"You know my authority's only two hundred thousand. I won't be able to sign off on a bigger settlement than that. Not without going upstairs."

"Big fucking deal. You're looking at a multimillion-dollar demand letter. The whole landscape's changed."

"What do you mean? You're double-crossing me?"

"Listen to you, 'double-cross.' No, I'm not cutting you out, I'm just saying the landscape's changed. For one thing, Mack's going to have to get a bigger percentage. He has to. Fucking guy might be impotent the rest of his life." J.T. swallowed some more wine. "On top of which I'm pretty sure his Coast Guard dream is fucked now."

"But what does that have to do with me?"

"Okay, listen. Until five minutes ago, you were going to be happy with what, forty, fifty grand? I'm saying you're covered, okay? This thing settles, you won't need to risk the heat inside GSAC anymore and you can afford to quit, just like you wanted."

J.T. could hear Al breathing on the other end of the line. *Impervious to good news, this guy.* "If this thing gets anywhere near what I think it'll get, I'll work it out with Mack. You'll get your fifty K plus a nice bonus."

Al sighed. "You really think so?"

"Believe me, this is all good, man."

TWENTY-NINE

When J.T. stopped by Eisenhower Medical Center at 8:30 a.m., Mack was still zonked out on what drugs J.T. couldn't begin to imagine. Wanda got him on the list so he could talk to the doctors and get an early preview of the charts and prognosis.

He drove to El Fuente Dorado with the windows down, the volume from the stereo maxed, and singing with Andrea Bocelli at the top of his lungs, grinning at the heads turning as he flew past retirees walking their dogs on the sidewalks.

He wanted to see the fourteenth hole where the tractor had hit Mack. Unfortunately, given the looming litigation, he couldn't just walk up and interview witnesses from the pro shop. He had a monster on his hands, and he wasn't about to fuck it up with an ethics beef.

That didn't mean he couldn't scope out the course, though. He pulled the Mercedes up to the pro shop and left his clubs at the bag drop. He went out as a solo, so excited on the first tee that he yanked his opening drive almost to the same spot Mack had.

He'd forgotten how much he used to love playing these desert courses. The big brown mountains surging up in the distance. Not smack on the fairway like at Mira Chiste. Hell, when this thing settled, he might look into joining a club out here himself.

He took his time, enjoying the round, his pulse quickening the closer he got to fourteen, where he could get out and do a little investigating. There was no one on the course, so he wouldn't be holding anyone up.

When he reached the fourteenth tee, he got out and went down the hill to where he saw the jagged fragments of what used to be the hunter green portable toilet. The moisture had burned off in the desert dryness, but the stench remained. He half expected to see a chalk outline where Mack had been writhing on the ground, grasping his johnson and wailing in pain.

The tractor had been moved, but not that far—just across the fifteenth fairway. J.T. climbed back in his cart and played out fourteen. When he got to the fifteenth tee, he deliberately stroked a four-iron short and left to where the tractor was. There were grounds crews at work, but the tractor sat idle near the grassless desert rough. J.T. got out and examined the tractor's wheels. The bits of green fiberglass were small, but they were there.

He peered up at the slope from where the tractor had initially rested before barreling downhill. He shielded his eyes from the sun and stared at the hill. He looked back at the blue-green Rorschach pattern on the edge of the fourteenth fairway directly opposite where he stood.

He picked up his ball and climbed back in the cart. He started whistling the tune he'd been singing in the car and drove back to the clubhouse without stopping. He'd give himself pars on the remaining four holes.

He finally had a winner.

THIRTY

Hector Aza got a call from Sid Stewart, associate general counsel at GSAC, about a demand letter received several weeks before from John T. Edwards.

"I know of him," said Hector. "Never had a case against him."

Hector had seen J.T. at the occasional bar association golf tournament. Tipping cart girls twenty bucks for a screwdriver; bragging about playing seven courses in a single week in Scotland; yammering about how the greens break at Spyglass.

"Guy's been on our radar for years," Stewart explained. "Made shitloads in asbestos, fen-phen, and every quicksilver class action fad you ever heard of. He's pretty much on the skids now. Partners kicked him out of their big-time class action practice. Rumor was they had enough ethical dirt on him to cock-block all his scorched-earth threats. Second wife left him after that."

According to Stewart, Edwards also had a string of dramatic financial reversals unrelated to his legal career. "His practice has gone to shit, but he still keeps up the façade. Half a floor in the Inland Empire Tower. Hot young receptionist. Big Mercedes."

Stewart yawned near the phone. "He's a paper tiger. From anyone but J.T. Edwards, this demand letter almost has a whiff of legitimacy, but because it's him, I just can't get over a nagging feeling there's a bullshit claim behind it."

"Slip and fall?" asked Hector.

"Guy gets into a freak accident on the Tesoro course at Fuente Dorado. A tractor rolls down a slope and runs over him while he's taking a leak in a portable toilet."

"Ouch."

"Broke his dick."

"What?"

"Yeah—penile fracture. And get this: on his honeymoon."

"You think the medical's legit?"

"Got pictures from Eisenhower Medical in Rancho Mirage. I'll have the file sent to you. Don't look at the pictures if you haven't eaten breakfast."

"That bad?"

"Hollywood couldn't come up with special effects like that."

Hector turned around in his chair and reached into the mini refrigerator he kept under the scratched table serving as a credenza. He pulled out a Diet Coke, pointed it away from his desk, and opened the can. "So what's the angle?"

"Looks to be about sixty degrees."

Hector cleared his throat. "I meant the claim angle."

"I can't see if there is one. Edwards may just be due to get lucky, I don't know. I do know that these assholes are looking to settle this thing for big dollars, no questions asked."

"How big?"

"Demand's for nine mil. These guys are talking about offering eight seventy-five right now."

"Nothing's been filed yet?"

"I bet Edwards hasn't gone to trial in at least five years. Maybe longer. Certainly nothing bigger than a DUI defense."

"That's a lot of money for someone not to try a case."

"Look, if the guy's really hurt, and if the policyholder really was negligent, sure, I'd rather settle the case than lose at trial. But c'mon. No discovery? No medical eval? No witness interviews?"

"So you want to make him file first."

"At a minimum. He doesn't want to try this thing, he just wants to turn a quick buck. I don't think he's got the money to try it, frankly. I can live with a settlement. I just don't want to be hustled."

Hector wrote up the engagement letter and budgeted for discovery, motions, and trial. If Stewart was right and the case was going to settle anyway, Hector knew he might be able to keep the price tag down with a little digging and discovery. First, however, Edwards would have to file.

Al Boyle's nerves felt like they'd been raked over a cheese grater. The deadline for the Weed transfer was looming. He'd heard nothing more about the internal investigation into the database breach. That was unsettling enough. Making matters worse, the vig to Frankie Fresh that had once seemed so insignificant was now running $300 a week. The only silver lining was that Frankie didn't know about the new legitimate claim. He was still under the impression it was a $100,000 scam. If they could hurry up and settle for even a fraction of what the case was worth, the vigorish would be nothing more than a minor annoyance.

His imagination fueled by relentless coffee drinking, Al surfed the web, looking at comps for his house. He thought about the husks of abandoned would-be four-bedroom homes standing desiccated in the hot dust blowing in from the desert. He was fucked. How could his house still be worth $97,000 less than his mortgage note?

J.T. Edwards was pissed. It was just like those GSAC cocksuckers to string him along. It was all the more infuriating in that he had a legitimate claim. Horrific injury. Unimpeachable medicals. Unquestionable negligence.

Probably.

J.T. knew if his case had one fly in the ointment, it was causation. Having used some of Frankie Fresh's cash to buy chemicals for the Jacuzzi that had long sat inert on his deck, J.T. sat in the tub with a bottle of wine, trying to think like GSAC's in-house lawyers. They had to be hung up on the causation. There was no way to fake a broken dick. As for the medical opinion, a guy who'd been Lew Wasserman's urologist was no Sonu Chugh.

J.T. had been so excited about Mack's real injury, he'd soft-pedaled any self-doubts about *how* it happened. The tractor really did roll down the hill. The toilet really did shatter. He'd seen for himself the tractor with pieces of green fiberglass in the wheels. Wanda confirmed the assistant pro and the clubhouse kid saw Mack covered in shit and cloacal solvents.

Buddy. He needed to get to Buddy and get a thorough debriefing. What if there had been a minor earthquake that started the tractor rolling? It was possible. J.T. made a mental note to check on the website of the U.S. Geological Survey when he got out of the tub. Probably just some Mexican forgot to put the tractor in gear.

Yeah, the simplest explanation was usually the right one.

Mack moped in Wanda's apartment. He'd avoided the de-gloving procedure but had needed surgery to regain the use of his penis. The catheter had been nearly as bad as the accident itself. Wanda had gone back to work at the club, but Mack was still housebound and still afraid he'd never get another boner.

He couldn't believe his string of luck. He was all but sure to be unfit for the Coast Guard now. He didn't want to call the recruiter to ask. He'd defer any more bad news until he was better able to digest it. Sure, he'd probably get the truck now—a new one—and even the flying lessons, but then what? Wanda seemed to think their case was worth a hell of a lot more than what J.T. had promised when it was just a slip and fall in the lobby. Mack hoped so. She also warned him about giving J.T. too much of the claim now.

It was one thing when the claim was a scam, she said, but now he was really hurt. Hell, they could hire any personal injury lawyer in California and walk away with a fortune. Mack gave it some thought. He was sick of being called a dumbass by J.T. Edwards. He had lost his desire to be one of J.T.'s *associates.* Still, as long as there was going to be a lawsuit, it did seem kind of shitty to walk away and leave J.T. hanging after he'd been the one to approach Mack in the first place. Yeah, he'd stick with J.T., but there'd have to be a new understanding about how Mack was going to be talked to.

Al was daydreaming in front of a computer screen when his district manager, Marino Vargas, stepped up to Al's cubicle. Vargas picked up a foam stress ball on Al's desk, worthless swag from an adjuster's convention in San Diego.

Vargas leaned against the fabric-covered wall of Al's cubicle and squeezed the ball absently. "Just got a call from Sid Stewart in legal. They don't want to settle yet on that broken dick claim at Fuente Dorado."

"You serious?"

"Yeah. Stewart's not sold. He doesn't think this guy Edwards has the stones to try the case."

"No shit?" Al leaned back in his chair. He picked up a pencil and chewed on it. "But the guy's got a broken cock. How do you fake that?"

"I don't know. Fucking lawyers, right?"

"Jesus, if this thing goes to trial, we could get waxed."

"Hey, you know what? Serves 'em right. Fuck it. It'll be SAICO's problem by that point anyway."

Al chewed on the pencil again. "So the merger's definitely going through?"

"I'm pretty sure. You realize, once they announce it formally, you're going to have to shit or get off the pot on the Weed thing, right?"

"I know, I know." Al rubbed his ribcage. The little scabs had long since flaked off, but sometimes he felt a phantom rash. He wanted to change the subject.

"So who'd they hire on that Fuente Dorado claim?"

"Hector Aza. You ever work with him?"

"Never heard of him. One of your homeys?"

"You kidding? Guy's probably more Anglo than you." Vargas bounced the ball on Al's desk. "I think his father was born in Spain but moved here when he was a kid."

Vargas bouncing the ball annoyed the shit out of Al, but he didn't say anything.

"Anyway," continued Vargas, "you know the drill. Just send him the file and whatever else he needs." He tossed the ball to Al. Al caught it and stuffed it behind his monitor to make sure some other mook didn't come by and start bouncing it on his desk.

"Yeah, okay."

"And think about the Weed thing. Seriously, okay? If you don't want it, I got plenty of people who do."

Vargas thumped the cubicle wall a couple of times and walked away. Al slumped in his chair. No settlement. Not for a while, at least. *J.T. was too fucking greedy.* He'd priced his demand out of settlement range, which was almost impossible with a legit claim like this. Al hadn't realized the degree to which J.T. was a known quantity at GSAC. He should've been tipped off when J.T. was complaining about how the company dragged its feet settling cases. If the guys in legal were scared of J.T., they'd be plenty happy to settle and in a hurry. Their stance meant only one thing: they weren't worried about J.T.

But Al Boyle was worried. He'd hitched his wagon to this turd in the hope of scoring a quick and dirty forty grand. Now he was under the thumb of a shylock with a sixty-five-inch waist. Worse yet, J.T. didn't seem to be in any hurry to settle. Frankie's vig was mounting, and J.T. kept saying how a multimillion-dollar verdict would make it seem like nothing.

J.T. was living in fantasy land. Al wondered if he was on drugs. Frankie had sniffed out their scam when it was a simple slip and fall. Did J.T. really believe that Frankie wouldn't put two and two together when Mack started driving around Riverside in a new Corvette? If only Al could get J.T. to buy him out of his end now.

J.T. had given GSAC until Friday to call him back with a settlement offer or he would go ahead and file. Friday came and went and J.T. filed his case against Fuente Dorado in superior court on Monday. Although Fuente Dorado was the nominal defendant, GSAC was driving the bus on the claim. J.T. knew that even though the case was still unlikely to go to trial, once he filed, any settlement would be drawn out. On the other hand, the longer he waited to file, the more confident GSAC would become. More emboldened, they'd be less inclined to part with the significant dollars the claim was worth.

When J.T. returned to the office after lunch, Shari gave him a message that a lawyer named Hector Aza called regarding his representation of GSAC in Mack's case. J.T. began perspiring. He grabbed a bottle of water off the serving tray in the reception area, dusted every morning by Shari for clients that never came. He fumbled with the plastic cap, spilling a little on his shirt as he brought the slightly shaking bottle to his mouth.

"Are you okay?" asked Shari.

J.T. wadded up the message and stuffed it in his pocket. "Yeah. I think too many chilies in the *pico de gallo* or something." He pulled the pink message slip back out of his pocket. "I need to give this guy a call."

GSAC wouldn't have had time to get the complaint yet. That meant the in-house guys hired Aza even before the claim was filed. *That* meant they weren't looking to settle. *That* meant GSAC thought the claim was bullshit.

J.T. looked around for something in his office to break. Something inexpensive. He picked up a stapler and slammed it down hard on a Scotch tape dispenser, shattering the clear plastic. *Fucking cocksuckers!* He had to get under control before he returned Aza's call.

J.T. didn't know Aza. He vaguely recognized the name, but then again, he could have been confusing it with some other Mexican. They all had *z*'s in their names anyway. J.T. decided to Google Aza's website before he called. A shitty, one-page embarrassment. Didn't even have the guy's picture. Just a phone number and a map of how to get to his office, an office J.T. imagined next to a nail salon in some rundown strip mall. And this chump was going to take money off J.T. Edwards? *In your fucking dreams, pal.*

J.T. dialed the number and reclined in his chair.

"This is Hector Aza."

The guy didn't sound Mexican.

"Mr. Aza, J.T. Edwards. I'm returning your call about the McMahon claim against El Fuente Dorado Resort."

"Oh, yes, thank you for returning my call."

J.T. could sense Aza sitting up at attention now. Good.

"I was just calling as a courtesy, actually," said Aza, "to let you know I'd been retained by Golden State Assurance in the matter."

"Okey-doke. You get a copy of the complaint yet?"

"I wasn't aware a complaint had been filed."

Of course you weren't, you dumbfuck. "Yep. Filed this morning. I expressed to GSAC my willingness to negotiate a settlement, but no one got back to me, so I filed the complaint as I promised I would."

"I see."

"Would you like me to send you a copy?"

"That would be great, thanks."

Of course it would, you clueless bastard.

THIRTY-ONE

An unfamiliar phone number appeared on the caller ID of Al's desk phone. Only after Hector Aza had been talking for ten seconds did Al realize he was the lawyer Marino Vargas had told him about.

"Anyway," said Hector, "now that a complaint has been filed, I was hoping—"

Al coughed. "They filed already?"

"Yeah. I just got off the phone with opposing counsel a little while ago."

"How about that? I tried to tell Sid the case was pretty strong. You see the pictures of the guy's pecker yet?"

"Uh, no. Actually, that's kind of why I was calling. Sid said you could e-mail the file to me."

"Sure, no problem." Al's head was spinning. "I'm still surprised they didn't want to settle this one. It could be a huge verdict if things go south."

Al searched on his computer for the electronic file on Mack's claim.

"There's always a chance it could settle," said Hector. "But I don't know that it's a mistake not to get a little more information before the company just opens the checkbook."

"Mm-hmm." Al took one more look at the picture of Mack's broken joint, then scribbled down Aza's e-mail address.

"By the way," said Hector, "do you have contact information for the witnesses out at Fuente Dorado?"

"Witnesses? I thought no one was around."

"Well, there had to be someone around at the resort, right? Someone that saw the plaintiff when he came in from the course? Hotel manager? Somebody?"

"Oh, yeah. I think it's in the file." Al's fingers rattled across his dingy keyboard. "Okay, I just e-mailed you everything I have."

"Thanks. I'm going to head over there this afternoon. We'll see if we get any questions answered."

Al felt his rash returning. He took one of the disposable phones out to his car and called J.T. "What the fuck? You filed the complaint already?"

"Yup. How'd you find out?"

"The lawyer—what's his name, Raza?—he called me and had me send him the file."

"It's Aza, not Raza, and don't worry about it. I checked the guy out. He's a bum. I'll eat him alive."

"What are you basing that on?"

"First of all, I know for a fact you guys don't pay shit for insurance defense, so that's Exhibit A. Second, the guy's a lawyer in Riverside and I never heard of him. Third, I checked out his website. Looks like it was designed by a retarded Albanian kid. I'm telling you, I've got it under control. Unlike some people."

"What's that supposed to mean?"

"You're supposed to be the hotshot claims manager, and you can't even get a settlement negotiation going for a guy whose dick looks like it got caught in an elevator?"

"I told you my authority's only two hundred thousand."

"So you didn't suggest they settle?"

"Of course I did."

"So then clearly GSAC doesn't think much of your opinion."

"Actually, they don't think much of you."

The line went silent on both ends.

"What?"

"Nobody doubts Mack's hurt. The guys in legal apparently just all know something I didn't."

"What's that?"

"That you're full of shit. That they can drag this out forever and you couldn't afford to finance the case, even if you weren't afraid to go to trial."

"Those assholes said I was afraid to try this case?"

"'Like a cockroach with the light on,' I believe was the quote." Al made that up, but he wished someone really had said it.

J.T. was breathing hard through his nose and Al could hear it through the phone.

"This shit just got punitive, my friend," said J.T.

"You know what? Spare me. I've heard enough bullshit to last me a lifetime."

"Okay, just think about something, you simpleminded fuck. You got any idea how many jury verdicts I've had in my career? How many multimillion-dollar cases I've won or settled? You're letting the tough talk of some third-rate, in-house hacks make you think there's a chance in hell GSAC's not going to get their asses handed to them on this. Ever wonder, if these guys are such great lawyers, why are they working for GSAC? Why aren't they out there making millions, huh? They're fucking drones, man. Ciphers. Guys like me shit out guys like that every morning with a bran muffin."

Al blinked quickly but said nothing. This was the most pissed off he'd ever heard J.T.

"You saw those pictures. What's the jury going to say when the doctor testifies? The doctor who treated President Ford, Walter Annenberg, and Bob Hope, and who says Mack's dick was broken in that accident and that the guy will never have sex again, huh?"

Al hated it when J.T. was right. Even if J.T. was a shitty lawyer, a housewife in Temecula could walk into court and win on the medical evidence alone.

"You know, if you want to bail on this thing, be my guest. When you could authorize a settlement, you had some use to me, but without it, who the fuck needs you?"

"I didn't say I wanted to bail." Al turned the car on and cranked up the air conditioning. "I'm just telling you what these guys said. They don't want to settle." Al looked inside his shirt to see if the blisters were returning. "Not yet anyway."

"That's just it. They will settle. They'll settle because they'll have to. Between Mack's broken dick and the loss of consortium claim, I'll squeeze every fucking dime out of that place. And we haven't even begun to talk about the pressure from Fuente Dorado when the publicity machine gets ramped up."

"What do you mean?"

"You think the resort's going to want this story popping up on the Drudge Report and the Smoking Gun, showing Mack's busted schlong? The fucking Emperor of Japan stays at Fuente Dorado. The Prince of Wales. Little billionaire arbitrage creeps. Fuente Dorado does not want to be known as the place where you go to get your dick mangled on the golf course."

"I guess you're right. I hadn't thought about that."

"Don't take this the wrong way, because I am *not* patronizing you, I promise." J.T. sighed. "I *know* you hadn't thought about that. You know why? Because it's not your job to think about things like that. It's my job."

Al closed his eyes and rested his head on the steering wheel.

"Everybody makes lawyer jokes," J.T. continued, "because lawyers are the ones who think about things like this. Looking four, five, eight moves ahead. It's a fucking chess game, man."

Al thought about that. Maybe those guys in legal really weren't as sharp as they acted. What if they were just bluffing themselves? Shit, it wasn't their money. They could talk tough in the office, but J.T. had a point. If they were such hotshots, why weren't they in court themselves?

"Look, I apologize for blowing up a minute ago," J.T said. "I know what it's like to have people turn your head with a bunch of shit. Let me ask you something. You know all those asbestos settlements? Tobacco settlements? Do you think the defense lawyers or insurance company lawyers weren't telling the plaintiffs their cases were bullshit? But think about this. If those cases were bullshit, why did the defendants end up paying out so many billions of dollars?"

"I guess you're right." Al looked at his watch. "I gotta get back to my desk."

"Listen, if you're still in, you can still be of some use."

"How?"

"Just keep me posted. Stay in touch with Aza. Let me know what he's thinking. What he's doing."

"Well, I know he's going out to Palm Desert today."

"Seriously?"

"Yeah, why? Is that a big deal?"

"Not at all, Al. Not at all. Just keep me in the loop, okay?"

Mack's depression deepened. He was still recovering from the operation. His dick had returned more or less to a normal shape, but he couldn't get an erection. A part of him was afraid to even try, afraid it might snap in half or explode or something. Making matters worse, even though Mack's penis was useless, his balls were still working. The doctor told him the recovery would be long and that there was a chance of regaining sexual function, but there were no guarantees.

Exacerbating Mack's pessimism was the fact that he was now legally married and living in Wanda's apartment. Wanda only had a double bed, which she kindly let Mack have during his convalescence. She slept on the couch when she was home, which was seldom, as she'd gone back to picking up as many shifts as she could at the club. She was nice enough to Mack, but now that they were away from the Fuente Dorado, she'd dropped the honeymoon act. She'd certainly never called him "baby" as she had after the accident.

Was it really an accident? He'd been so out of his mind when everything happened, he never really stopped to question just how the tractor had started moving. He'd barely noticed the thing at all as he jogged down the slope to use the toilet. Buddy had said J.T. talked to him about hurrying things along. Had J.T. put Buddy up to mowing him down with the tractor?

Tired of being pent up in the apartment, Mack occasionally went by the club to say hi or grab lunch. Everyone at the club seemed genuinely concerned about his injury. He could feel them treating him differently too, since he was now married to Wanda. People in the office smiled and waved when they saw him in the parking lot or the clubhouse. The other waitresses in the 19th Hole gave him free iced tea.

When he'd gone into the greenskeeper's shed, he'd pulled the tarp off the McMahon 3000. He creaked and groaned as he folded himself into the driver's seat. When he was on the job he'd never crank it up during work hours, but he wasn't working, and with all the other racket from the mowers outside, it wasn't like it was going to bother anyone.

Mack was surprised at how smoothly the engine ran. Tommy must have been starting it for him once in a while for it to be sounding so clean. *Man, I can't wait to take this fucker out in the desert.* The thing was going to be indestructible. A four-inch-thick roll cage welded onto the chassis, crisscrossing overhead. He'd ripped out all the Mini's ruined interior and put some new knobby-tread tires all around. Looked like a fucking moon rover, if a moon rover was badass.

The doc had said while he should take it easy, he could go back to light work whenever he felt ready. J.T. had told Mack to stick his ass in the apartment and stay there. He was supposed to be injured, not out fucking around fixing golf carts and mowers. Besides, as J.T. had explained, he'd get all those lost wages on the back end anyway.

But Mack was getting close to his boredom redline.

THIRTY-TWO

Hector introduced himself to the resort manager and politely asked if he might interview Winfred Bailey, the assistant pro, as well as the kid who'd been there when Mack rolled up after the accident. In front of Hector, the manager called Bailey and told him to extend to Hector every accommodation. The manager also dispatched Anna, an assistant hotel manager, to accompany Hector and ensure the resort's employees were cooperative.

Anna drove Hector in a golf cart out to fourteen, where the tractor had been perched at the top of the slope. Bailey followed in a separate cart. There was no evidence of the shattered fiberglass in the area between the fourteenth and fifteenth fairways. Anna drove down to where a handful of guys were reshaping the sand traps and laying new sod in some areas on the sixteenth that had been torn up in the process of reworking the irrigation system.

The foreman of the crew, wearing a faded yellow golf cap, showed Hector exactly where the tractor had come to rest.

"You leave the key in the tractor?" asked Hector.

"During the day, yeah."

"You're not worried it'll disappear?"

"A couple years ago, one of our guys got picked up on his lunch hour by *la migra*," said the foreman. "They trucked his ass back to Mexico with the tractor key in his pocket. Since then, we leave the key with the tractor until we're done for the night."

Anna handed Hector a bottle of water from a cooler on the golf cart.

"And when you found the tractor in the fairway here?"

"Key was in it. Just not in gear. Whoever was driving it last must've left it in neutral, I guess."

Hector took a sip of water. "Who was driving it last?"

"Chuy was, but he swears he had the thing in gear."

"You believe him?"

"Yeah, I guess."

"Just seems weird that it could start rolling on its own," said Hector.

"I dunno," said the foreman. "Maybe there was an earthquake or something."

"It's possible, I suppose. I don't remember one, but then again, it's been a few weeks."

"Maybe a little one? Just enough to rock it?" said Bailey. "Might've been so small nobody felt it."

"Could be," said Hector.

They rode back to the pro shop and Hector asked to meet with Tripp Wallace, the kid who'd seen Mack.

"Yeah, he was pretty messed up," said Wallace.

"And talk about stink," said Bailey.

"He wasn't playing by himself, was he?" said Hector.

"No, there was a black dude with him."

"You get his name? The black guy?"

"Nah," said Bailey. "The one who got hurt, McMahon? He was comping his greens fees. Even bought him some shoes and a hat and stuff."

"He was staying at the resort with him?"

"No, McMahon said he was on his honeymoon," said Bailey. "I teased him about it being with the black guy. McMahon said he was his homeboy from over in Moreno Valley."

"Can you describe him?"

"I don't know. Regular size. Early twenties. More on the dark-skinned side, I guess. Seemed like an okay dude."

Hector looked at Anna still sitting in the cart.

"Pretty good player, I think," said Wallace.

"Why do you say that?" said Hector. "You see him play?"

"No, but after they pulled up and McMahon's wife came out, everybody left in kind of a hurry. They left the scorecard on the cart. I remember wondering if they were any good. The McMahon guy, I'm guessing it was him—one player had an M, the other a B—anyway, I think M was plus-seven and B was plus-five, if I remember."

"You still got the card, by any chance?"

"You're kidding, right?" said Wallace. "That was, like, how long ago? I just threw it away when I cleaned out the cart."

"Yeah, of course, sorry," said Hector.

"Cart was a mess," said Wallace. "Guy was covered in shit, excuse me, but—"

"It's okay."

"Anyway, he was a mess and there was beer spilled everywhere, cans in the basket, and just nasty from the toilet, you know? I hosed the whole thing off. It was disgusting."

"You mentioned his wife. Did she say anything?"

"She seemed pretty upset," said Bailey.

"Yeah?"

"I think she'd come directly from the spa. She was big. Like, almost like a dude. Kind of a pretty face, though."

"You think she was a tranny?" asked Wallace.

"I didn't say that," said Bailey.

"But were you thinking that?" said Wallace.

"No, dickhead, I wasn't thinking that. She was just a big lady, that's all I'm saying."

"But you have seen chicks like that that turned out to be dudes, right?"

"Well, yeah, like on TV. I never tried to pick one up in Hollywood or anything."

"So you can't really be sure," said the kid.

"What are you talking about? You think somebody's gonna shell out the kind of bucks it costs to play here and bring some tranny hooker to pretend he's his wife?"

Anna looked at Hector and rolled her eyes.

"Guys," said Hector, "I really appreciate it. You've been very helpful." Hector turned to Anna. "Can we go talk to housekeeping, please?"

Anna led him to housekeeping, where the manager determined that Beatriz had been responsible for the McMahons' casita. Rather than send for her, Hector said they could go talk to her where she was.

The girl was pushing her cart along the breezeway. She jumped when Hector and Anna approached her from behind. Anna said Hector had a few questions to ask her.

Hector held a little notebook but didn't open it. "The housekeeping manager said you cleaned casita twenty-one a few weeks ago."

"Jess."

"Do you remember hearing about someone getting hurt on the golf course?"

"Jess."

"Do you remember those people?"

"Jess."

The girl's eyes kept shifting between Hector and Anna.

"Yo no soy policia," Hector said. *"Soy un abogado del hotel. No se preocupa*, okay?"

"Okay," said Beatriz. She blinked three times and cracked a tiny smile.

"Now, the people that stayed in the casita," said Hector, "was there anything unusual?"

"No." Beatriz waited a beat. "The minibar, I think."

"The minibar?"

"I think they drink a lot from the minibar. Also, they don't..."

"Don't?"

Beatriz blushed and looked down at her shoes. *"La cama."* She looked up at Hector.

"The bed?"

"Limpia," Beatriz said. *Clean.*

"Gracias," said Hector.

"De nada," the girl said, and resumed pushing her trolley down the breezeway.

THIRTY-THREE

J.T. had never gotten altogether comfortable with where Buddy fit into the big picture, and he wanted to get his version before somebody like Aza dug him up. As J.T. suspected, he found Buddy in the greenskeeper's shed, pumping up tires on the carts with a compressor that looked to be mounted onto a moving dolly.

"Buddy, how we doing, my man?" asked J.T.

"Okay."

"I told Tommy I needed to ask you some questions about Mack's case. How 'bout we step into the 19th Hole and get a Coke or something?"

Buddy nodded and pulled the plug on the compressor, leaving the contraption in the middle of the floor next to the cart. He followed J.T. across the flagstones set in the painted-bark ground cover and through the parking lot and into the clubhouse.

J.T. asked Wanda for a Coke for Buddy and an Arnold Palmer for himself, and the two sat down at the corner table where they'd first met earlier in the summer.

"So listen," J.T. said, sipping his drink and looking up at the TV, "when you were out at Fuente Dorado, did you give anyone your name? Hotel? Golf course? Anyone?"

Buddy was also watching the TV. "Naw, man. Nobody talked to me I can remember. Wanda, that's it."

On TV the guy with the huge head was arguing with the guy who was smiling. A ticker scrolled beneath the split screen.

"Okay, good. So nobody saw you there that could point to you as a witness."

"Well, the dudes from the pro shop saw me. I didn't say nothing, I don't think. No, wait." Buddy turned from the TV and looked at J.T. "You ever heard of...what'd that guy call it...IBS?"

"IBS? Like, irritable bowel syndrome?"

"Yeah, that's it. It's a real thing?"

"Yeah, it's a real thing. What's that got to do with Mack?"

"Nothing. The assistant pro said something when we pulled up at the clubhouse. He asked me if Mack had it."

"Why?"

"Why? 'Cause the motherfucker was covered in shit from head to toe, that's why."

"Right. So what else did you talk to them about?"

"That's it. Wanda came out just as Mack went in to hose off. I gave her the money like you said and I got out of there."

J.T. looked up when a couple of retired players came in. Jesus, these guys had to be here every single day. "Okay, I think we're going to be good, then. I was afraid somebody there was going to track you down and talk to you about what happened out on the course."

Buddy continued to stare at the TV across the room.

J.T. waited for Buddy to volunteer some information, but Buddy was too caught up following the Fox News ticker. "So what did happen out on the course?"

"Tractor hit the toilet."

"Yeah, I know. How did it happen? I mean, nobody else was around, were they?"

Buddy sipped his Coke. "Nope." He craned his neck toward the TV and squinted.

"So the thing just started rolling by itself and happened to hit the toilet just as Mack went inside."

"Pretty much."

The door to the 19th Hole swooshed open. Sunlight and heat poured into the room. Tommy's hand went up to shield his eyes as he looked around the room. "Buddy!" he shouted. "C'mon, let's go! Those assholes ran over a sprinkler again. PVC's all fucked up on eight. We gotta git."

Buddy stood up slowly and slurped the last drops of his Coke through his straw. "Thanks for the Coke, man."

"Yeah, sure." J.T. held Buddy's wrist and leaned toward him. "Buddy, anybody does come looking for you to ask you questions about the tractor and Mack, you give me a holler, you hear?"

"Yeah, man. I hear you. I gots to go."

As he sat in front of his terminal, Al debated whether he should reach out to Hector Aza to check on the status of his investigation. He didn't want to appear too curious. On the other hand, the company was paying Aza, so by extension, Al had a right to know what was going on. Al figured he'd give Aza another day or two to get back to him, otherwise, he'd call on his own.

What Al really wanted to do was go out to the range and hit some balls. J.T. told Al that being anywhere near the course now was a bad idea. While the scam was being set up, Al hadn't even wanted to play; now that he couldn't, his desire to go hit balls was beginning to consume him.

But then there was the flabby specter of Frankie Fresh. A sweaty film spilled over Al whenever he thought about bumping into Frankie. Every time he handed over another $300, it gnawed at Al's insides. He couldn't understand how J.T. could be so cool about it. What if this thing went to trial? What if it dragged out for two years like most of these cases? Two years' worth of vigorish on thirty grand at a point a week…*Thirty-one grand! And that's assuming J.T. doesn't do any more freelance borrowing.*

An e-mail from Marino Vargas popped up on the screen. The subject line said “FWD: Re: ROGER ELLIS.” Just as Al was about to open the e-mail, Ellis himself walked past Al’s cubicle carrying a cardboard box and followed by the building’s uniformed security. Al’s eyes darted back to his screen and he opened the message from HR to GSAC’s Inland Empire senior staff, explaining that Roger Ellis would no longer be with the company.

Al pushed away from his desk and, as casually as he could, walked over to Vargas’s desk via the kitchen.

“What the hell happened?” asked Al.

“You remember that hack job where somebody breached the database? It was Ellis.”

“No shit?”

“No shit.”

“He cop to it?”

“You kidding? Fucking guy acted like he was totally surprised. Nobody bought it, though.”

“What do you mean?”

“Just too suspicious. The IT dorks tracked it down to a computer on this floor. Everybody on the floor has been here for years. Ellis was the only new hire. He was only probationary anyway at this point. That’s why they were able to get rid of him and he couldn’t say shit about it.”

“Why do they think he did it?” Al bit the inside of his lip. He knew he shouldn’t have gone any deeper. The last thing he needed was to trigger his own manager’s suspicion about Al’s interest. Fortunately, Vargas seemed oblivious.

“Who the fuck knows?” Vargas said. “Maybe he was a mole from GEICO or something. Maybe he was trying to get into a more valuable database and just didn’t know what he was looking for. Anyway, he’s gone. Just as well. I never really trusted that guy, you know?”

“Yeah. I barely talked to him myself.”

Al had caught a break. Ellis was fired. Good luck getting another job in the industry with that reference. Ouch. Al felt kind of bad for the guy. Then he realized just how close he'd come to getting caught himself. He wondered if he should take that as a sign. A sign to get the hell out of GSAC.

With a hard copy of the McMahon file on the front seat of his Crown Victoria, Hector thought he might drive past the Mira Vista Golf Club on his way back to Riverside from Palm Desert. The file said McMahon worked at the club. Maybe his golfing partner, the guy who was five over after thirteen holes at Fuente Dorado's Tesoro course, worked at Mira Vista too.

Hector pulled the Crown Vic into the lot and entered the pro shop. A sign above the window behind the counter said STEVE ESTEP, PGA PROFESSIONAL. A guy with a name tag that said "Steve" and "Head Pro" was restocking a golf balls display.

"Can I help you?" asked Estep.

"I hope so. My name's Hector Aza. I'm a lawyer for GSAC. Do you know Mack McMahon?"

"Sure. He works in the greenskeeper's shed, but he's not working now though, I don't think."

"Oh, that's okay. Actually, for ethical reasons, I can't speak with Mr. McMahon without his attorney present." Hector hefted a Scotty Cameron putter from a display case and looked at the price on the sticker. "I understand when he was injured, that he was playing golf with a friend of his at El Fuente Dorado. Black guy from Moreno Valley?"

"Oh, that'd be Buddy, I'm sure."

"Buddy?"

"Yeah. He works with Mack in the shed over there," Estep said, pointing to a warehouse-like building with a green metal gambrel roof.

Hector walked over to the building. A radio was playing inside, but Hector couldn't see anyone. There were carts lined up against two of the walls, all but two of them plugged into battery chargers. In the far corner, a canvas tarp covered some kind of go-cart with knobby tires. Hector walked toward what looked to be an office, but in spite of music blaring from a radio, he found no one inside the shed.

Hector looked at his watch. No wonder his stomach was growling. He walked back over to the pro shop, where Estep told him he could get a hamburger at the 19th Hole. A table next to the smoked-glass window gave him the closest thing to a view of the greenskeeper's shed he was able to find. After a quick rundown of the menu, he told the beautiful waitress towering over the table that he'd have the Reuben with fries. The waitress smiled and blew away a curl that had dangled into her eyes.

She gave him another friendly smile when she returned a minute later with an iced tea.

"You know, I'd heard of this place, but I'd never made it out here," said Hector. "You been working here long?"

"A couple of years now, yeah."

"You know anything about the course? Is it any good?"

"I guess so. I'm not a golfer. I do know that it was originally supposed to be a championship-level course. They were going to wrap a resort around it. Try to siphon off some of the Palm Springs traffic."

Hector laughed. The idea of a resort on this bristly bole snatch of unincorporated Riverside County competing with La Quinta and Rancho Mirage was as ludicrous as the name of the club itself. The only vista to be seen was that of the rocks the color of almond shells surging vertically from the edges of the fairways. Still, Hector could imagine that the terrain alone might make for some challenging golf. With the surrounding land relatively useless, he could see where somebody looking to throw up some spec houses around a golf course during the boom might have seen this as a diamond in the rough. No doubt whoever was behind the idea vastly overpaid for the land and improvements.

Hector sipped his tea, mesmerized by the girl's dimples. "I'll have to come out and play a round sometime."

"You should," said the waitress with a wink.

Hector sat alone in the middle of the room, facing the TV. The sound was turned down, which was fine with him. A sweaty guy walked in and headed straight for the locker room, removing his hat and wiping his forehead with the back of his wrist. The waitress came back and asked if Hector needed anything.

"So you've worked out here a long time," said Hector, "do you know a guy named Buddy that works with the greenskeeper?"

"Yeah, sure. He was just here about thirty minutes ago, why?"

"Not a big deal, I just wanted to talk to him. You know his friend Mack that works with him?"

Wanda raised an eyebrow. "What did you say your name was again?"

"I'm sorry, I don't think I did. Hector Aza. I'm a lawyer for Golden State. I'm actually working on a matter involving Mr. McMahon's injury. I just had a couple questions for Buddy." Hector looked up at the waitress, who was no longer smiling. "I guess I didn't get your name, either."

Wanda pursed her lips quickly. "It's Wanda."

Hector cocked his head. "Wanda? Like—"

"Yeah. Like Wanda McMahon." Wanda exaggerated a grimace and raised her eyebrows. "The wife."

"Oh my gosh. I had no idea. Listen, I'm really sorry, but under the circumstances, I'm afraid I can't talk to you. Ethical reasons, you understand."

"Sure, I understand. Adverse party, right?"

"Exactly. Anyway, sorry to bother you. I'll find Buddy on my own. I'll give J.T. Edwards a call and explain that I bumped into you by accident."

"It's okay. Not a problem."

Hector left fifteen dollars on the table and walked back toward the greenskeeper's shed. He called J.T. Edwards's office, and the receptionist put Hector through.

J.T. answered his phone with the confident bonhomie of a lawyer in control of his case. "Ah, hello, counselor," J.T. said. "How goes the fight in the GSAC trenches?"

"It's going okay. The reason I'm calling is that I just unwittingly ran into your client and I wanted to let you know right away. We didn't discuss the case, but—"

"You *unwittingly* ran into my client? What, are you shitting me? How do you *unwittingly* run into an injured guy at his home?" Hector heard J.T. gasping on the other end of the line. "I'm gonna have your ass in front of the bar before you can say *carnitas, amigo.*"

"I think there's been a misunderstanding."

"You're goddamn right there's been a misunderstanding. You misunderstand the ethical rules about talking to an adverse party represented by counsel. You won't be able to get a job picking lettuce when I'm through with you."

"Are you finished?"

"Not even."

"Before you exhaust your vault of Mexican insults, you might let me explain. I didn't talk to Mr. McMahon. It was his wife, Wanda, that I ran into. She served me lunch at Mira Vista Golf Club. I had no idea who she was. She didn't identify herself until after I'd said I was working for GSAC on this matter."

"This is bullshit."

"I don't want to tell you how to run your practice, but if you don't believe me, I'd suggest you call her yourself. In any event, the meeting was entirely accidental. No particulars of the case were discussed. There was no ethical breach whatever. If, after you speak to Mrs. McMahon, you still feel like reporting my completely innocuous conversation to the ethics committee, well, that's your prerogative. I'm sure you have the number."

Hector hung up.

THIRTY-FOUR

J.T. couldn't breathe. He loosened his tie. He felt like his neck was going to explode. *What the fuck was Aza doing at Mira Vista?*

J.T. called Wanda, who confirmed Aza's version of events.

"What were you doing even speaking to that clown?"

"What are you talking about? He was just a guy ordering a sandwich. I didn't know he was a lawyer for GSAC. It's not like either of us said anything about the case anyway."

"Well, what the fuck was he doing there, then?"

"I think he was looking for Buddy."

"Buddy!"

"He asked if I knew him. That's how it came up that he worked for GSAC. Said he had some questions to ask him."

"Are you shitting me?" J.T. wanted to throw something through his floor-to-ceiling plate-glass window. "Wanda, you see Buddy, you tell him to give me a call right away, okay?"

"Fine. I got a customer. I gotta go."

Wanda's insouciance did little for J.T.'s anxiety about Hector Aza.

Al.

Al would be able to find out what Aza was looking for and what he knew already. J.T. called him, but there was no answer. J.T. was torn between staying in the office or going back out to Mira Vista. Maybe he should call Mack. No, no sense getting him riled up. J.T. took a couple of deep breaths. His pulse slowed. What was the big deal, anyway? Even if Aza talked to Buddy, what could

Buddy tell him? He could talk to Al and Mack later. What was he worried about? *I'm J.T. fucking Edwards. Everything's under control here.*

J.T. picked up his file on the *Fuente Dorado* case and tucked it in his briefcase. He'd work it out in the hot tub with a bottle of that pinot noir from Sonoma.

Mack paced around the apartment. Aside from lingering post-op discomfort, he felt fine. He procrastinated as long as he could hold out, but he finally broke down and called his Coast Guard contact. The recruiter confirmed Mack's injury was fatal to his chances of joining the Guard.

Having run through every program on HBO at least twice, Mack sulked on the couch and flipped through a couple of off-road magazines he'd picked up at the Kwik Stop. One of them had a feature story about Pete Fruccione and his customizing business in Fontana. Frooch, as he was known, was standing in his spotless garage the size of an airplane hangar, his bare arms sleeved in tatts, a radically customized dune buggy in the background. The reflection from the chrome in the photograph looked so vivid, it almost hurt Mack's eyes.

Mack took the magazine into the kitchen with him as he mixed up a batch of margaritas in the blender. He missed the sounds of engines. He mashed the turbo button on the blender, the tiny motor shrieking as it crushed ice at 1,000 RPM. He poured a third of a bottle of Cuervo Gold into the sea-green vortex and watched it coast to a stop when he turned off the blender. He filled a stadium cup and went back out to the couch.

Mack continued to flip through the story on Frooch. *Not much of a story, just a bunch of pictures.* There was one picture of Frooch with his arm around Johnny Ho that led to another story, an interview with Johnny Ho himself.

Johnny Ho was the godfather of extreme desert sports in Southern California. Motocross, ATVs, dune buggy rallies... what Tony Hawk was to skateboards, Johnny Ho was to desert motorsports. Mack read the story, scrutinizing the sidebars, looking for tips. There was a picture of Johnny strapped into an ultra-light as he flashed the shaka sign, his signature dragon helmet covered in sponsors' decals, and the snow-capped peak of Mt. Baldy in the background. Johnny claimed his next goal was to get a drone, but fly it himself from the inside. Mack wondered how much a drone cost and where you got one.

Al hated this part of the day, the part where he pulled into his driveway. The warping trusses and dusty studs of abandoned homes leered at him, his house standing out like a depressing afterthought. It reminded Al of those pictures in the paper when a tornado wipes out an entire town in Kentucky except for one house.

Noticing a missed call from J.T., Al took a deep breath and rang back. When J.T. answered the phone on the third ring, it sounded to Al like J.T. was cooking spaghetti or something.

"Saw a missed call," said Al. "Left the phone in the car, sorry."

"That's the least of our problems."

Al tossed his keys on his kitchen counter. "What now?" He opened a Coors Light from the refrigerator and sipped the foam escaping from the tab.

"You talk to your friend Aza lately? Seems like he's been sniffing around at Mira Vista."

Al choked on a mouthful of beer. "Are you serious?"

"I thought you GSAC guys stayed on top of things. I'll have to remember that next time I'm looking for a policy."

"Are you fucking with me? Aza was really out there?"

"Heard it from Wanda herself."

Al couldn't believe how calm J.T. was about this development. "He was talking to Wanda? Without you? Can he do that?"

"Hell no, he can't do that. Unfortunately, neither he nor Wanda seemed particularly concerned about it."

"You're not concerned?"

"You're goddamn right I'm concerned. The thing is, even if I bring a beef to the ethics committee, if it went down like he and Wanda say it did, it's not a violation. Neither one of them claims to know the other one was connected with the case."

"And you believe them?" Al rubbed his side where the rash felt like it could be coming back.

"You're missing the bigger picture." J.T. expired one of his patronizing sighs on the other end. "Let's give Aza the benefit of the doubt and say it was an innocent misunderstanding, that he really didn't know it was Wanda he was talking to. Do you not see the problem?"

"Why was he out there, then?"

"Ah, so you do see it."

"Well?"

"I was hoping you could tell me. That's why I called you in the first place."

"How the hell should I know? If he's not allowed to talk to Mack or Wanda, what was he doing out there?"

"He was looking for Buddy."

"Buddy? How would he know about Buddy?"

"I don't know, Al. That's why I called." Another sigh. "I'm thinking maybe somebody at Fuente Dorado tipped him off."

"His name wasn't in the file, was it?" Al lifted his shirt and held his beer can against his skin. "I'm sure it wasn't. I'd remember if it had been."

"Aza probably pieced it together. Buddy was with Mack when he pulled up in the golf cart. You don't think maybe a couple of jamokes from the pro shop would remember a redneck and a black dude playing golf together on a course that costs three hundred bucks a round? Especially when the redneck gets his dick maimed by a tractor?"

"So how does that lead Aza to the club?"

"Jesus, where would you start if you wanted to look for a friend of Mack's? It's not like Aza's a fucking mind reader. It's a logical place to look."

"I guess you're right." Al shook the little remaining beer in the can. "So you think Buddy told him anything?"

"I met with Buddy this morning. I asked him how the accident went down, but he said it just happened. Guy's not much of a raconteur."

"So then everything's okay? Jesus, you gave me a heart attack for nothing."

"Not so fast, my friend. First off, we don't know if Aza talked to Buddy. If he has, there's no telling what he might pick up."

That's what Al had been worried about. Why was J.T. making him out to be such a dumbass?

"Second, what we need to be doing is coordinating on what Aza's strategy is. You see what I mean? Does he think causation's the hook? He's got to. The medicals are immaculate."

"I don't know."

"I know you don't know. What I'm telling you is that you need to find out. Aza's not going to tell me, not yet anyway. You need to talk to him, figure out what weak spots he's probing. Then we go to work on him. Convince him he's off the mark and that this thing needs to settle before I go thermonuclear on his ass."

J.T. hung up. Al flopped on his living room sofa.

Why couldn't he have just gone to Weed?

Unable to find Buddy in the greenskeeper's shed, Hector returned to the pro shop and left his business card with the pro. After seeing a stack of scorecards by the register that showed a slope rating of 137 for the course, Hector also made a mental note to schedule a tee time in the near future.

Hector drove the Crown Vic back to his office at the strip mall on Archibald. He lifted the file from the front seat and carried it into the office with him. He couldn't deny that the injury was gruesome. Pictures aside, it was an awfully thin file on which to pay out nearly a million dollars.

He waved at the Filipina girls in the nail salon as he opened the door to his office, converted from a former pet shop. Hector's partner, Manu Kakar, sat at his desk, a desk like all the furniture in the office, picked up secondhand at a bankruptcy auction in San Bernardino. Manu was transfixed by the computer screen and didn't react to Hector's entry.

"No news, I'm guessing, Manu," said Hector.

"No news," said Manu, staring ahead at his screen.

Hector thought about the guys at Fuente Dorado and their earthquake theory. He couldn't deny it was conceivable. Tractor left in neutral on a hill. Minor seismic event starts the tractor into motion. Conceivable, maybe. But was GSAC really willing to pay out without even interviewing the only witness?

"Manu," said Hector. "You got a minute to research something for me?"

Manu didn't look up. "Yes."

"You follow earthquakes and hurricanes and stuff, right?"

"Yes."

"There's got to be some website that has all kinds of earthquake data, right?"

"U.S. Geological Survey. USGS.gov."

"Would you mind looking up for me whether there was an earthquake—even a minor one—on June tenth? Anywhere in Southern California."

"Okay." Manu didn't look up from his computer.

Hector sat down at his desk with its chipped veneer. He spun around in his chair and pulled a Diet Coke from the mini refrigerator. He opened the file on the desk and flipped through the pages, ignoring the photographs of Mack McMahon's disfigured penis.

"No."

"I'm sorry?" said Hector.

"No seismic activity in Southern California on ten June. Quake in Iran. Temblor in Chile. Tremor in China. Nothing in California."

"Just like that? You already checked? You sure?"

Manu was chewing on a plastic ballpoint pen and still staring at his computer screen that was again showing a giraffe stretching his tongue to reach leaves on a Joshua tree. "Yes."

While Manu's Asperger's syndrome had put him at a disadvantage in job interviews, his monomania and laconic small talk made him the ideal partner for Hector Aza.

THIRTY-FIVE

The bottle of Cuervo was nearly empty by the time Wanda came home on Saturday evening. Mack had Willie Nelson blaring on the CD player when Wanda opened the door.

"Jesus, turn that down, will you? What about the neighbors?"

"Aw, fuck the neighbors," said Mack. "This is Willie."

Wanda stepped over to the console and turned the volume down herself. "C'mon, it's inconsiderate."

"Awright. Hell, you sat around this motherfucker by yourself all day, you'd be losing your mind too."

"Well, if I hadn't been on my feet since five-thirty in the morning, I might be able to appreciate what a burden it is watching TV all day."

"Oh, I get it. This shit's my fault."

"That's not what I said." Wanda pulled a glass, fork, and plate from the sink and loaded them into the dishwasher. "You talk to J.T. today?"

"No, why?"

"A lawyer for the insurance company came by the club today looking for Buddy."

"You serious?"

"Of course."

"How do you know?"

"Because he told me."

"Told you? You talked to him?" Mack took a long sip from his tequila.

"Yeah, I talked to him. The guy ordered lunch and we started talking. That's when he said he was working for GSAC and investigating the claim."

"Investigating? He said investigating?"

"No, he didn't say investigating. *I* said investigating. It's called paraphrasing. The guy wanted to talk to Buddy. You think he was looking for tips on how to charge a golf cart?"

"Jesus."

"Maybe you should call Buddy. Find out if he talked to the guy." Wanda finished wiping down the kitchen counter and spread the dishtowel over the faucet. "I'm going for a swim."

While Wanda changed in the bedroom, Mack dialed Buddy's cell phone. "Yo, man, you talk to that lawyer from the insurance company?"

"Naw. I heard he's looking for me, but I never saw him. Been out fucking with the irrigation all day. I ain't called him yet."

"Look here," Mack said, looking down at the pool from the kitchen window, "why don't you swing by the crib? Wanda's getting ready to go down to the pool. I'll make us up some margaritas and shit."

"You serious?"

"Shit yeah. Why not?"

"Awright then."

"Oh, and Buddy...stop off and get a bottle of tequila, would you?"

Wanda was still swimming laps when Buddy arrived with a bottle of some off-brand silver tequila. Mack shook his head. *That's what I get for asking a black guy to pick up tequila.* Mack mixed up another pitcher of margaritas and filled three stadium cups to the rim. He and Buddy carried them down to the pool, and Mack set down one of the cups on the mottled safety-glass table near the rubber-banded chaise lounges.

Wanda glided into the wall on her final lap and stood up in the waist-deep water of the pool's shallow end. She shook her head and waved when she saw Buddy sitting with Mack by the table. There was no one else at the pool.

"Brought you a margarita," said Mack.

"Thanks," said Wanda. She crossed her arms and leaned on the edge of the pool. Her maroon bathing suit was stretched taut front and back. She laid her head on her arms and blew out her cheeks. "Getting old," she said.

"Not hardly," said Buddy, grinning.

Mack picked up Wanda's drink and carried it over to where she kicked her legs gently in the pool. Her legs were long enough that her lampshade thighs were still in proportion. Her back and shoulders were clearly bigger than either Mack's or Buddy's.

Buddy shook his head as Mack walked back to the chair. "Man, I still can't believe you wound up with that," Buddy said out of the side of his mouth.

"Yeah. That and a broke dick."

"I hear you," said Buddy. "Still, you finish your rehab or whatever, you gonna be sitting pretty, you know what I'm saying?"

Mack shook his head. "Shit. She didn't want nothing to do with me before. Only thing I'm getting from this is out of the fuckin' Coast Guard."

Wanda climbed out of the pool and wrapped herself in a light blue bath sheet. She bent down to pick up her drink.

Buddy clucked his tongue. "Unh!"

"Shit, maybe you shoulda married her 'stead a me."

"I know that's right."

"'Course you'd have to get a new wardrobe when she stretched all your clothes out."

Buddy frowned at Mack as Wanda approached. "Man, you need to shut the fuck up," Buddy whispered.

Mack took a quick sip off his margarita. "Hey, you see the latest copy of *Off-Road*?"

"I'm around golf carts all fucking day. What I want to look at a bunch of trucks for?"

Wanda sat on a chaise lounge and adjusted the back. The sun was setting and lightning bugs were starting to appear.

"They got a big fuckin' spread of Johnny Ho in there. Guy's gonna get himself a drone, man. Just fuckin' buzz all around the desert and shit. Probably start a whole drone-racing circuit."

Buddy was staring at Wanda's cleavage as she unwrapped her bath sheet and toweled off her hair. "Uh-huh."

"Shit, man, now that the Coast Guard's fucked, maybe that's what I'll do. Open up a customizing place like Frooch."

"See?" said Wanda. "There you go."

"Anyway," said Mack, "I get Johnny Ho wearing some of my decals and shit and I'll have motherfuckers coming out of the woodwork. Hell, I already got the McMahon 3000. That can be my launching pad."

"Uh-huh," said Buddy, smiling at Wanda as she again wrapped the towel around her torso and tucked the remaining bit between her breasts.

"That sounds like a great idea," said Wanda.

"Yeah," said Mack, sipping his drink. "So did getting married."

"Wow," said Wanda, "you *did* have a tough day at the office."

"Yo, man, chill," said Buddy.

"Fuck that, man. What do I have to chill about? That asshole J.T. don't want me to leave the house. Stuck in a fucking one-bedroom apartment all day with a broke dick, and now my *wife* wants to bust my balls about not working?"

"Relax," said Wanda. "I'm sorry if I hurt your feelings."

"Yeah, well, fuck that. You think I asked for this shit? Goddamn, man." Mack shook his head. "I just wanted to join the fucking Coast Guard, not wind up married to some dude and be a fucking cripple." Mack threw back the rest of his drink.

Buddy looked at Wanda. She tucked her lips within her teeth for a second, then offered a wounded smile to Buddy before she stood up and walked through the gate and back to the apartment.

"Man, that shit was uncool," said Buddy.

"What? Shit, man, she thinks I like sitting home all day? I ain't no fucking bum, man. I work."

"Why you want to say that foolishness about her being a dude, man? That shit was not nice."

"Aw, hell, ain't like she's never heard that before."

"That don't make it right." Buddy stood up. "I gotta get going anyway."

"C'mon, man, stick around. I'll make some more margaritas. It'll be cool, don't worry."

Buddy shook his head. "Naw, I gotta pick up my auntie anyway." Buddy slapped hands with Mack and slipped through the gate, leaving Mack alone on the pool deck with three empty plastic cups.

THIRTY-SIX

Marino Vargas leaned on the wall of Al's cubicle. "You've got to give me an answer. They're going to announce today that the merger's going through."

Al rubbed at his side. God, it sure felt like the shingles were coming back. "I know, I know."

"Just tell me: What's holding you back? Are you interviewing somewhere else or something? You can tell me."

Al's shoulders slumped. "No, it's not that. It's just the fucking house, man. I'm underwater by a hundred grand, and I know I'll never rent it for enough to cover my nut."

"I hate to do this, but time's up, man. Shit or get off the pot."

As he rubbed his ribs, Al thought about trying to start his Camry in the dead of winter in Weed, California. Fuck it. He'd have to get a 4x4. In those mountains? With that snow? Before he'd started with J.T., he'd thought about looking into a short sale, but he'd given up on that once he'd convinced himself that a $50,000 payday was just a month away. Now it was too late for a short sale to make a difference.

"I guess I've got to pass. I'm sorry."

"Hey, don't sweat it. Stuff works out. It's not like SAICO's closing down the office tomorrow."

Later that morning, Al received an e-mail copy of the press release issued by corporate and filed with the SEC announcing the merger. The press release e-mail was followed by a blast e-mail to hundreds of GSAC employees, informing them of a reduction in force upon completion of the merger with SAICO and including a link to the GSAC's outplacement services webpage.

Al had felt that Frankie's involvement had been a point of no return. He now realized he could probably have found a way to pay off Frankie and just walk away. Take the job in Weed. Run the claims office. Start over. Hell, the cost of living up there was probably nothing. His ribcage felt scalded.

J.T. called Hector's office using the pretext of questions about discovery and pretrial motions. He wanted to get a sense of Hector's doubts about the case and what GSAC really thought the settlement value of the suit was.

"Hector, this is J.T. Edwards. Do you have a minute to talk about discovery in the McMahon case?"

"I've got a meeting in a few minutes, but I'm free right now."

J.T. leaned back in his chair and propped his feet up on his desk. "Listen, first I wanted to apologize for blowing up the other day over the contact with my client. It's just that I've been burned before by insurance company lawyers, including GSAC lawyers, talking to my clients without authorization."

"I see."

"I shouldn't have gotten emotional, though." J.T. tried to use the most contrite voice he could muster. "I was out of line with some of my comments and I wanted to apologize."

"Consider it forgotten."

J.T. was hypnotized by a plane descending in the distance. He snapped awake. "So, I was going to send you my interrogatories, and I just wanted to give you a heads-up. I know you haven't prepared a witness list yet, obviously, but just in terms of calendaring, I was wondering if you wanted to talk about blocking out some time for depositions."

"Well, I suppose," said Hector. "As you said, I really haven't had an opportunity to develop a witness list yet." J.T. could hear Aza's keyboard clicking. "I have a trial scheduled for October, but I have a feeling that's going to be pushed back." More clicking. "I have depositions scattered throughout the rest of August, but there are a few open days I could work with in September. Again, a lot will depend on what happens with my October trial."

"Don't I know it," said J.T. "That's why I like to try to block these things out as early as possible. Anything comes up, we've got options built in."

"Of course."

"So, my end's pretty straightforward: a representative from El Fuente Dorado's landscaping company; the assistant pro; the surgeon that operated on Mr. McMahon's mangled penis…" J.T. let that hang in the air, hoping the visual effect would be unsettling for Hector. "So did you have a ballpark idea of how many we might be looking at from your end?"

"Well, again, don't hold me to this, but, um…well, the plaintiff, obviously, Mr. McMahon. His wife. His friend, Buddy Cromartie, who I understand played golf with him that day and witnessed the accident."

So Aza definitely knew about Buddy. Okay, it wasn't a surprise. J.T. still wondered if Aza'd talked to Buddy firsthand and Buddy hadn't called J.T.

"Right," said J.T. "So have you met with Buddy yet?"

"You know, I'm really not in a position to get into that right now," said Hector.

J.T. bit his lip. The guy was tight as a clam. "Sure, I understand."

"Oh, and the doctor, most likely."

"The doctor?" So much for being a clam. "I'm sorry. I thought I just said I was calling Dr. Morris."

"Oh, not the surgeon. I'm talking about Dr. Garvey. The physician who first saw Mr. McMahon at EMC."

"Garvey?"

"Uh-huh."

J.T. didn't bother suppressing a chuckle. This guy Aza was a clown. Why would the defense depose a doctor who was so clearly a favorable witness for the plaintiff? "Really? I mean, it's your call, but I must say I'm a little surprised."

"Oh, yeah?"

"It's just that the medical evidence is so overwhelming. I'm curious what he'd have to say that could possibly help your case."

"Well, when I talked to him—"

"You talked to him? You talked to Garvey already?"

"Like I said, I'm not going to get into my work product. Of course, as I'm sure you know, Dr. Garvey mentioned that Mr. McMahon had quote-unquote 'fucked up' his shoulder just before the incident at El Fuente Dorado."

J.T. bit at a piece of cuticle on his thumb. How the fuck could Mack have mentioned the shoulder to Garvey? More troubling, how had Aza tracked down Garvey and gotten that information? Of course. The release was for Eisenhower Medical Center. J.T. had been so excited by Morris's notes, he hadn't even thought about anyone else at the hospital.

And who was this fucking guy Aza, anyway? J.T. noticed that when he said El Fuente Dorado, he said it like a white guy, not a Mexican.

J.T. wondered how long he'd been breathing into the phone. He leaned forward in his chair. "Oh, yeah, Garvey. I'd forgotten about him. I tell you, I was so caught up in the pictures and the medical report by Dr. Morris, the guy that was *President Gerald Ford's urologist*, that I really hadn't focused on Garvey myself."

J.T. leaned back in his chair again and let that sink in.

"Anyway," said Hector, "don't hold me to it, but that's all I can think of right now."

J.T. thought he heard a little bell jingle. Guy was probably working out of a fucking pet shop.

"Now if you'll excuse me," said Hector, "it looks like my meeting's actually going to start on time for a change."

J.T. could hear Aza's chair squeaking. Must be standing up.

"I'll have to get back to you on the discovery," said Hector.

J.T. resumed gnawing on his cuticle. "Sure, no problem."

No problem my ass. Fucking Mack.

With the blender going full bore, Mack hadn't even realized Wanda had left the apartment until he felt the rattling of the cheap construction when the front door closed. As he flopped on the couch and started looking for something on TV, he felt kind of bad about calling Wanda a dude. But who the fuck was she to call him a bum? He had a job. It was that asshole J.T. told him to stay home. Hell, if Mack had it to do over again, he'd never have signed on for even the first fall with the shopping carts. Shit, he'd be in Cape May this very minute, probably being recognized as the top candidate in his class, and with his choice of any assignment he wanted—even Hawaii.

Sitting in front of the TV, Al surfed through a hundred channels, searching in vain for anything to distract him from the miserable turn his life had taken. He stepped into the kitchen to freshen his vodka when he heard an explosion, then another, bigger blast. He walked back out to the living room expecting to see Bruce Willis or Mel Gibson rappelling from a flaming skyscraper. A commercial for fabric softener was on the screen. From the corner of his eye, some movement from the window caught his attention.

The house behind his, the only other completed house even remotely close by, was on fire. He'd read about these assholes—cooking up crystal meth and always blowing themselves up. As Al watched the scene from his dining room, the hot summer wind stoked the flames that were already pouring out of the second-floor windows.

As if his day hadn't been shitty enough.

Al stared out the patio door, feeling the fire's warmth through the glass. He wondered if anyone had called the fire department yet. Then he realized, of course not. If the junkies in the house hadn't already been incinerated, they were probably halfway to Mexico. No way were they sticking around to answer a bunch of cops' questions. There weren't any other neighbors anyway. Al was the only one who could call.

Not that it was going to do any good, he thought as he picked up the phone. With all the furloughs, sequesters, RIFs, and layoffs, the fire departments in the Inland Empire had been decimated. By the time anyone got out here, the fire would have destroyed the house. Probably Al's too.

Jesus Christ. Al dropped the phone on the counter. *Could it?* He opened the patio door and felt an instant blast of heat. Odd bits of flaming debris floated over into Al's scraggly backyard. The fire, however, while still blazing on the other side of the wooden fence, looked like it might be burning itself out.

Al watched the flames for a minute, transfixed. He thought he heard a siren in the distance, but it was just the fire whistling through the studs. Was he going to get this close only to have the fire die out? He looked at the gas grill on the patio. He opened the glass door wider and felt the rush of hot wind pour into his house. He stepped out onto the concrete, grabbed the grill's handle, and dragged it out into the yard almost all the way to the fence. He opened the gas jets and threw the lid back, then ran back to the house. He'd give it another minute for the gas to catch, then another five for the house. It would take the fire department fifteen minutes to arrive in the best of times; now it might take thirty. Judging from the way the first house went up, in twenty-five minutes, his place would be cinders.

The way the first house went up. The meth lab. The cops and fire marshal would figure that out in about two seconds. Al looked out at the yard, the grill spewing invisible liquid propane into the night sky. If they could figure out a meth lab, they could damn sure figure out a gas grill in the middle of the yard with the jets on.

Al sprinted back out to the grill. He could feel the heat from the fire intensifying. *God, don't blow this up while I'm trying to get the jets off.* He dove on the ground to get to the tank. Even the dirt was hot. He reached up for the tank, fumbling for the knob. When he found it, he turned it one way, then the other. *God, don't let me shit my pants while I'm trying to get the jets off.* He could hear the flames screeching through the cheap shingles next door. Completely discombobulated, he lay face down in the sandy patch of scrubby grass. He pulled himself up to his knees, confirmed the tank was closed, and then dragged the grill back to the patio. If the tank blew up once it was on the concrete, well, that'd be too bad.

Sparks were still floating over the fence when the wind freshened and a gust blew down off the San Bernardino Mountains, showering Al's roof with embers. Al was standing in the yard, his fists clenched, his knees bobbing like he was watching a Tiger Woods putt circle the cup at Augusta. Thirty seconds later his own house was officially on fire.

Al walked back inside and grabbed a six-pack from the fridge and the bottle of vodka from the counter. He put his hand on the doorknob to the garage. He'd have plenty of time to move the car to a safe place away from the fire. *Hold on. Fuck that.* He topped off his vodka one more time, adding extra ice and pouring it all into a big cup from Qualcomm Stadium. He scooped up the cell phones and threw them into a biodegradable plastic bag with the beer and the vodka and strolled out to the front yard to call 911 and wait for the fire department.

When, as Al predicted, the fire department arrived half an hour later, there was no chance the house could be saved. It had gone up like a movie set. Al watched the firefighters attempt to water down both houses, but like the firemen, Al knew it was futile. His biggest disappointment was that his beer had gotten warm while he watched his house burn.

Once it was obvious there was nothing to do for the house but contain the embers, one of the firefighters strode over to Al, who told him about the explosion he'd heard and his suspicion about a meth lab in the unoccupied house.

"Yeah, we're seeing this a lot these days. Cheap houses. Assholes playing chemist. Fire departments gutted by the fucking tax rolls evaporating. Only a matter of time until the whole Inland Empire is one giant bonfire."

"Yeah."

"Our guys aren't finding any bodies in the house over there, so at least that's something," said the firefighter.

Al was almost delirious from his newfound freedom. The white elephant was no more. "Yeah."

"Glad you made it out, pal," the fireman said, extending his hand. "It's the insurance company's problem now, am I right?"

The smile that Al had been suppressing finally emerged. "Well, I guess that's something, isn't it?"

The firefighter returned to his truck, talking into the radio Velcroed to his suit. Al was free. Free from having to go to Weed with its bullshit snowy winters. Free to stay in Southern California. Free to play golf whenever he wanted as his own boss, running his own consulting business.

Al stared at his house. Tears began to gather in the corners of his eyes.

With the steam and smoke rising from the creosote ruins, Alvin Boyle was now free to watch his computer—containing all the stolen GSAC information he'd risked his job, loan sharks, and prison to exploit—melt in the dying embers of the white elephant's ultimate revenge.

THIRTY-SEVEN

Buddy backed into a spot in the parking lot of the apartment complex where Wanda stood outside waiting for him. He unhitched the trailer before pulling away and parking his Monte Carlo in a nearby space. Wanda walked around the McMahon 3000, the buggy itself strapped down on the trailer and covered in a tarp bungeed onto the roll cage.

"Thanks for bringing it out," Wanda said, as Buddy walked toward her from his car.

"No problem," said Buddy. "Sure nice a you to get him that. He been wanting one forever. What it set you back?"

"Guy in Banning was asking eleven hundred on Craigslist. I got him to bring it to the club for a thousand cash."

Buddy couldn't believe it. Not only was Mack getting paid to be married to this fine woman with that killer body, she bought him thousand-dollar presents, even though he acted like an asshole to her. Shit, if he'd known Wanda was going to be part of the package, he would've made that first trip out to J.T.'s office after all.

"Look here," said Buddy, "Mack say anything to you about investin' in my business when he get his check?"

"Not really. You know he's onto that dune buggy–customizing idea now. Of course, he can only focus on something for so long before he gets distracted."

Buddy shook his head. "I know that's right."

"So your invention? It's some kind of golf ball–retrieving contraption, right?"

"Yeah." Buddy hadn't thought about it before, but maybe Wanda was the way to go. If she was married to Mack, she'd be getting some of that settlement check too, right? "I got it rigged up so you can get all the balls off the bottom of the lake without having to go dive in there."

"Sounds like that would save a lot of time."

"Save a lot of gator and moccasin bites too. Not out here, maybe, but back home? Shiiiit. You won't catch my ass jumping in no Florida lake for no golf ball. My cousin, Donnell? Fuckin' gator hopped out the water and ate his dog whole, man."

Wanda laughed and sat down on the trailer's fender. She was still almost as tall as Buddy.

Buddy had been completely serious, but when he thought about it, it did seem kind of funny—especially out here, where they wouldn't know a gator from a possum. *Is she not wearing a bra?* "So J.T. say when y'all can expect your settlement?"

"Nah. These things take a while sometimes. When I used to be a paralegal, we had some claims that took years if they went to court." Wanda looked at the bungee cords that secured the tarp. "So what's the story with your invention? You got a company set up and everything?"

"I got a shell LLC. Set it up as a Subchapter S. I ain't done nothing with a patent yet, though. I was hopin' Mack would invest when he got his check, but if it's gonna be years, then…"

Wanda stood up from the fender and unhooked the bungee cords on the tarp.

"You never know," she said, dragging the canvas off the McMahon 3000 in a smooth veronica.

Mack woke to the sound of Wanda cleaning up the mess from the margarita mix and tequila bottles.

"Jesus, what time is it?" he asked, stretching his arms and walking into the kitchen. He'd learned his lesson the first couple of days after the surgery and conditioned himself not to instinctively grab his junk the first thing upon waking.

"Almost noon."

"Whoa."

"Yeah."

"Listen, about yesterday. I'm sorry. I didn't mean nothing."

"Forget it. I know you didn't plan on any of this. I know you'd rather be working. I'm sorry I said anything. How about we call it even?"

"All right then. Works for me."

Wanda tied up the plastic garbage bag, hefted it out of the can, and shook open a new one. "Okay, put a shirt on. I've got something to show you outside."

Pulling a T-shirt over his head, Mack grabbed a cap and followed Wanda out to the parking lot where in an empty parking space the McMahon 3000 sat perched on a white trailer.

"Holy shit!"

"I was feeling bad about everything, even before last night, so I bought the trailer so you could take the McMahon 3000 out to the desert."

Mack ran his hand along the wire mesh sides as he walked around the trailer.

"Sorry it's used," said Wanda. "I couldn't afford the new one."

Other than during his marriage blackout, it was the first time Mack had actually hugged Wanda.

"Man, that's awesome! How'd you get it up on the trailer?"

"Buddy."

"That fucker," Mack said, smiling. "He musta cleaned it up too."

"Yeah."

"Wow. I wish I could take this sumbitch out right now."

"What's stopping you?"

Mack looked around the parking lot to see if anyone was watching. "J.T. said I'm supposed to stay home."

"J.T. wants it to look like you can't work. So you're not working. Look, you're not claiming your injury keeps you from driving a car. It just means..." Wanda looked down at the ground. "Sorry."

"It's okay. You know what? Fuck it. I believe I will take this sumbitch out today. You want to come with me?"

"I would, but I've got a shift in a couple hours. You go have fun, though."

"I will. Hey, really, thanks again for the trailer. It was real thoughtful."

"Forget it." Wanda smiled. "Hey, can I ask you a question?"

"Sure."

"Why do you call it the McMahon 3000?"

Mack put his foot up on the trailer and pushed his Mira Vista golf cap back on his head.

"It just sounds badass, darlin'. It just sounds badass."

Mack hitched up the trailer to his Firebird and headed east on the 10 out toward Joshua Tree. He was getting a later start than he would ordinarily have liked, but it was just a shakedown cruise, a test run for the McMahon 3000 about to be unleashed on the hot Mojave sands.

The buggy itself performed even better than Mack had hoped. The suspension ignored rocks and potholes; the tires rolled over the loose sand like it was pavement.

Fuck you, Frooch. The competition just drove up.

Al checked into a Holiday Inn Express while his insurance claim was being sorted out. As much as he'd resented the lid GSAC had placed on his advancement within the company, he had to hand it to them for taking care of their own when it came to a claim. He'd lost everything in the fire, so while he got out from under the mortgage note, he still had to replace everything he owned, down to his golf clubs. The company had cut him a check for ten grand the morning after the fire, an advance against his overall claim. Even though it would be deducted from the proceeds, considering Al didn't even have a change of underwear with him when he watched his house burn, it was a welcome windfall.

He'd picked the motel because of its proximity to the GSAC office. After two days he realized there was no real benefit in being close to a job he was going to lose anyway. He decided he ought to move to a motel closer to the club. At least that way he could go hit some balls in the morning. It was too bad they never got around to putting rooms in at Mira Vista. That would've been nice. Get up, hit a bucket of balls, grab some breakfast, and roll into the office. J.T. didn't want him hanging around the club, but if Al wanted to hit balls at 6:00 a.m., who was J.T. to tell him he couldn't?

As he walked out into the parking lot of the Holiday Inn Express with a Styrofoam cup of coffee and a nylon duffel bag, Al noticed a white BMW in corner of the lot. Even though it had been almost ten years, Al still felt a tinge whenever he saw a white BMW. The BMW of the guy Michelle left him for had been white.

Al hadn't been crushed when she left. He hadn't even been hurt that she left him for a guy from her gym she'd been fucking. What really stung Al was that she didn't even go for alimony. He knew he was lucky, but it wounded his pride that she never expected he'd make enough money to bother with. That Sunday, parked down the street, he'd watched her load her stuff into the back of the guy's car.

Arriving at his desk now, Al was torn between discouragement and giddiness. He was demoralized to have lost not only his job, but also the ill-gotten foundation of his consulting business. On the other hand, with no unsalable house to anchor him to

Riverside, he was now free to go anywhere his imagination took him. His problem was his imagination didn't really take him anywhere else.

He needed a hobby. He decided to get back to playing golf. He'd have Steve Estep fit him for a real set of clubs—not some off-the-rack, 3-PW set of pot metal irons from Wal-Mart, but a real set of sticks. He'd try out every new driver in the shop. If a new driver was $500, so what? It was time to turn his life around.

Thinking about his new purchase gave Al Boyle's outlook a conspicuous boost. People in the office who ordinarily walked by without saying a word stopped to ask a smiling Al how everything was going. Like a robot he processed the foot-high stack of files on his desk, intermittently checking the Internet to compare the ratings of irons, drivers, and putters on various golf magazine websites. They had some neat bags now. He hoped Mira Vista's pro shop carried them.

After stopping by In-N-Out Burger for dinner, Al drove his loaner Honda straight to Mira Vista. Estep was only too happy to get Al set up with $3,500 worth of new equipment, from clubs and shoes to bags, clothes, balls, and tees. As he loaded his new purchases into the trunk of the Honda, he noticed another white BMW off near the range where a handful of guys were hitting balls. There seemed to be a lot of them on the road now. Maybe once his check came in, he'd have to take a look at getting one himself.

THIRTY-EIGHT

J.T. was more than a little annoyed that Buddy had never called him about meeting with Aza. On the phone Aza had been so cagey, J.T. couldn't tell if the two had talked yet or not.

On top of that, Al was making him nuts. *Guy complains nonstop about how screwed he is with his worthless house; then when he finally catches a break and the fucking thing burns to the ground, he's still finding something to whine about.* J.T. wondered if any meth dealers might move into *his* neighborhood. Shit, even Stephanie's would be a help.

Shari brought in a cup of coffee and laid the *LA Times* on the desk. She had an ass the size of a volleyball, and J.T. watched it float out of his office and into the hallway. *Soon.*

Smoothing out the paper, J.T. noticed a two-column bar below the fold with a photo of Meshulam Razin and the headline "Meshulam Razin, 'Keeper of Secrets,' Dead at 90."

> BEVERLY HILLS—Legendary attorney and long-time Angeleno Meshulam Razin, 90, died in his sleep last night, according to a press release issued by his son-in-law, Dr. Michael Rosenstein, of Bel-Air.
>
> As an attorney, Meshulam Razin's formidable trial skills often had him mentioned in the same breath with America's legendary lawyers such as John W. Davis, Edward Bennett Williams and Johnnie Cochrane. But perhaps Mr. Razin's most lasting legacy is that of a behind-the-scenes power broker.

> Long considered one of the most powerful men in the nation, Razin was known as "The Keeper of Secrets," and his influence throughout the entertainment industry was unequaled in the late twentieth century. Razin famously exploited his personal relationships to rescue seemingly troubled projects. Shunning the spotlight, Razin consistently declined numerous appointments to public office, including a reported ambassadorship to Israel during the Reagan administration.
>
> While many attributed his publicity aversion to personal shyness, Razin could never shake whispers of darker explanations. In addition to studio heads and film stars, Mr. Razin's relationships with reputed underworld figures were also tabloid fodder....

J.T. dropped the paper on the desk. *Son of a bitch.* He knew Razin was old, but somehow he'd never actually believed he was mortal. Now that he was gone, would all those secrets really go to the grave with him? Would the kids try to cash in with a tell-all book?

One thing J.T. did know: Meshulam Razin would never have gotten jumbled up with this posse of assclowns.

When Hector arrived at the office, Manu was already there. Upon closer inspection, Manu appeared to be wearing the same clothes as the day before.

"Manu?"

"Yeah."

"Did you go home last night?"

"I got caught up in an online discussion about *The Matrix.*"

"All night? Why don't you go home?"

"Okay." Manu closed up his laptop and collected his phone from his desk. "McMahon has a bench warrant."

"What? What are you talking about?"

"McMahon is the plaintiff in your GSAC case."

"I know that. What's this about a warrant?"

"I did a background check. He was cited in Moreno Valley a few days before his accident at El Fuente Dorado. He never responded to the citation. The court issued a bench warrant for his arrest."

"No kidding?"

Manu began walking toward the glass office door that opened onto the strip mall's parking lot.

"Um, Manu? Can I see this?"

"I saved a PDF and e-mailed it to you. There's also a hard copy on your desk. See you later, Hector." Manu walked out the door.

Hector dropped his briefcase behind his desk and pulled a Diet Coke from the mini fridge. He sat down and picked up the pages Manu had left on his desk. Hector called the duty supervisor at the sheriff's office in Riverside.

Hector had defended two deputies in a §1983 action brought by a twenty-five-year-old who'd gotten the shit beat out of him outside a Circle K convenience store. The media framed the story as two fascist jackboots ganging up on a defenseless young black man, Jamal Blake. Hector had shown at trial, however, that the multiply fractured victim had, in fact, turned not one, but two pit bulls loose on Sam Roper, a uniformed deputy who'd told the guy to "get those fucking dogs away from the store." Had it not been for a passing deputy who witnessed his colleague writhing in the parking lot under 188 pounds of canine rage, Roper would have been killed. One of the dogs had Roper's right wrist in his mouth; the other was tearing at Roper's left biceps. As it was, Roper received ninety-two stitches. The dogs were not so lucky.

Deputy Don Tinny radioed for backup as he raced into the parking lot. Tinny leapt from his car and shot the first dog as Deputy Brent Sowell's cruiser screeched around the corner. Tinny ran around his car to get a shot at the second dog. Out of nowhere and swinging a chain leash, Blake charged Tinny. Sowell, skidding into the parking lot, slammed his car into Blake, knocking him into the store's wall. Tinny shot the second dog and was prying its dead jaws loose from Roper's arm when an injured but cranked-up Blake, still holding his chain, picked himself up from the sidewalk and charged Sowell. A former defensive lineman at Auburn, Sowell, and Tinny, the one-time martial arts instructor at Marine Corps Base Camp Smedley D. Butler in Okinawa, "ensured the suspect had been fully subdued before taking further action."

In spite of Hector's occasional DUI work, obtaining a defense verdict for Tinny and Sowell had earned him a lifetime of goodwill with the Riverside sheriff's office. The duty officer took a message for Brad Fojtik, the deputy who'd written up Mack McMahon. Fojtik returned Hector's call and agreed to meet Hector at the Costa Coffee shop in the strip mall.

Hector had blown up a copy of Mack's driver's license and took the printout detailing the bench warrant down to the coffee shop. Fojtik walked in a few minutes later.

"I *do* remember this asswipe," said Fojtik, laughing. "He had a busted headlight and was heading straight to Hooters in Moreno Valley. You know, the one off the Sixty?"

"Yeah. You remember anything else?"'

"He gave me some line of shit about how it had just happened five minutes ago at the Van Slaters. I only remember because it was so stupid. Like you get run over by shopping carts and you go to fucking Hooters?"

"He said he got hit by shopping carts?"

"Yeah. He said that's what fucked up his headlight and his shoulder."

"He mentioned his shoulder?"

"Kept rolling it over, you know, dramatizing it to try to get out of the citation."

"Anybody with him?"

"No, he was by himself." Fojtik took a sip of coffee. "I did notice him in my rearview talking to some guy while he was going into Hooters."

"You get a look at him?"

"Nah. Black kid. It was dark. Nothing suspicious or anything." Fojtik sipped his coffee. "What kind of case you got going?"

"It's nothing. Just running down some details for an insurance claim." Hector arranged the papers in the folder and closed it. "No big deal."

Al checked into the Best Western on Sunnymead in Moreno Valley. After sitting alone in his motel room alone for ten minutes, all Al could think about was his brand-new clubs in the trunk of the Honda. He slid his electronic room key into his pocket and strode down the hall, thrumming the window as he waited for the elevator. Out in the parking lot, as soon as he opened the trunk, he was hit by the smell of the new bag. He loved the way the clubs jangled in the bag softly with their new head covers—not like his old set of irons that sounded like a ring of car keys. As he slammed the Honda's trunk, he stopped whistling. Across the street in the parking lot of the Sunoco was a white BMW. Al froze. After fifteen seconds, the BMW started up and pulled onto Sunnymead and out of view.

Al ran back to the lobby, his new clubs bouncing in their new padded bag, the bag itself beating against his calves. *Fuck. Fuck. Fuck. J.T. Call J.T. Fuck.*

Al called J.T., gasping. "We got a problem," he said, hyperventilating after his sprint from the parking lot. "Somebody's following me."

"Who? Why?"

"I don't know. Maybe because of the house. Maybe they're following me because they suspect arson."

"Then it sounds like *you* got a problem, Al, not *we* got a problem."

"C'mon, I'm serious."

"Is there any reason they'd suspect arson?"

"Shit, I don't know. Hundred grand underwater. Suspicious explosion."

"If that was the case, the cops would be pulling up in paddy wagons for every fire in the Inland Empire. Everybody's underwater. Don't worry about it."

"Shit."

"What?"

"Vargas."

"Who's Vargas?"

"My boss. I told him I couldn't take the job in Weed because of the house. That was right before the fire. Shit."

"First of all, have you ever had a thought that you didn't just blurt out? Jesus."

"I'm having one now."

"Listen, relax. Worst case—*wooorrrrst* case, they investigate. So what? You didn't blow up the house next door, did you?"

"No."

"The cops found the meth lab, didn't they?"

"Yeah."

"So let them investigate their asses off. Big fucking deal. I'm telling you, if you really didn't burn your house down, you got nothing to worry about."

Al wanted to calm down. Maybe J.T. was right. *Still.*

"Then who the fuck is following me?"

"You're sure you're not being paranoid?"

"You told me I was supposed to be paranoid, remember?"

"And you're making me proud, son."

"Quit fucking around. I'm not kidding. Somebody in a white BMW was at my motel this morning in Riverside. I saw him again at—" Al caught himself. He didn't want to hear J.T.'s shit about being at the club.

"At where?"

"At least two more times today that I know of, including just now at *this* motel in Moreno Valley." Al was starting to hyperventilate again.

"Okay, here's what you do. Tomorrow morning, you keep your eyes peeled. If you're being followed, the guy's going to follow you to work. Get a plate number and we can take it from there."

Al jumped when he heard something thump the wall outside. Then he heard a vacuum cleaner and realized it was just the maid.

"You don't know anybody with a white BMW, right?" said J.T.

"Michelle's husband had one."

"Michelle?"

"My ex."

"Well, shit, there you go. That's probably it. He's probably just looking to dump her and get you to take her back."

"Very funny."

"Would you lighten up? The FBI doesn't drive German cars. You're not a drug dealer. You didn't burn your house down. I really think you're overreacting."

"I hope you're right."

"Just take it easy. What's the worst thing it could be?"

THIRTY-NINE

Mack pulled into the parking lot of Wanda's complex totally pumped. The McMahon 3000 had outperformed even his wildest expectations. Shit, if all Mini Coopers ran like this, he was going to have to reconsider the whole King Ranch pickup idea.

He was still jacked when Wanda came home at 9:00 p.m., and he ambushed her as she opened the front door.

"Hey! Guess whose McMahon 3000 just kicked some desert ass?"

"No kidding? That's great."

"Goddamn right. That sumbitch out there is a *machine*, baby. A fucking *machine*."

"That's great, really." Wanda dropped her purse on the dining room table. "Listen, I don't want to blow you off, but I want to go down and get a swim in, okay?"

"Sure. Hell, I'll whip us up some margaritas and I'll join you."

"There you go."

Mack poured the entire pitcher into three stadium cups and carried them down to the pool, where Wanda's long body cruised through the water like a mako. Big as she was, Mack couldn't get over how gracefully she moved in the pool. He'd finished one of his margaritas and was nearly through the other when Wanda pulled up. She stretched herself out and rested her head on her arms the same way she'd done the other night when Buddy was there.

"Here's your drink, darlin'."

"Thanks, but you go ahead. I'm just taking a little breather."

"You sure?"

Wanda nodded and ducked underwater and came up smoothing her hair. Mack took a big slug of the margarita. He'd already had two pitchers while he was sitting around the house waiting for Wanda. Now he wished he'd taken a leak before he came down.

"I saw that guy Johnny Ho on TV back at the club," Wanda said.

"Oh, yeah?"

"He was with your pal Pete Fruccione."

"Frooch ain't no pal of mine. Hell, I don't even know the man. He might be looking over his shoulder this-a-way 'fore long, though." Mack leaned back in the patio chair and stretched his legs. "What were they talking about?"

"They were saying that nobody had ever scaled Joe Frey Hill in an ATV before."

"That the place over by Twentynine Palms?"

"Yeah. People hike up to the top all the time, but the Frooch guy was saying nobody could ride up the trail in an ATV." Wanda kicked gently in the shallow water. "Then that guy Johnny Ho goes, *'That sounds like a challenge, bro!'*"

"Shit. The McMahon 3000 could take that fucker. Guaranteed."

"I don't know. Frooch was going to customize this special ATV for Johnny Ho."

Mack sat up straight. "Did he do it on TV? Get to the top?"

"No, they were just going over the design of the ATV. I think they're going to wait and keep showing Frooch building the thing, then go for it at the end of the season."

"So nobody's climbed that thing yet?"

"Nope. Still a virgin."

"Not for long, darlin'." Mack drained the last of the margarita he'd brought for Wanda. "I got a date tomorrow mornin'."

The next morning when Al carried his clubs down to the car, there was no sign of a white BMW. J.T. was right. All his paranoid bullshit had finally gotten to Al.

Al was the first non-employee to arrive at Mira Vista. He hit a large bucket of balls, but he was so excited by the way the balls jumped off the clubface, he bought another small bucket. Thoroughly satisfied, Al took his clubs back to the car and went into the 19th Hole to get some breakfast.

When he returned from washing his hands in the men's room, he saw someone sitting at a table with his back to Al, and opposite him, the unmistakable bulk of Frankie Fresh. Al wheezed as he tried to catch his breath. He wiped his hair with his damp right hand. Something felt weird. He looked down and the palm of his hand had at least thirty hairs stuck to it. Panicked, Al wiped the other side of his head with his left hand. Same result. The burning sensation again torched Al's ribcage as he approached the table.

"Frankie."

"Hiya, Al," said Frankie with a wave of his meaty hand. "Long time no see."

"Yeah."

"Hey, listen, I understand you know my new friend here." Frankie pointed to the guy with his back to Al. "Rog?"

Al coughed when Roger Ellis turned around.

"Hiya, *Al*."

Hector hustled out to Van Slaters in Moreno Valley first thing to have a talk with the manager. After identifying himself as an attorney for the company's insurance carrier, the manager, as Hector suspected, told him he wasn't on duty the evening the accident had happened in the parking lot. There was, however, an incident report written up by the night manager according to corporate policy in the event a claim was filed. The report said that a blond man driving a Pontiac Firebird had been hit by a cluster of runaway shopping carts in the parking lot. The man had refused to give his name but had threatened legal action. The night manager, Jenny Calloway, did get the names and contact details for several witnesses and included the information in the report.

The plate number matched the one from Manu's research into the bench warrant. Hector couldn't necessarily put everything together, but maybe the night manager could fill in the gaps.

Hector called Al's office, but the phone rolled into voicemail. Hector looked at his watch. It was early, but not so early that he couldn't call Al's cell phone.

"Have a seat," said Frankie. "Join us for some breakfast and fellowship."

"Yeah, thanks, but I've got to get moving. I just popped in for a cup of coffee."

"Back to the office, eh?" said Frankie.

"You know how it is."

Ellis sniffed. "Actually, Al, I don't. Why don't you tell us how it is?"

"Are you the one who's been following me around in the BMW, Ellis?"

"Seems like a coincidence, I'll bet," said Ellis.

"Seems like fucking stalking is what it seems like," said Al. "What is your deal?"

"My deal? My deal is I got fired from GSAC for some bullshit that you pulled. That's my deal. What's yours?"

"I don't know what you're talking about." Al's cell phone rang. He ignored it.

"Boys, boys," said Frankie. "There seem to be some raw emotions here at this little conclave. Wanda," Frankie bellowed, "can we get some bloody marys over here, please?"

Al's cell phone rang again. Again he ignored it.

Wanda pulled three jumbo Styrofoam cups from beneath the counter. "Sure thing."

Al's cell phone rang again. He looked at it. It was Aza.

"I've got to take this," said Al. "Work."

Frankie waved an imaginary pest away from the table. "Of course. Of course. Business before pleasure, I always say."

Al stood up from the table. "This is Alvin Boyle," he said, and walked out to the parking lot. As soon as he got outside, he positioned himself out of the eyeline of Frankie and Ellis, but so he'd still be able to see if the door moved an inch.

"Hi, it's Hector Aza. You got a minute?"

"Um, sure. Quick one." Al wondered if Aza could hear Al's pulse thumping through the phone. "What've you got?"

"McMahon. When I was out at Eisenhower, the doctor, Garvey, mentioned that McMahon had complained he'd hurt his shoulder."

"Uh-huh." Al was pacing back and forth, hoping he'd get Aza off the phone in time to call J.T.

"So it turns out that McMahon was injured in what I'd call a borderline suspicious incident at Van Slaters only a couple of nights before. In addition to El Fuente Dorado, guess who also insures Van Slaters?"

A tiny croak escaped from Al's throat. Dried spittle clogged the corners of his mouth. He tried to swallow but it was like he had a neck full of sand. "Ohmigod."

"Don't get too excited. I mean, at this point it's just a coincidence, but I thought it was interesting, how about you?"

"Jesus."

"Like I said. Still too early to know much, but I'll keep you posted."

"Yeah," Al gasped. "Thanks."

He hung up the phone. He wanted to call J.T. but realized the dispose-a-phone was in the car. If Frankie saw him go to the car, it would be bad. Calling J.T. from Al's own cell phone would be bad. If Al didn't warn J.T., that would be pretty fucking bad too.

Being Al Boyle, he split the baby and jogged to his car. He reached in and grabbed the phone to call J.T. He started walking back toward the 19th Hole as slowly as he could, hoping he could buy a few more seconds before he had to go back inside. J.T. answered on the second ring.

"What's up?"

"Shit storm. Frankie's got me collared here at the club. The guy that was foll—"

"Wait a minute, what the fuck are you doing at the club? Didn't I tell you to stay away from that fucking—"

"Jesus, not *now*, J.T.! Just listen. The guy that's been following me is the guy that got fired from GSAC. Ellis? Remember the internal investigation? They found the breach into the database and blamed Ellis. Now the fucker's got me in his sights for losing him his job."

"Okay, slow down, Al—"

"J.T.! Listen! He's here with Frankie! That means Frankie knows about Mack's dick! That means he knows we've been holding out on him!"

"Jesus. How the fuck—"

"*Christ, J.T.! Shut up and listen!* That's not all. Aza just called. He found out about Van Slaters." The door opened slowly, with Frankie's enormous frame filling the space. "Okay, thanks, Lidia," Al said, nodding. "I'll call him back when I get in. No, no, no problem. Okay, hon. Bye." Al shook his head as he glanced up at Frankie's alligator smile. "Always a crisis."

J.T.'s head was spinning. How had something so right turned so quickly to shit? Al Boyle had to be cursed. Everything the guy even remotely touched just melted into a surging, white-capped river of feces.

J.T. looked at the gas gauge of his Mercedes. Not for the first time, he wondered: What if he liquidated everything—just got all the cash he could scrape together—and took off like O. J. toward Mexico? How far could he get? How much to buy a new identity and just disappear? Shit, he could be a bartender in Cancún or something.

Aza knew about Van Slaters. How the fuck was this possible?

Fucking Mack. What kind of asshole goes to Hooters with the guy who mowed him down? If only he'd been killed by that fucking tractor. No. Only devoutly religious people got that kind of luck, and it was too late for J.T.

How to neutralize Frankie? That would take some finessing. Depending on what he knew, it could be played off as mission-critical to maintain absolute secrecy. After all, Frankie was in for eight points, right? Eight points on seven hundred grand was a lot more than on a hundred. J.T. could lay the whole thing off on trial strategy. Tell Frankie he didn't want to disappoint him with the news that this thing could go to trial; not so long as there was a real chance the thing could settle before that.

J.T. had only filed a few days ago. He could just explain to Frankie he hadn't had a chance to tell him personally. He hadn't been anywhere near the club, not that he could remember.

Buddy. He'd forgotten he'd come by that day to talk to Buddy; J.T. had made a point of getting the hell out of there expressly to *avoid* Frankie. That would make for a tougher sale if Frankie knew about J.T.'s visit. One thing about Frankie: he acted like an idiot, but the guy was two steps ahead. So long as J.T. could stay five steps ahead, everything would be okay.

Al. It always came back to Al. *Heading over Diarrhea Falls in a fucking barrel.*

FORTY

Beneath the scorching August sun of Twentynine Palms, Mack released the straps securing the McMahon 3000. He reached over the driver's seat, dropped the machine into neutral, and pushed it gently backward until it rolled off the parallel ramps.

As he put his fingers on the key to turn the motor over, he thought he heard artillery fire in the distance. For all the glory that would come with being the first vehicle to scale Joe Frey Hill, getting blown to shit by U.S. Marines would clearly suck all the fun out of it. Mack thought about it and figured with all the civilians out this way, it would take a colossal clusterfuck for some kind of ordnance to land that far off course.

He was disappointed that no one was around to witness his feat. On weekends the place was crawling with dune buggies, hippies, bird watchers, and thirsty Mexicans dumped out of semis. He looked up the path to the hill's first switchback. For something supposed to be a tough climb, the trail looked awfully fucking wide to Mack. The next level up the path got narrower, but looked doable. Given the slope of the hill, though, the McMahon 3000's independent suspension, the clingy knobby tires, and the vehicle's proven balance, Mack realized what his geometry teacher had been trying to explain back at Pershing High in Van Horn: the shortest distance between two points was indeed a straight line.

Mack walked halfway around the hill's northeastern slope. There didn't look to be any boulders in the way. A few rocks, but nothing to knock the McMahon 3000 off its wheels. Shit, he wished Wanda were here with a video camera or something so they could send this to CNN.

When he turned the engine over, the buggy barely made a sound. *Like a Prius or something. Quiet. Almost scary-quiet.* Mack started up the hill in first gear. The McMahon 3000 just walked up the side of the 2,200-foot-high mountain like Spider-Man. Mack rose halfway out of his seat to look for rocks or holes, bracing himself with his right hand on the roll bar and his left on the steering wheel. He was making great progress. He looked over his right shoulder at the switchbacks bent like bobby pins cutting the slope from the hill. *Bunch of pussies.*

With the vehicle still in first gear and no visible obstacles, Mack felt his pulse quickening. He was almost at the top. *Goddamn, I wish Wanda was here with a camera.* He saw condors circling above, riding thermals in big lazy arcs. He turned his head quickly to look directly behind him. Things looked smaller, but not like ants. He couldn't believe that the baddest extreme motorsports expert in California was afraid of this little hill.

"*Fuck Johnny Ho!*" Mack yelled to the condors. His voice boomed over the roll bar; it soared above the coloratura whine of the McMahon 3000's tiny engine. His proud cry floated over the abrupt peak of Joe Frey Hill and down the 260-foot sheer drop of the hill's *southwest* slope, with the McMahon 3000 and Mack McMahon himself hurtling through the fading echo.

Frankie laid a beefy arm on Al's shoulder and steered him back toward the table. "I haven't seen our friend the counselor around the club of late, have you?"

"No. Not lately."

Ellis sat in his seat watching his coffee cool as Al and Frankie approached the table and sat down. The three bloody marys Wanda had brought over sat untouched on the table.

"Listen," said Al, "I really do have to get into the office."

"Lot of activity over there, is there?"

"Just trying to wrap things up before the merger's finished."

"You know, it's funny," said Frankie, splashing a few drops of Tabasco sauce in his bloody mary, "I understand things have been really interesting over there at GSAC."

"Well, it's a big merger."

"I was thinking more in the field of interesting personal injury claims."

"I don't follow you."

"Young Roger here was telling me of a recent claim in which a young fellow was traumatized by a—what was it, Rog? A penile fracture?"

"Yeah," said Ellis, glaring over his bloody mary at Al.

"Yeah, that's a very interesting claim," said Al. "Problematic, but a potentially large payout."

"Problematic?" said Frankie, sipping his drink. "How so?"

"Listen, I'd love to tell you all about it, but I really have to go."

"Relax," said Frankie, "they're not going to fire you."

Al turned to face Ellis, even though he was talking to Frankie. "They already did." Al turned back to Frankie. "What, Wonder Boy didn't fill you in on that? Yeah, I lost my job. I'm out. My fucking house burned down three nights ago. I'm getting laid off at the end of the month, and now I've got this nutjob driving around stalking me like a teenage girl."

"Jesus, Al," said Frankie, "I had no idea. I'm really sorry about that."

"Thanks, but can we pick this up later?"

"Sure, sure." Frankie turned to Ellis. "Rog, you'll excuse us for a minute, won't you?"

Ellis nodded and got up from his chair and took his drink out toward the pro shop.

Al leaned in toward Frankie. "What the fuck? What does he know?"

"Don't worry about him. He's just pissed about losing his job. Thinks you set him up to get fired."

"He got fired because he's obviously a dumbshit. Not that it would matter anyway. I been there seventeen years and I'm getting laid off with the rest of them."

"Sorry to hear that. Really and truly. Makes it a little awkward, but you know what's coming up, right?"

"Yeah. I don't have the vig on me right now," Al lied, "but I'll bring it out tonight after work."

"That's terrific," Frankie said, laying his swollen paw on Al's shoulder. "Then maybe you can fill in the blanks on how our young maintenance man is walking around with a million-dollar wound, and your good friend and partner, Frankie, is the last to find out about it."

That afternoon, for the second time since the sun came up, Hector found himself crawling in traffic along the 60. He finally reached Moreno Valley, pulled off at the Perris Boulevard exit, and made his way back to the Van Slaters parking lot.

The night manager, Jenny, recognized Mack's photograph from the file. A piece of paper slid out of the folder Hector held, and Jenny picked it up. She jumped when she saw the photo of Mack's deformed penis. She gasped, squeaked, and looked up at Hector.

Hector gently took the paper from her hand. "Sorry about that. Should've left that one in the car."

Jenny confirmed that Mack had indeed been hit by the carts. "He was still on the ground when I came running out. A couple of witnesses claimed they saw a black guy give the carts a shove before driving off."

Hector raised his chin. "So you didn't see the guy yourself?"

"No. I couldn't even say whether it was intentional or just an accident." Jenny was unconsciously looking at the folder in

Hector's hand. "I've been telling these guys it was only a matter of time until this happened." She shook her head. "The bag boys think it's fun to stack ten carts together and come hauling ass down that slope. Not going to be so funny when some old lady gets knocked over and killed."

Hector thanked her, climbed back into his Crown Victoria, and drove back up onto the 60 and headed home. He'd wait until the morning to call Al. The guy sounded like he could use some good news.

Al's heads-up, while panicked, had given J.T. a chance to digest what was happening. Aza was onto the Van Slaters fall. Not good. Not good at all, but not prima facie evidence of fraud. They'd never filed anything. The only thing Aza had was that Van Slaters was a GSAC policyholder and that Mack was a jerk-off. If there were a law against being a dumbass, J.T. would have long been California's leading bounty hunter.

Unless someone saw Buddy in the grocery store parking lot. That would be a real pig-fuck. J.T. didn't even want to consider that possibility, so he turned his focus to his more immediate problem.

Frankie.

The Frankie thing was disturbing. J.T. couldn't quite follow Al's convoluted story about being followed by a disgruntled ex-GSAC employee who thought Al had gotten him fired but Al hadn't and....It gave J.T. a fucking headache.

J.T. left the office early and beat the traffic home. He opened one of his last two bottles of the thirty-nine-dollar cabernet from La Bodega, cranked up the volume on KCBS on the sixty-inch flat-screen, and climbed into the Jacuzzi.

As he poured the last third of the bottle into his balloon glass, J.T. heard the news mention Meshulam Razin's funeral the following day at Forest Lawn. J.T. reached over and picked up one of the disposable phones and called Al.

"Where are you right now?"

"On my way back to the club to give Frankie the vig."

"Pull over. This is going to take a minute to explain."

FORTY-ONE

Hector went online to check out the Mira Vista Golf Club and Resort. The website had clearly not been updated since the club opened. He thought about Wanda McMahon's smile when she'd brought him his lunch. She was just his type. Tall. Athletic. Dark-complected, with those gorgeous dimples. Why did she have to be married to the guy that fixed golf carts?

He'd still never heard back from McMahon's friend, Buddy. He wanted to try the club one more time in person, but if he were to bump into Wanda again, J.T. would go nuts. But there was no rush. Hector still had weeks to get J.T.'s discovery back to him. There was time.

"Here's what you're going to do: you're going to pay Frankie his vig, and you're going to tell him everything's still a go."

"I am?"

"Yes, you are."

"But I'll be laid off before this thing gets anywhere near trial. How am I supposed to convince him to hang on? I already told Frankie I was losing my job."

Fucking guy cannot keep his mouth shut about anything. "Listen to me. You're going to tell him everything's a go. You're going to tell him it was me, J.T., who *expressly* told you not to mention the new development to a soul. You're going to tell him how I, J.T., knew that if even a whisper of this leaked out, we'd lose any chance at all of settling short of trial."

"Okay."

"I'm not done. You're going to tell him now that the cat is out of the bag, now that your big-mouth friend Ellis has opened his fucking yap, this thing is going to trial. You can't sign off on a settlement—hell, you can't even convince the company they should settle. See? You're totally telling the truth."

J.T. wondered if Al caught the dig buried in there. "Now listen: this is the critical part, okay? You're going to take your cell phone and leave it in your shirt pocket, you got me?"

"Yeah. Why?"

"I'm getting to that. Now stay with me, okay? I need you to record your conversation with Frankie using the cell phone. Can you do that? Can you figure out how to record a conversation with the cell phone?"

"Sure, I guess."

"Guessing will not be good enough this time. I don't want you to get stressed out, but I gotta tell you, this gets fucked up, we're both looking at careers in landfill, and I don't mean shoveling it, you hear me?"

"Yeah. Hang on, let me try it." Al picked up one of the other disposable phones and fumbled with the buttons. "Testing…testing…one, two, three."

J.T. threw his head back against the wall of the hot tub. *Fucking knew he'd say that.* "So did it work?"

"Yeah."

"Okay, this is the very, very important part."

"Okay."

"I need one hundred percent of your concentration right now, okay?"

"Okay, *fuck*!"

"Good, now here's what you're going to do. You need to get Frankie to start talking shit about Vinnie Fangs."

"Vinnie Fangs."

"Vinnie Fangs." J.T. sighed loudly and turned off the jets to the tub. "You're going to tell Frankie that you've lost your job and that you can't influence the case anymore."

"He knows that."

"Just fucking listen, all right? Trust me, I'm trying to help us both out of this." J.T. climbed out of the Jacuzzi and sat down in a patio chair. "You tell him you're worried about Vinnie Fangs. You do *not*, under any circumstances, call him Vinnie Fangs. You call him *Mister Fegangi*, you got it?"

"Got it."

"I don't want you to try to memorize anything else. I know this is a lot, buddy, all right? Just try and follow me." J.T. topped off his glass of wine. "Your objective—your only objective—is to get Frankie to talk shit about Vinnie Fangs. You know Frankie. He's a loudmouth. Give him enough rope and he'll hang himself."

J.T. sipped a big mouthful of wine. He was thinking so fast he wasn't paying attention to what he was doing. He paused while he swirled the wine around in his mouth. *Not bad.*

"You need to steer the conversation to getting Frankie to say, effectively, 'Fuck Vinnie Fangs.' You want him to admit he never told Vinnie Fangs about the scam."

"That's it?" said Al.

"That's enough."

"But isn't this illegal? How are the cops going to be able to use this?"

Once again, J.T. counted to five in his head. "Of course it's illegal. We're not—never mind." He looked for the wine bottle. He'd already forgotten it was empty. He tossed it over his head and out into the yard, where it landed in the soft Bermuda grass with a thud. "I need you to do one last thing for me and then we're done."

"What's that?"

"First, how much cash can you get your hands on right now? Tonight?"

"I think I still have four grand from the insurance payout."

"Shit. That's not going to get us very far."

"I lost everything when the house burned."

J.T. craned his neck and looked at the sun growing buttery in the sky. "Fuck it. Keep it."

"Yeah?"

"Yeah. Listen, after you meet with Frankie, I need you to drive and meet me at the Der Weinerschnitzel on University. You know the one I'm talking about?"

"Yeah, but you said we were never supposed to meet."

"Did I also mention I didn't want to wind up tied to an engine block at the bottom of the Salton Sea?" J.T. started drying himself with a gold Ralph Lauren beach towel. "I'll be there in a booth, reading. Say eight o'clock. You come in; order something to go. Walk by my table, put the phone with the recording on it, and just keep on going. Can you do that?"

"Yeah, I can do that."

"Okay. Now, listen. Take a deep breath and relax. It's almost over."

FORTY-TWO

Al went into the office, but he couldn't focus on the growing mound of paperwork immigrating to his desk. He'd lost more hair to the point where his scalp was now visible. He thought about buying a rug.

After meeting with Frankie, Al had stuck around the 19th Hole for a couple of vodkas before he drove back to Riverside. He went in to the Der Wienerschnitzel and ordered a dog with kraut. He walked over to the condiment station, got some extra napkins, and laid the phone on J.T.'s table on his way out the door. Alone in his motel room, Al ate his hot dog with kraut, drank some more vodka, and watched *Sahara* on TV. When he saw Matthew McConaughey moving his fingers from left to right pretending to read Arabic script, Al chuckled out loud.

At least I'm not the *dumbest asshole in the world.*

Traffic backed up off the 5 onto the Glendale Boulevard exit. As limousines inched up Glendale toward Forest Lawn, J.T. felt like an extra at Vito Corleone's funeral. He knew there would be a turnout, but he hadn't counted on quite this overwhelming an outpouring of...*relief.*

With the demise of J. Edgar Hoover, no individual—not the president, not the head of the CIA, not the foremost computer hacker in the country—had access to the kind of information

Meshulam Razin had stored in the nautilus chambers of his craggy, white-thatched head.

J.T. parked the rented Taurus behind what seemed like a mile of black limousines. He hung his head, thinking about how far he'd fallen. He'd focus on losing the Mercedes later. He trudged up a hill and down the other side, following the herd of mourners and gawkers to Meshulam Razin's final resting place. As much as J.T. hated standing around at funerals, for once he was hoping the thing would run long, long enough anyway for him to find, isolate, and approach Vincenzo Fegangi.

He wouldn't be easy to spot. There had to be two thousand people there. All in dark suits. Men wearing yarmulkes. J.T. had cut a circle out of an old pair of bicycle shorts and affixed it to his hair with a paperclip. It didn't have to be perfect. It just had to stay on for a few minutes until he could get clear of the crowd.

He hoped Fangs wouldn't be too close to the casket; otherwise J.T. would never get through. After five minutes of looking, bobbing up and down as he circled the gathering, he still hadn't seen him. He was just about to climb up on Alan Ladd's headstone when he spotted Fangs flanked by two younger men built like file cabinets.

J.T. watched. The two guys occasionally said something to Fangs with their hands covering their mouths. Vinnie Fangs either nodded or looked away. J.T. moved a little closer, a few feet at a time, never drawing their attention.

At least he didn't think he had drawn attention to himself, until he felt someone squeezing his left triceps from behind.

"Who the fuck are you?" a gravel voice whispered from behind.

"My name's Edwards," J.T. said. He lifted his chin slightly as though not only was he not surprised, but as if people grabbed him from behind all the time. "I'm a lawyer. Mr. Razin was a kind of mentor of mine."

"What are you doing creeping over this way?" Still no face. Still a firm grasp on J.T.'s elbow.

J.T. knew this was the point where he needed to pull away or he'd never get close to Fangs. J.T. jerked his arm from the grip of the guy behind him and turned around. "I told you." J.T. scowled at the guy, who was about his size but years younger. "I'm a lawyer. Here." J.T. pulled a loose card from his pants pocket. "I have something urgent I need to talk to Mr. Fegangi about."

"You don't get to decide what's urgent—"

"Look, I don't know who you are. I'm sure you're doing your job. But do not fuck me on this, you understand?" J.T. stared at the guy the way he had at a thousand hostile witnesses. "I told you who I am. I told you I've got some important business that I need to share with Mr. Fengangi."

"Tell me what it is and I'll go tell him."

"What am I, an asshole?" J.T. saw Vinnie Fangs turn his head to look at the minor disruption. J.T. knew this was his shot. If he didn't get to Fegangi right here, right now, he never would. "Gimme that." J.T. yanked his business card out of the guy's fingers. J.T. tore it in half twice and threw it at the guy's chest. "Just remember: I tried to reach out to warn Mr. Fegangi, and it was *you* that fucked him, not me."

J.T. stomped off in the opposite direction of Vinnie Fangs and his associates. He made sure that he also walked in an indirect path leading nowhere near the Taurus. He zigzagged around the perimeter of the crowd like he knew where he was going until he heard "excuse me" from behind.

One of the two file cabinets that had been standing with Vinnie Fangs walked briskly up to J.T. "Come with me."

J.T. followed the guy, who didn't say a word. The service was over and the mourners started to break up, the crowd slowly, thickly dispersing down the path leading to the bank of limos over the hill. Well back of the crowd, Vinnie Fangs and the other file cabinet were walking toward him. The guy J.T. had yelled at was three steps behind them.

The file cabinet walking with J.T. stopped, so J.T. stopped with him. Vinnie Fangs looked at him and didn't say anything. J.T. knew this move. It was the same polonaise he'd been through with Frankie Fresh. It was designed to throw someone off balance; get him to start talking, say something he didn't mean to say.

Vinnie Fangs blinked first. "So you came here to warn me about something?"

J.T. smiled slightly. It had worked. "Yes, sir."

"So who are you?" asked Fegangi.

"My name's Edwards, Mr. Fegangi. J.T. Edwards. I'm a lawyer."

"Uh-huh."

Fegangi had just reversed the gambit and stared ahead. J.T. knew he needed to have Fegangi maintain face. "You know we're being watched here, right?" J.T. said.

"You came to my friend's funeral to warn me I'm being watched? Thanks, pal, but I got drones flying over my patio twenty-four hours a day. My grandson shoots his BB gun at them. You couldn't have come out here for that."

"No, sir. It's just that I want to tell you up front that I'm here in my capacity as an attorney. The subject matter of what I have to discuss with you is highly confidential."

"You billing by the hour, counselor? Get on with it."

J.T. pulled a cell phone from his pocket. "What I need to discuss with you is recorded on here, Mr. Fegangi. Now," J.T. said, returning the phone into his jacket pocket, "is there somewhere I can play this for you where we won't be disturbed?"

The guy who'd grabbed J.T. held the limo door open for Fegangi, who got in the car, followed by the two file cabinets opposite him.

Fegangi slid over to make a space for J.T., then nodded at the guy outside the car, who closed the door.

"As I was saying, Mr. Fegangi," said J.T., not wanting to try his host's patience, "I have a client who is concerned—deeply concerned—that a recent indiscretion of his may not have had your full sanction."

Fangs picked a leaf from the cuff of his pants.

"Anyway, this client of mine has just been laid off from an insurance company where he worked. Just before his exit, however, he—rather unwisely, if you ask me—participated in a settlement of a personal injury claim that may have been...*less than wholesome*."

Vinnie Fangs sucked his teeth and raised his eyebrows.

"My client, as I said, had been told that his participation in this venture had your implicit approval. He later learned, as you're about to hear, that it had not."

Fangs shifted in his seat. He didn't say anything, but J.T. now had his unalloyed attention.

"My client had been told that the Inland Empire fell within your quote-unquote 'sphere of influence.' He's worried that your associate—"

"What associate?" said Fangs.

"A Mr. McElfresh. I understand Mr. McElfresh is a sportsman."

Fangs looked across the limo's open space at File Cabinets One and Two, then back to J.T. "Maybe you'd better play me what's on that thing."

"Of course." J.T. turned the phone on, hoping that the battery had been charged; that he hadn't picked up the wrong phone; that his edits to the conversation weren't noticeable. "One of the voices is my client's; the other I'm sure you'll recognize as being that of Mr. McElfresh."

—Well, what does Mr. Fegangi say about all of this?

—Mr. Fegangi don't say anything about all of this 'cause Mr. Fegangi don't know about all of this.

Fangs shot another quick look at File Cabinets One and Two.

—But I thought you worked for him. What's he going to say when he finds out? I got no money and no job, Frankie.

—I see where you're confused. You think I work for Vinnie Fangs. I don't.

J.T. watched Fegangi's molars grinding in his cheeks at the sound of Frankie calling him "Vinnie Fangs," a name he was known to despise.

—This is my deal out here. The day I start asking some diaper-wearing old guinea for table scraps…

Fangs stared at the cell phone, but J.T. noticed File Cabinets One and Two look at each other with eyes as big as CDs.

—Listen, boyo. I'm telling you—you ain't gotta worry about Vinnie Fangs. He's never gonna find out. Who you do *have to worry about is your good friend Frankie. You hear what I'm saying?*

After two seconds of silence, J.T. switched off the phone. "And that's it. That's what my client gave me."

File Cabinet One shook his head and set his jaw tight.

"From what I understand from my client," J.T. continued, "he himself was under the impression that the settlement of the claim in question was to be several hundred thousand dollars. Mr. McElfresh insisted on a 'finder's fee' of fifteen percent."

"That greedy fuck," said File Cabinet Two. Fangs scowled at the younger man.

"Yeah, well, there were serious defects in the claim that turned out to make it not such a gold mine after all. The claim was a dog and the company settled it for nuisance value. A total of twenty-four thousand dollars."

J.T. looked around the limo for a reaction. Getting none, he resumed his story. "My client paid Mr. McElfresh his fifteen percent finder's fee off the top—thirty-six hundred dollars.

Mr. McElfresh, however, apparently had been expecting a far greater fee. You don't need me to do the math, of course, but a fifteen percent finder's fee on a mid-six-figure claim..."

"You're right, counselor. I don't need you to do the math."

"Right. Anyway." J.T. cleared his throat. "My client, in addition to being unemployed and not particularly clever, is now very much afraid that Mr. McElfresh wasn't being forthcoming when he said that he hadn't told you about the scam, and that you would likewise be expecting a finder's fee for a half-million-dollar claim."

J.T. reached into his jacket and pulled out an envelope. He started to hand it to Fangs, but Fangs tilted his head toward File Cabinet One, who reached across the limo's open space to take the envelope.

J.T. knew Vinnie Fangs was his only chance to get out of this thing with that malignant walrus, Frankie Fresh. He also knew that showing up empty-handed to talk to Fangs would be suicide. Fangs or one of the File Cabinets would call Frankie and Frankie would hold a mirror in front of J.T.'s face while he stuffed J.T.'s testes down his throat.

He needed what the French called *une douceur.* He couldn't take it from Al. Not after the poor bastard lost his house and everything in it, not to mention his job. An envelope with cash, even though it was small potatoes to Vinnie Fangs—*especially* because it was so embarrassingly light—was J.T.'s only hope to convince Fangs of his story's truthfulness.

So J.T. had sold the Mercedes. He still owed $18,000 on it, but he was able to net a quick twenty grand in cash from the dealer that had sold it to him almost five years ago.

"There's sixty-eight hundred dollars in there. I told you the claim settled for twenty-four thousand. After Mr. McElfresh's fifteen percent, that represents my client's full one-third split of the settlement."

File Cabinet One flipped through the envelope and tilted his chin as he looked up at Fangs.

"Why?" Fangs asked.

Seeing Al at Der Wienerschnitzel, J.T. knew he'd done the right thing. The guy looked like Death's syphilitic cousin. His head was the color of newsprint, dull gray paper beneath dark wisps of hair. His shoulders were bony. J.T. could only guess how much weight Al had lost, not that he could afford to lose any in the first place.

"I told you, he's scared. He's a weak man, Mr. Fegangi. He got caught up in something bigger than himself. He just wants to walk away and not be afraid. He's terrified that this meeting will get back to Mr. McElfresh and that.... You appreciate what a delicate position he's in."

Fangs looked at the file cabinets seated across from him; then he turned back to J.T. "How'd you know to look for me here?"

"Meshulam Razin was kind of a hero of mine. I didn't know him personally. When I was in law school, and later, when I was working in the DA's office, I used to go to court and watch him. He wasn't a young man, but he was just..." J.T. surprised himself when his voice caught. "Just the best lawyer I ever saw."

Fangs nodded.

"I'd read somewhere that you and he were close. I thought you'd come by to pay your respects."

"He was a good friend," said Fangs. "A very misunderstood guy."

"But he made that work for him in the end, didn't he?" said J.T.

"I guess you're right, counselor." Fangs extended his hand to J.T. "Now I don't mean to be impolite, but I'm afraid I have some things..."

File Cabinet Two tapped the window twice with his pinkie ring, and the door opened from the outside.

FORTY-THREE

It was after 9:00 a.m. when the green-and-white cruiser pulled into the parking lot at Mira Vista. The two Riverside County sheriff's deputies, Johnson and Reyes, pushed their sunglasses back in unison as Johnson reached to open the door to the 19th Hole. There was no one behind the bar and no patrons in the grill, so they just stood waiting and looking around until Wanda came out of the kitchen with two oranges.

"Ohmigod, did you find him?"

"Yes, ma'am, we did," Johnson said. "I'm really sorry."

Wanda took a deep breath. Her eyes filled. She put the oranges on the bar and rubbed her eyes against the sleeves of her pink golf shirt. She pinched her nose and sniffled. "I'm sorry," she said, her dimpled chin trembling.

"Hey, c'mon," said Reyes. "It's okay. Come out here and have a seat."

Wanda walked from behind the bar, wiping her hands on her apron. "Where did you find him?"

"Twentynine Palms. Just like you said."

"Ohmigod."

"We pulled up this morning and there was the Firebird and the trailer, just like you'd described."

"So where was—"

"There's no nice way to say this," said Johnson. "He was smashed up halfway down the southwest side of the hill. Must've just gone over the top. No other way he could've gotten there, short of being dropped from a plane."

"You're kidding."

"For what it's worth," said Reyes, "he was killed instantly."

Johnson nodded. "It took a helicopter an hour to get him out of there. Looks like he just shot over the top and landed upside down."

"He wanted me to go with him."

"Good thing you didn't," said Johnson. "You'd have been killed too."

There was a rush of noise from the hand dryer's motor down the hall as the door opened to the men's locker room.

"So what happens now? Where is his body?"

"Because of where the accident occurred," said Johnson, "they took him to a mortuary in Blythe that the county uses to hold remains until autopsies or whatever."

"They don't need to do an autopsy, do they?" Wanda asked.

"On what?" said Reyes. Johnson backhanded him in the chest. Reyes winced. "Sorry. This is my first time doing this."

Johnson shook his head. "No, ma'am, I can't imagine there'd need to be an autopsy. You don't have any reason to believe he was on drugs, do you?"

"No chance," Wanda mumbled. "He'd had an operation a while back, but he wasn't even taking pain meds anymore." She looked down at the table. "He'd wanted to be in the Coast Guard." Wanda sniffled and dabbed her eyes with a cocktail napkin.

A couple of patrons came in and stood at the bar. Wanda made no move to get up.

"You'll want to call a funeral home to make the arrangements. They can take care of everything," said Johnson. "Again, I'm really sorry."

Hector was surprised to get a call from Brad Fojtik, the deputy he'd met with only days before.

"You're not going to believe this. That guy we were talking about? McMahon? The dumbass with the busted headlight?"

"Uh-huh."

"Dead."

"What?" said Hector. "You're kidding. How?"

"Asshole drives some kind of dune buggy up a mountain out by Twentynine Palms. Crashed the fucking thing going over the top."

"I would say this is unbelievable, but then again it totally sounds like the guy's MO, doesn't it?"

"I don't want to speak ill of the dead or anything, but what a fucking dumbass."

"And there's no question of foul play, as they say?"

"I guess you've never seen this thing. It's called Joe Frey Hill. It's not the Matterhorn or anything, but hippies like to go down there and smoke dope and pretend buzzards are condors."

Hector leaned back in his chair and tossed the file he was reading onto his desk.

"There's a hiking trail with a lot of switchbacks that you can walk up to the top," Fojtik continued. "It's only a coupla thousand feet high."

"So why drive?"

"Exactly. This shitbrain obviously never re-conned the hill. The slope's easy enough to get up in low gear, that's not the point. The problem is there's no way to turn around once you get up there. From below it looks like there's a little area at the summit, but it drops off like three hundred feet down into a bunch of jagged-ass rocks. What I heard was the guy just flew right over the top." Fojtik chuckled. "What an asshole."

Wanda was walking out the door to the parking lot with her purse when Frankie Fresh wedged through the door with his new sidekick, Ellis, behind him. Frankie gave Wanda his usual bluff morning greeting. Wanda nodded and wiped away a tear as she stepped past him.

"No breakfast today, hon?"

"No, I've got to go," she said over her shoulder. "Sorry."

Dee, Wanda's replacement, came out from the kitchen carrying a rack of glasses. "Hey, Frankie. You having breakfast?"

"I was. Where's Wanda going? She can't be taking a second honeymoon this soon, can she?" Frankie's gut rose and fell, his man-tits flapping like windsocks.

"Don't be an asshole."

"What?"

"Mack's dead."

"What?"

"He was killed yesterday out in the desert. Riding his dune buggy or something."

Frankie looked at Ellis. Ellis's mouth was open. Speechless.

Frankie put his hands on his hips. "Tell me this is some kinda joke."

"You're a sick man, Frankie," said Dee as she carried the empty rack of glasses back to the kitchen.

Al was on his way to the office. He wasn't getting any closer to getting rid of his stack of paperwork. Why did they keep giving him work when he had no incentive not to fuck it up? His cell phone rang. *Frankie.*

J.T. had warned him that under no circumstances was he to go back to the club until further notice. Then, after Al had agreed, J.T. made Al *swear* that he should get ass-raped by every member of the Oakland Raiders, dead or alive, should he go back to Mira Chiste without J.T. giving him the okay.

"I swear."

"Not good enough. I need verbatim."

"J.T." Al whined.

"*In haec verba*, Al. I am not fucking kidding."

"I swear that I should get ass-raped by every member of the Oakland Raiders, dead or alive, should I go back to Mira Chiste without J.T.'s okay."

J.T. had kept Al in the dark about all the cloak-and-dagger stuff with the recording. Al couldn't figure out J.T.'s angle. He couldn't take it to the cops. He couldn't blackmail Frankie with it—J.T. was in the scam even deeper than Frankie himself. Al had no choice but to believe J.T. when he said it was going to work out. Either way, Al was sure he'd be felled by a heart attack or a perforated ulcer soon enough.

Al debated whether to answer Frankie's call. What if he insisted Al come back to the club? The hot breath of Frankie McElfresh on his neck, or an eye-patched John Matuszak mounting him from behind with a machete in his teeth?

Al let the phone ring out.

Thirty seconds later it started ringing again. *Frankie.*

Al let the phone ring out.

When the phone rang a third time a minute later, and a fourth time a minute after that, Al felt like he was losing his vision. Everything seemed cloudy. Blurry. He pulled off the 60 and into the parking lot at Jack in the Box. He hyperventilated for about thirty seconds until he felt like he might black out. He rolled down the window. That helped.

Al stared at the phone. *Fuck it. Be a man.* He called Frankie, determined not to get pushed into going back to the club.

"Jesus, Frankie, what is it? I'm on the highway with the CHP riding right next to me. I had to pull off the highway to call you back."

"Number One, who the fuck do you think you're talking to? I gotta call you four times to get *my* call returned? You fucking kidding me?"

"I just told you. I couldn't talk on the phone because the CHP was either right behind me or right next to me. What is it? What's so important it couldn't wait till I got to the office?"

"Mack's dead."

Al sensed he was going to pass out again. He opened the door wide and swung his legs out of the Honda.

"What? What? What do you mean?"

"What do you think dead means? He's gone. Flipped a fucking jeep off a mountain in Coachella or something. Anyway, he's dead, so you're going to need to get back here pronto so we can talk strategy."

"I can't. I've got meetings all morning. I've got to have all my shit cleared out by Friday."

"Al? Get back here."

"I can't, I'm sorry. Now I've got to go." Al hung up.

Frankie called back in three seconds.

"Listen to me, cocksucker. You hang up the phone on me and I'll go Hannibal Lecter on your ass. You got me, motherfucker?"

"Frankie, I—"

"*Shut up and listen.* Our newest team member, Jolly Roger here, tells me Mack's claim on the busted dick from the golf course will survive even though Mack didn't. You beat that?"

"Frankie—"

"No wonder GSAC dumped your ass. You don't listen real well. Try again."

Al gasped for air. He rubbed the side of his head. His palm was covered in hair.

"Okay," said Frankie, "now if the claim is still alive as far as his estate's concerned, we're still in business. Rog says your settlement authority is two hundred K. Settle the fucking thing for two hundred K and get my money."

"It'll never work."

"It *will* work. By the way, that sportsman's discount you got when we started this? You lost it when you hung up on me. *Fifteen* points, motherfucker. That makes thirty large from the score; another thirty for the principal you cocksuckers borrowed. That's sixty grand you owe me, asshole. First dollar payout, remember? Plus, you're giving fifteen percent of *your* end to our friend Roger here for getting this fucking thing out of the ditch."

"Frankie, I can't come back to the club."

"Oh, don't worry about that anymore. Rog and I are coming to meet you."

Al heard one car door slam, then a second. "What?"

"Yeah, we're on our way. We're leaving right fucking now, so don't let me down again. We'll meet you across from GSAC's office at the Starb—"

The call dropped.

Al leaned out of the car, put his head between his knees, and threw up.

FORTY-FOUR

J.T. turned on the TV in his office just for some background noise. Shari happily took the day off when he insisted. He was too bummed out about the Mercedes to feel like talking to anyone.

He took it on faith that Vinnie Fangs wouldn't tell Frankie about the visit or even give Frankie a chance to talk his way out of the shit storm that was about to befall him.

When J.T.'s disposable phone rang, he reached for it, hoping it was Mack. J.T. was bothered that he'd never gotten to the bottom of whether Buddy had talked to Aza, and now Buddy was MIA. J.T. looked at the phone. *Al.*

J.T. fell back on his telephone patter, as much to distract himself from the loss of the Mercedes as anything. "Al, what's the good word, my man?" J.T. could hear coughing, retching, and spitting in the background, along with what sounded like trucks zooming past. "Al?"

"It's bad. It's fucking bad."

"C'mon. Get a grip. What's the problem?"

"Mack. Frankie."

J.T. heard Al throwing up. "Are you okay?"

"Frankie's coming after me."

"What are you talking about?"

"Mack's dead." Al retched again.

"Al. Al. Listen to me. What's going on? What about Mack?"

"He's dead. I don't know, I don't know, he's just dead."

"Who told you that?"

"Frankie."

J.T. heard more coughing and spitting in the background. "How does he know?"

"Shit, I don't know. Maybe he fucking ate him." Al retched again.

J.T. grimaced at the sound effects. "Why do you say he's coming after you?"

"Because he said *'I'm coming after you!'* J.T., I'm telling you, I don't know what to do. I've been sitting here in the Jack in the Box parking lot for half an hour puking my guts out. That asshole Roger Ellis has Frankie convinced I can still sign off on a two-hundred-thousand-dollar settlement. It's all so fucking crazy I can't believe it."

A breaking story on the TV across the room caught J.T.'s attention. A helicopter was flying over a plume of black smoke from a parking lot below. Something looked familiar to J.T. The camera panned across the lot. EMTs stood in front of a warehouse with a green gambrel roof. The greenskeeper's shed. Mira Chiste. The bird's-eye zoomed in to show a blown-up yellow Lincoln Navigator with jagged strands of metal peeling from the dark center like a black-eyed Susan. He recognized the car. Fat fucking Frankie Fresh.

"Al? You still with me, Al?"

"Yeah."

"Okay, I want you to take a deep breath."

J.T. heard him hyperventilate.

"I'm looking at the TV right now. Frankie Fresh is not, I repeat not, coming after you."

"What?"

"What was it your granddaddy used to say? 'Pigs get fat; hogs get slaughtered'?"

"Yeah."

"Get yourself in front of a TV. We're looking at one slaughtered hog."

Having talked Al off the ledge, J.T. needed to cut the shit and find out what was going on with Mack. He called Wanda's cell phone. She didn't even say hello.

"It's true," she said.

"How?" J.T. was puzzled. He'd seemed like such a healthy kid. Maybe the doctors at Eisenhower had fucked up the surgery. *Oh, shit! Wouldn't that be a fucking coup?*

"He took that dune buggy out to the desert to climb Joe Frey Hill."

"That place where the hippies go to drop acid and shit in the bushes?"

"Yeah."

"A dignified exit, I'm sure."

"Don't be an asshole."

"Gimme a break. I mean, I feel bad for the kid, but let's face it, the ol' gene pool just dodged a riptide."

"I'm hanging up."

"Wait. We have to talk about the claim. It may have taken a hit—okay, a huge hit—but it was filed before he was killed. There's still at least some value there."

"Do what you have to do. I need some time to sort things out, J.T. Goodbye."

What a bitch. She ought to be kissing my ass. Her nightmare of a sham marriage evaporates and I'm the asshole? Stupid fuck robs me from beyond the grave and I'm the bad guy?

He scrolled through his cell phone for Aza's number, then called him from the office line.

"Hi, it's J.T. Edwards. I'm afraid I have some unfortunate news."

"I'm guessing this has to do with your client's death."

Who is this fucking guy? "Yes, tragically, I'm afraid. Young man like that. In his prime. Newly married to a beautiful wife and his last month spent in agony."

"So much agony that he went off-roading in the desert."

Maybe there was a wrongful death angle with the dune buggy manufacturer! No, of course not. That dipshit fabricated the thing himself. "Hector, what do you say we just hack through some of this bullshit right now?"

"I'm all for that."

"The dollar value of my case has taken a significant hit. We can agree on that, can we not?"

"I don't see why not."

"Conversely, the sympathy factor for my surviving client, the Widow McMahon, coupled with the unspeakable gruesomeness of her late husband's injury, makes for an acutely compelling narrative when I put it in front of a jury."

"I don't know about acutely compelling, but I'll grant you she might be a sympathetic figure."

"Well, now, you do know Wanda's maiden name, right?"

"No, and I'm not sure I understand what that's got to do with anything."

"I should have thought it obvious that given the Riverside County demographic, that Wanda Maria *Ortega*-McMahon," said J.T., enunciating the *t* in Ortega like he'd just hopped over the fence from Sonora, "newly widowed, sole support of her wheelchair-bound mother...do you really think the rich gringo resort is going to get off scot-free?"

J.T. leaned back in his chair. Shit, when he said it like that, it didn't sound like such a dog after all.

"J.T.," said Hector, "you sound like you have a number in mind."

J.T. held the phone against his stomach, bit down on his lip, and pumped his fist three times. He wanted to throw something, but in a good way this time, like a spike after a touchdown. He relaxed and smiled. "You don't expect me to bid against myself, Hector."

"You called me, J.T. Maybe you have more free time than I do. If you don't have a number I can take back to my client, I'm afraid I have a bunch of deposition transcripts I have to read for my upcoming trial."

"Fair enough, Hector. Fair enough. Our complaint asked for nine million." J.T. sat up in his chair now. "I appreciate that this was predicated on a worst-case scenario, with actuarial tables projecting a lifespan of roughly eighty-seven years…impotence, etc." J.T. cleared his throat. "Given that some, but not all, of the damages have been extinguished along with Mr. McMahon, I think a one-point-nine-million-dollar settlement would make you an absolute *hero* at GSAC."

J.T. heard Hector laughing on the other end.

"That sounds like a cry for help, J.T." Hector chuckled again. "Listen, I played the Westin PGA with a therapist from Betty Ford. Gave him at least six putts. I can't make any promises, but maybe he could get you an urgent admission."

Now J.T. laughed. "Too bad we couldn't have played together. A guy who gives away that many putts…" J.T. leaned back in his chair again. "So you're not impressed with one-point-nine."

"No sale."

"So what did you have in mind?"

"Gosh, J.T., I hate to throw a wet blanket on things, but I'm afraid when I think about the strength of your case, only one number flashes in my mind."

"What number's that?"

"Eight-five-oh."

"Eight hundred and fifty grand? For that kind of injury? With a Latina widow going against a resort where a glass of room-service orange juice is thirty bucks? I don't think there's any way she'll go for it, Hector, if we're being candid. I'll take it to her, but frankly, I will not be recommending settling at that figure."

J.T. was ready to jump up on his desk and start beating off like a chimp.

"No, no, I think you misunderstood. I didn't mean eight hundred and fifty thousand dollars. I meant eight-five-zero." Hector paused a beat. "You know what that is, right?"

"What are you talking about?"

"Eight-five-oh. It's the area code for Jackson County, Florida. I suppose technically I should say Two Egg, but I think they're pretty liberal about geography down there."

"What?"

"Buddy. You know his mother lives down there, right? She was so excited about how they got the Internet—she calls it the inner nets—but I knew what she meant. Anyway, this might surprise you, but did you know she likes to Skype?"

J.T. closed his eyes in the tightest squint he could stand and bounced his head on the back of his chair.

"J.T.?"

"No. No, I didn't."

"Now, as you said, as long as we're being candid with each other…As an officer of the court, I'm not going to misrepresent that I know where Buddy is at this very moment. I will, however, submit to you that his permanent unavailability is not something I would tell your client to count on."

"I don't know why she would count on that, or why she would even care."

"Well, great. So that's where we are."

"So you'll take my one-point-nine offer back to your client."

"I promise it will receive all the deliberation it deserves," said Hector.

"Very well. I'll wait to hear back from you then."

Fuck.

FORTY-FIVE

Marino Vargas caught Al as he was shuffling toward his desk from the elevator. "Jesus, are you okay?"

"I've been better."

"You hear the news? Roger Ellis? That dude we shit-canned? He got blown up in a car bomb with some Mob guy!"

Al blinked. "What?"

"I knew there was something about that guy."

"Ellis was killed? You sure?"

"Yep. It's been flying all over the office. I told you he was a dick."

"I think he was stalking me."

"What? Why didn't you say anything?"

"I wasn't a hundred percent sure." Al was breathing easier now. He felt almost relaxed. "Did he drive a white BMW?"

"Fuck yeah, he did! That son of a bitch!"

"Figures."

"You know he tried to pin that shit on you about the data breach."

"You're kidding."

"I told you. I knew there was something wrong about that guy." Vargas seemed genuinely pissed off.

Al felt like he'd downed a dozen Vicodin. "So you think he was working for the Mob? Like a mole or something?"

"All fits together now, doesn't it? Get inside. Get proprietary information. Feed it to the Mob. Finger you when it goes south."

Vargas covered his mouth. “You don’t think it was him torched your house, do you?”

“You know, the cops said they were running a meth lab in the empty house next door, but Jesus, who knows what to think now.” Al almost giggled he was so relieved.

“Listen, man. Everybody here really feels bad. The guys upstairs are going to go batshit when they find out Ellis was stalking you.”

“Let’s just let it go.”

“See, that’s what I mean. I don’t think the company, even SAICO, should lose a guy like you. A guy with your experience, you know?” Vargas looked around to see if anyone might be listening. He leaned in toward Al. “I had to post that job in Weed, but I know for a fact we haven’t hired anyone yet. If you were serious about the house being the only thing holding you back, I’m telling you, I’ll make this shit happen.”

After batting away the offer again and again over the past weeks, Al thought about how two hours earlier he’d have sold his soul to get to Weed and away from Frankie Fresh. He hadn’t come through this fiasco without learning something.

“That would be terrific, thanks, Marino.”

Weed had begun to grow on Alvin Boyle.

J.T. had been so despondent over the crumbling of his case, he’d all but forgotten about his flanking movement on GSAC and El Fuente Dorado. As soon as he got the pictures of Mack’s fractured penis, including stills of the surgery itself, he’d used an e-mail account from one of the dozen dummy web domains he bought every year and had sent the complaint and photos to the Smoking Gun. El Fuente Dorado Resort and Spa had been inundated with calls from Tokyo, Shanghai, Dubai, and London. The board duly relayed these inquiries to GSAC's general counsel, Joel Neuman, who kicked them downstairs to Sid Stewart.

Hector had expected Sid would laugh in his face when he called him with J.T.'s one-point-nine offer. When Sid said he'd have to get back to him, Hector had been shocked. When Sid did get back to him and told him to settle the thing for 350 grand and a gag agreement, Hector was floored.

Mindful of not wanting to discourage repeat business, Hector nonetheless insisted to Sid it was a mistake. The suit was not only winnable for GSAC, the dollars were nuts.

"This is coming from upstairs," said Stewart. "They're getting pressured from the resort. The publicity's horrible. The policyholder wants this over, and the board wants this out of the reserve before SAICO takes over."

Hector Aza's jaw felt as heavy as a beer keg. He reached for the wastebasket and swallowed hard, trying not to vomit. Not since his own divorce had he felt so defeated, even though he knew this time it wasn't his fault. The client insisted he settle the claim. An asinine waste of money. He sighed and dialed J.T. Edwards.

"Hello, Hector," said J.T. "Let me guess: you're calling with a settlement offer."

Hector felt another reflux bubbling up. "Against my advice, GSAC's willing to settle the case. One-time offer." He spat in the wastebasket and set the can back on the threadbare carpet. "Take it or leave it."

"What's the number?"

"Three fifty."

"Are you kidding? Three hundred and fifty K for that—"

Hector cut him off. "One-time offer, J.T. No negotiation." At least on that one point, GSAC had listened to him. "Take it or leave it." Hector loosened his tie. "You should leave it, J.T. Please. I'm begging you. *Please* take this to trial."

J.T. chuckled on the other end of the line. "As much as I'd look forward to that combat, Hector, in the interest of judicial economy, I know I speak for my client when I say we will, with no little regret, accept your offer of three hundred and fifty thousand dollars and just try to get on with our lives as best we can."

Hector reached for the wastebasket again. He really thought he might yak this time. He could practically feel J.T.'s grin oozing through the phone. "I'll get you the paperwork next week."

"You have a nice weekend, Hector."

"Yeah."

Reclining on his couch with a glass of scotch, J.T. watched Shari walk in and out of his office with her volleyball ass. First thing he was going to do was fly that out to Kauai. Second thing he was going to do was get another Mercedes.

J.T. Edwards was back.

FORTY-SIX

Her skin a perfect crème brûlée, Shari glided topless across the lanai with a spliff the size of a rolling pin in her fingers. A hibiscus-print batik sarong wrapped around her waist just above where her hips would've been if she'd had an ounce of fat below her breasts.

J.T. relaxed, his head resting against the top of the bungalow's Jacuzzi as the early-afternoon breeze freshened off the Pacific. He took a slow drag on the Montecristo No. 2 the concierge in the grand lodge had procured for him. Swirling three fingers of Green Label in his sweating glass, the soft tinkle of the ice cubes punctured the dull hum of the tub's motor. Given the occasion he'd have popped for the Blue Label, but Jesus, as it was, these guys were already getting an 800 percent markup on the Green in this clip-joint.

With his credit cards either maxed out or in collection, Shari had had to book the trip on her card. He'd scrounged what remained of his Mercedes proceeds to reimburse her with cash. Fortunately, his gold status on Delta wouldn't expire for another month, so they were able to upgrade for the flight to Honolulu.

The cheap flip phone vibrated on the edge of the tub. Before Mack's death, things had gotten so bad that AT&T suspended his smartphone data plan. He had his office line forwarded to one of the shitty disposables left over from the scam. He'd get that sorted and back onto his iPhone as soon as he returned to Riverside.

Ordinarily, he'd have had Shari answer it, but she was now sitting on the edge of a hammock, smiling at him as she took a long unhurried toke. She raised her eyebrows, an unmistakable invitation to what would be their third go in the past twelve hours. He was so hard he could see the end of his cock for the first time in months. *Thanks, Cialis.*

He fondled himself briefly under the water, smiling back at Shari before he answered. "J.T. Edwards."

"J.T.? It's Hector Aza."

"*¡Hector, mi amigo!*" Even though he was a GSAC hired gun, and thus the enemy, J.T. felt a soft spot for a guy who took a punch so gracefully. "Let me guess. You're calling to set up a tee time. Going to give me some of those putts like your pal at Betty Ford? *¿Que pasa, hermano?*"

"Um, actually, J.T., just a courtesy call with a minor housekeeping matter. The client's going to forego the counterclaim."

J.T. laughed. "Well, of course they are, Hector. That would clearly fall under the umbrella of the settlement."

"J.T., I'm not sure—"

"Speaking of which, I'm still waiting on your paperwork. Don't tell me those GSAC assholes are giving you the runaround too?" J.T. glanced over at Shari, still smiling, her eyelids drooping into provocative slits. "Listen, I'm actually out of town at the moment." He held the phone over the tub to let Hector hear the bubbles. "I should be back in a couple of days, though." Shari stretched her arms upright and arched her back, her bare twenty-three-year-old breasts lunging forward. "Maybe three." J.T. looked down into the tub. Still rock hard. "Have to see how my negotiations go out here."

"J.T., I think there's a misunderstanding. I'm talking about the tab your clients had at El Fuente Dorado. It was over forty-eight hundred dollars, but under the circumstances, the resort's decided not to pursue it."

Shit! That's right! He'd been so excited about getting his one-third split of the settlement, he'd forgotten that the expenses he'd fronted Mack and Wanda were coming off the top. There was also the 2K from Vegas. Nice little windfall. Hell, maybe he'd pop for the Blue Label after all.

"Not sure you what you mean by 'under the circumstances,' Hector, but as I said, that was already assumed. Not to mention a deal breaker." Shari lay back on the hammock and pointed a toe to the thatched roof above the lanai. Her sarong fell back, flashing J.T. a glimpse of a creamy tan-line and black landing strip. "So, Hector, I'm afraid I need to bounce. I don't have my computer here or I'd have you just e-mail the paperwork to me."

"You're serious. You really don't know?"

"Know what?" J.T. turned off the motor and stuck his cigar in his teeth. He hauled his dripping pink ass onto the side of the tub as he reached for one of the resort's enormous white bath sheets.

"Your client dismissed your case." Hector laughed. "You really didn't know. Man, this is just too classic."

The cigar dropped from J.T.'s mouth and bounced off his wet chest back into the tub. "What the fuck are you talking about, Hector?"

"Your client? The grieving Widow McMahon? She dismissed your case. With prejudice, J.T." Hector laughed again. "With prejudice."

This wasn't possible. *Nobody walks away from two hundred and thirty grand! Why the fuck would Wanda pull the plug on the case?* And with prejudice meant it couldn't be re-filed. There had to be a mistake. J.T. leaned on the side of the tub to steady himself. "But she, she…she can't—"

"But she did, *amigo*. Apparently she used to be a paralegal. Knows her way around the clerk's office. Oh, Jesus, this is too priceless."

"This is bullshit!" *Fuck!* There had to be some way to re-open this shit. Maybe somehow through estate law. God, when was the last time he'd tramped through that swamp? "I'm filing a fucking motion first thing tomorrow morning!"

"That's great, but I don't know what relief you'd be seeking. Settlement offer's gone, J.T. As in, for good. Why do you think the client was being so generous about the hotel bill?"

J.T. slipped off the tub and landed onto the lanai with a thud. "Listen, we can still work this out, Hector." He scrambled to his feet, naked, still dripping, with a huge smear of Montecristo ash in the middle of his chest.

"*Se acabó, hermano.* It's over. *Nos vemos.*"

J.T. looked down at his fleshy damp gut. The line wasn't the only thing that went dead.

FORTY-SEVEN

Buddy had seen enough episodes of *Shark Tank* to know that the $50,000 cashier's check he'd gotten from Wanda for 25 percent of his company was a win-win. At first he was a little surprised that the offer was contingent upon his going back to Florida to set up the company's headquarters. There were plenty of golf courses in the Sunshine State, Wanda explained, and a lot fewer people who might have questions about shopping carts and tractors.

Having found a reluctant but desperate buyer for the Monte Carlo, Buddy bought a small used pickup truck, packed up his prototype for the Magic Wanda ball-retrieval system, and headed east across the desert in the early dawn hours.

The case had ended a month ago, and Hector Aza had moved on. After shooting a seventy-seven, he was feeling good enough about his Friday afternoon to pull up a barstool next to J.T. in the 19th Hole at Mira Chiste. J.T. was wearing street clothes and already appeared half in the bag. Unfashionable gray stubble peppered his face and neck just above his grimy collar.

"J.T.," said Hector, "how's it going? You get out today?"

J.T. stared straight ahead to the kitchen behind the bar, crunching some ice from his near-empty glass. "Nope."

Hector leaned on the bar and ordered a draft Dos Equis. Carrie, the former cart girl, back at UCR after a summer abroad, smiled at him when she set the glass on a faded red cardboard coaster. He sipped his beer and turned on his stool to look through the window at the putting green outside. Heat waves shimmied behind doughy retirees trying to squeeze in a twilight round. Hector's stomach rumbled when he smelled the basket of fries cooling at a table in the dark corner opposite the TV.

J.T., still staring straight ahead, stopped crunching the ice in his glass. "You ever hear of anything like that?" He swallowed the last of the ice. "I mean, fuckin' A, the money's right there." He shook his head. "Right fucking there."

Carrie dumped some more ice in a fresh glass and poured J.T. another double Dewar's. J.T. threw back his drink and gulped the whisky in one shot. He started crunching the ice in his glass again and motioned to Carrie for another. He tottered on his barstool, swirling ice cubes in the bottom of his glass, a greasy hank of hair hanging down his forehead like a plumb bob. He stifled a burp and got up from the bar, holding the stool to steady himself. He picked up the check lying next to the bowl of bar snacks and squinted at it. He drew a Montblanc pen from his jacket pocket and scribbled on the check, then pulled a ten from his wallet and dropped it on the bar. He staggered away from the bar and down the hall toward the men's locker room.

"Thanks, J.T.," Carrie hollered after him, a muffled thud coming in reply from the wainscoting in the hall. She swiped the bill off the bar and tucked it in her apron pocket.

"Man, he's a mess," Carrie said, wiping up the bar sweat from where J.T.'s glasses had rested.

"I had a case against him not too long ago," said Hector.

"Believe me, it's all he talks about."

"Really?"

"He's in here every night saying how Wanda screwed him."

"I only met her once. She seemed nice." The sound of a crowd roaring on the TV in the background got Hector's attention. Following a three-run homer by the DH, Baltimore was up by one over the Angels on the last night of the season. The Orioles had just recorded the first out in the top of the ninth. "Guess she's not working here anymore?"

"You didn't hear? She bought a place in Puerto Vallarta with the insurance money. She moved her mom down there and everything."

"What insurance money? She withdrew the claim. GSAC never paid out."

Carrie looked at Hector, confused, then rolled her eyes. "Not the thing when Mack got hurt." She leaned in toward Hector. "I heard about that. Totally gross. They said he was yankin' it in a Port-a-Potty when he got hit by a tractor. What a perv."

"What insurance are you talking about?"

"The life insurance. When they got married, Mack took out, like, a half-million-dollar policy. Wanda was the beneficiary."

Hector smiled, sipped his beer, and shook his head. The Amazon barmaid with the dimples and heart-melting smile had hustled them all.

Sid Stewart, now a hero within SAICO, had a tee time for the next morning with Hector, to whom he was ready to give all the business he could handle—even if he didn't know how Hector had pulled it off. Until now, Hector hadn't been sure himself.

J.T. emerged from the hallway, his trousers wet from where he'd half wiped his hands, and reached in his pocket for his car keys. He suppressed another burp, threw back his shoulders, and shuffled toward the door.

"J.T., you sure you're okay to drive?" Hector said.

"I will be. Once I get home."

"How about a taxi?"

J.T. looked at Hector, then at Carrie. He stepped back to the bar, reached over it, and grabbed three limes, his tie dipping into a puddle of maraschino cherry juice on the bartender's tray. He looked at Carrie and Hector again and sighed. He juggled the limes, tossing them each at least half-a-dozen times, then catching all three and returning them to the bar. He looked up at the ceiling and sighed.

"Three hundred and fifty grand," he said. Then he stepped through the door and into the twilight.

"Ohmigod," said Carrie. "Did you see that?"

From the parking lot a few seconds later, the flatulent combustion of a broken muffler seeped into the room as the pneumatic door to the 19th Hole closed. Through the wall's tinted glass, Hector watched J.T. drive away in a paint-blistered, two-tone, blue-gray Monte Carlo.

When he heard the commentators mention the Angels were down to their last at bat of the season, Hector turned his head to the TV. They weren't going to make the playoffs anyway, but it was going to be a long plane ride back to Anaheim if they didn't score. When the Angels' third baseman watched a called third strike to end the game, Hector turned around in his barstool. He tipped up his bottle to finish his beer.

Can't win 'em all.

ABOUT THE AUTHOR

As a trial lawyer, Jack Bunker has ridden the legal rails from a large international firm to solo practice, the U.S. Department of Justice, and a stint as a legal editor with Thomson Reuters in Dubai. He has the distinction of having both clerked for former Chief Judge Boyce F. Martin of the U.S. Court of Appeals for the Sixth Circuit, and played scout team tight end for Bobby Bowden's Florida State Seminoles. Jack received his law degree from St. John's University in New York, and he is (or has been) a member of the bars of New York, California, Georgia, and the District of Columbia, as well as the Virginia Cattlemen's Association. He splits his time between the home he shares in Northern Virginia with his wife and four children, and their family farm in Virginia's breathtaking Bluegrass Valley. This is his first novel.

CPSIA information can be obtained at www.ICGtesting.com
Printed in the USA
LVOW08s0005200516

489076LV00004B/195/P